泰戈尔诗文彩图馆

(印)泰戈尔 著
郑振铎·海宁 译

中国华侨出版社

中侨彩图馆

刘凤珍 主编

图书在版编目（CIP）数据

泰戈尔诗文彩图馆 /（印）泰戈尔著；郑振铎，海宁译．— 北京：中国华侨出版社，2015.12
（中侨彩图馆 / 刘凤珍主编）
ISBN 978-7-5113-5866-0

Ⅰ．①泰… Ⅱ．①泰… ②郑… ③海… Ⅲ．①诗集－印度－现代②散文集－印度－现代 Ⅳ．①I351.15

中国版本图书馆CIP数据核字（2015）第302717号

泰戈尔诗文彩图馆

著　者 /（印）泰戈尔
译　者 / 郑振铎 海宁
丛书主编 / 刘凤珍
总审定 / 江　冰
出版人 / 方　鸣
责任编辑 / 文　卿
装帧设计 / 贾惠茹 杨 琪
经　销 / 新华书店
开　本 /720mm×1020mm　1/16　印张：24.5　字数：439千字
印　刷 / 北京鑫国彩印刷制版有限公司
版　次 /2016年5月第1版　2016年5月第1次印刷
书　号 /ISBN 978-7-5113-5866-0
定　价 /39.80元

中国华侨出版社　北京市朝阳区静安里26号通成达大厦3层　邮编：100028
法律顾问：陈鹰律师事务所
发行部：（010）64443051　传真：（010）64439708
网　址：www.oveaschin.com　E-mail：oveaschin@sina.com

前言

罗宾德拉纳特・泰戈尔 (Rabindranath Tagore，1861–1941)，印度近代著名诗人、艺术家、社会活动家和哲学家，一生共写下诗作2000多首，出版诗集50余部。14岁时发表了第一首长诗《野花》。1913年，凭借《吉檀迦利》(英文版)成为第一位荣获诺贝尔文学奖的亚洲作家。他与黎巴嫩诗人纪伯伦一起并称为“站在东西方文化桥梁上的巨人”，被印度人民尊为“诗圣”，为印度近代文学的发展开辟了广阔的道路。

泰戈尔的作品被人们当作“精神生活的灯塔”，一个多世纪以来一直影响着世人。自20世纪20年代起，他的作品便由郑振铎、冰心等著名翻译家译介到中国，深受中国读者喜爱。他的诗歌文字优美、情感深刻，总是充满哲理的思考，弥漫着一种恬淡、静谧、飘逸、肃穆的意境，读来发人深思、让人陶醉。其蕴含的精深博大的人生哲理，总能令人振奋和鼓舞，在唤起人们对大自然、对人类、对世界上一切美好事物的爱心的同时，也启示着人们如何执着于现实人生的理想追求，让人生充满欢乐与光明。

《新月集》是泰戈尔的代表作，诗人用一支彩色神笔描绘了儿童纯净奇特的内心世界和绚丽多彩的生活画面，感人至深地表现了孩子与父母的骨肉亲情，语言空灵秀丽，形散而神聚。《飞鸟集》是一部富于哲理的格言诗集，深刻的智慧和简短的篇幅为其鲜明特色。在这部思绪点点的散文诗集中，白昼与黑夜，落叶与流萤，自由与背叛，无不在泰戈尔笔下化为一首首清丽的小诗，引人遐想而又耐人寻味。《故事诗集》是泰戈尔前期诗歌创作中一部极其重要的叙事诗集，被视为诗人留给人民的最优秀的精神遗产之一，主要取材于印度古代经典作品里的历史传说。《吉檀迦利》是泰戈尔中期诗歌创作的高峰，这部抒情诗集风格清新自然，带着泥土的芬芳。《园丁集》是一部“生命之歌”，它更多地融入了诗人青春时代的体验，细腻地描述了爱情的幸福、烦恼与忧伤，可以视为一部青春恋歌。《采果集》是一部现实主义作品，表达出对诚实淳朴的下层贫民的真诚同情，表现了诗人崇高的人道主义精神。

《泰戈尔诗文彩图馆》收录了泰戈尔最具代表性的《飞鸟集》和《新月集》，并精选《故事诗集》《游思集》《再次集》《最后的星期集》《尘埃集》《抒情集》《吉檀迦利》《园丁集》《采果集》等作品的精华内容。这些诗歌语言清丽，意味隽永，将抒情和哲思完美结合，给人以无尽美感和启迪。在编辑过程中，我们选配了与诗意相契合的精美图片，所配的图片能让读者在欣赏诗歌的同时获得美的享受；译文清新隽永、韵味悠长，完美展现出原作的精神与气质，具有很高的文学价值和收藏价值。

目录

1 新月集

105 飞鸟集

175 故事诗集

新月集

泰戈尔诗文彩图馆

译者自序

我对于泰戈尔（R·Tagore）的诗最初发生浓厚的兴趣，是在第一次读《新月集》的时候。那时离现在将近五年，许地山君坐在我家的客厅里，长发垂到两肩，很神秘地在黄昏的微光中，对我谈到泰戈尔的事。他说：他在缅甸时，看到泰戈尔的画像，又听人讲到他，便买了他的诗集来读。过了几天，我到许地山君的宿舍里去。他说："我拿一本泰戈尔的诗选送给你。"他便到书架上去找那本诗集。我立在窗前，四围静悄悄的，只有水池中喷泉的潺潺的声音。我静静地等候读那本美丽的书。他不久便从书架上取下很小的一本绿纸面的书来。他说："这是一个日本人选的泰戈尔诗，你先拿去看看。泰戈尔不久前曾到过日本。"我坐了车回家，在归程中，借着新月与市灯的微光，约略地把它翻看了一遍。最使我喜欢的是其中所选的几首《新月集》的诗。那一夜，在灯下又看了一次。第二天，地山见我时，问道："你最喜欢哪几首？"我说："《新月集》的几首。"他隔了几天，又拿了一本很美丽的书给我，他说："这就是《新月集》。"从那以后，《新月集》便常在我的书桌上。直到现在，我还时时把它翻开来读。

我译《新月集》，也是受地山君的鼓励。有一天，他把他所译的《吉檀迦利》的几首诗给我看，都是用古文译的。我说："译得很好，但似乎太古奥了。"他说："这一类的诗，应该用这个古奥的文体译。至于《新月集》，却又须用新妍流露的文字译。我想译《吉檀迦利》，你为何不译《新月集》呢？”于是我与他约，我们同时动手译这两部书。此后两年中，他的《吉檀迦利》固未译成，我的《新月集》也时译时辍。直至《小说月报》改革后，我才把自己所译的《新月集》在它上面发表了几首。地山译的《吉檀迦利》却始终没有再译下去。已译的几首也始终不肯拿出来发表。后来王独清君译的《新月集》也出版了，我更懒得把自己的译下去。许多朋友却时时催我把这个工作做完。他们都说，王君的译文太不容易懂了，似乎有再译的必要。那时我正有选译泰戈尔诗的计划，便一方面把旧译的稿整理一下，一方面参考了王君的译文，又新译了八九首出来，结果便成了现在的这个译本。原集里还有九首诗，因为我不大喜欢它们，所以没有译出来①。

我喜欢《新月集》，如我之喜欢安徒生的童话。安徒生的文字美丽而富有诗趣，他有一种不可测的魔力，能把我们从忙扰的人世间带到美丽和平的花的世界、虫的世界、人鱼的世界里去；能使我们忘了一切艰苦的境遇，随了他走进有静的方池的绿水、有美的挂在黄昏的天空的雨后弧虹等等的天国里去。《新月集》也具有这种不可测的魔力。它把我们从怀疑贪望的成人的世界，带到秀嫩天真的儿童的新月之国里去。我们忙着费时间在计算数字，它却能使我们重又回到坐在泥土里以枯枝断梗为戏的时代；我们忙着入海采珠，掘山寻金，它却能使我们在心里重温着在海滨以贝壳为餐具，以落叶为舟，以绿草的露点为圆珠的儿童的梦。总之，我们只要一翻开它来，便立刻如得到两只有魔术的翼膀，可以使自己从现实的苦闷的境地里飞翔到美静天真的儿童国里去。

有许多人以为《新月集》是一部写给儿童看的书。这是他们受

---

① 本书中的《新月集》为全译本。——编者注

了广告上附注的“儿歌”（Child Poems）二字的暗示的缘故。实际上，《新月集》虽然未尝没有几首儿童可以看得懂的诗歌，而泰戈尔之写这些诗，却决非为儿童而作的。它并不是一部写给儿童读的诗歌集，乃是一部叙述儿童心理、儿童生活的最好的诗歌集。这正如俄国许多民众小说家所作的民众小说，并不是为民众而作，而是写民众的生活的作品一样。我们如果认清了这一点，便不会无端的引起什么怀疑与什么争论了。

我的译文自己很不满意，但似乎还很忠实，且不至看不懂。

读者的一切指教，我都欢迎地承受。

我最后应该向许地山君表示谢意。他除了鼓励我以外，在这个译本写好时，还曾为我校读了一次。

郑振铎

再版自序

《新月集》译本出版后，曾承几位朋友批评，这里我要对他们表白十二分的谢意。现在乘再版的机会，把第一版中所有错误，就所能觉察到的，改正一下。读者诸君及朋友们如果更有所发现，希望能够告诉我，俾得于第三版时再校正。

郑振铎

家庭

我独自在横跨过田地的路上走着。夕阳像一个守财奴似的，正藏起它的最后的金子。

白昼更加深沉地没入黑暗之中。那已经收割了的孤寂的田地，默默地躺在那里。

天空里突然升起了一个男孩子的尖锐的歌声。他穿过看不见的黑暗，留下他的歌声的辙痕跨过黄昏的静谧。

他的乡村的家坐落在荒凉的土地的边上，在甘蔗田的后面，躲藏在香蕉树、瘦长的槟榔树、椰子树和深绿色的贾克果树的阴影里。

我在星光下独自走着的路上停留了一会儿。我看见黑沉沉的大地展开在我的面前，用她的手臂拥抱着无量数的家庭。在那些家庭里有着摇篮和床铺，母亲们的心和夜晚的灯，还有年轻轻的生命。他们满心欢乐，却浑然不知这样的欢乐对于世界的价值。

The Home

I paced alone on the road across the field while the sunset was hiding its last gold like a miser.

The daylight sank deeper and deeper into the darkness, and the widowed land, whose harvest had been reaped, lay silent.

Suddenly a boy's shrill voice rose into the sky. He traversed the dark unseen, leaving the track of his song across the hush of the evening.

His village home lay there at the end of the waste land, beyond the sugar-cane field, hidden among the shadows of the banana and the slender areca palm, the cocoa-nut and the dark green jack-fruit trees.

I stopped for a moment in my lonely way under the starlight, and saw spread before me the darkened earth surrounding with her arms countless homes furnished with cradles and beds, mothers' hearts and evening lamps, and young lives glad with a gladness that knows nothing of its value for the world.

海边

孩子们会集在无边无际的世界的海边。

无垠的天穹静止地临于头上，不息的海水在足下汹涌。孩子们会集在无边无际的世界的海边，叫着，跳着。

他们拿沙来建筑房屋，拿贝壳来做游戏。他们把落叶编成了船，笑嘻嘻地把它们放到大海上。孩子们在世界的海边，做他们的游戏。

他们不知道怎样泅水，他们不知道怎样撒网。采珠的人为了珠潜水，商人们在他们的船上航行，孩子们却只把小圆石聚了又散。他们不搜求宝藏；他们不知道怎样撒网。

大海哗笑着涌起波浪，而海滩的微笑荡漾着淡淡的光芒。致人死命的波涛，对着孩子们唱无意义的歌曲，就像一个母亲在摇动她孩子的摇篮时一样。大海和孩子们一同游戏，而海滩的微笑荡漾着淡淡的光芒。

孩子们会集在无边无际的世界的海边。狂风暴雨飘游在无辙迹的天空上，航船沉碎在无辙迹的海水里，死正在外面活动，孩子们却在游戏。在无边无际的世界的海边，孩子们大会集着。

On the Seashore

On the seashore of endless worlds children meet.
The infinite sky is motionless overhead and the restless water is boisterous.
On the seashore of endless worlds the children meet with shouts and dances.

They build their houses with sand, and they play with empty shells. With withered leaves they weave their boats and smilingly float them on the vast deep. Children have their play on the seashore of worlds.

They know not how to swim, they know not how to cast nets. Pearl-fishers dive for pearls, merchants sail in their ships, while children gather pebbles and scatter them again. They seek not for hidden treasures, they know not how to cast nets.

The sea surges up with laughter, and pale gleams the smile of the sea-beach. Death-dealing waves sing meaningless ballads to the children, even like a mother while rocking her baby's cradle. The sea plays with children, and pale gleams the smile of the sea-beach.

On the seashore of endless worlds children meet. Tempest roams in the pathless sky, ships are wrecked in the trackless water, death is abroad and children play. On the seashore of endless worlds is the great meeting of children.

来源

流泛在孩子两眼的睡眠——有谁知道它是从什么地方来的？是的，有个谣传，说它是住在萤火虫朦胧地照耀着林荫的仙村里，在那个地方，挂着两个迷人的胆怯的蓓蕾。它便是从那个地方来吻孩子的两眼的。

当孩子睡时，在他唇上浮动着的微笑——有谁知道它是从什么地方生出来的？是的，有个谣传，说新月的一线年轻的清光，触着将消未消的秋云边上，于是微笑便初生在一个浴在清露里的早晨的梦中了——当孩子睡时，微笑便在他的唇上浮动着。

甜蜜柔嫩的新鲜生气，像花一般地在孩子的四肢上开放着——有谁知道它在什么地方藏得这么久？是的，当妈妈还是一个少女的时候，它已在爱的温柔而沉静的神秘中，潜伏在她的心里了——甜蜜柔嫩的新鲜生气，像花一般地在孩子的四肢上开放着。

The Source

The sleep that flits on baby's eyes—does anybody know from where it comes? Yes, there is a rumour that it has its dwelling where, in the fairy village among shadows of the forest dimly lit with glow-worms, there hang two shy buds of enchantment. From there it comes to kiss baby's eyes.

The smile that flickers on baby's lips when he sleeps—does anybody know where it was born? Yes, there is a rumour that a young pale beam of a crescent moon touched the edge of a vanishing autumn cloud, and there the smile was first born in the dream of a dew-washed morning—the smile that flickers on baby's lips when he sleeps.

The sweet, soft freshness that blooms on baby's limbs—does anybody know where it was hidden so long? Yes, when the mother was a young girl it lay pervading her heart in tender and silent mystery of love—the sweet, soft freshness that has bloomed on baby's limbs.

孩童之道

只要孩子愿意，他此刻便可飞上天去。

他所以不离开我们，并不是没有原故[①]。

他爱把他的头倚在妈妈的胸间，他即使是一刻不见她，也是不行的。

孩子知道各式各样的聪明话，虽然世间的人很少懂得这些话的意义。

他所以永不想说，并不是没有原故。

他所要做的一件事，就是要学习从妈妈的嘴唇里说出来的话。那就是他所以看来这样天真的原故。

孩子有成堆的黄金与珠子，但他到这个世界上来，却像一个乞丐。

他所以这样假装了来，并不是没有原故。

这个可爱的小小的裸着身体的乞丐，所以假装着完全无助的样子，便是想要乞求妈妈的爱的财富。

孩子在纤小的新月的世界里，是一切束缚都没有的。

他所以放弃了他的自由，并不是没有原故。

① 同“缘故”。由于译者翻译时间问题，书中部分词汇与现今通行用法不一致。为了保持原译著风貌，编者未做更正，特此说明。

他知道有无穷的快乐藏在妈妈的心的小小一隅里，被妈妈亲爱的手臂拥抱着，其甜美远胜过自由。

孩子永不知道如何哭泣。他所住的是完全的乐土。

他所以要流泪，并不是没有原故。

虽然他用了可爱的脸儿上的微笑，引逗得他妈妈的热切的心向着他，然而他的因为细故而发的小小的哭声，却编成了怜与爱的双重约束的带子。

Baby's Way

If baby only wanted to, he could fly up to heaven this moment.
It is not for nothing that he does not leave us.
He loves to rest his head on mother's bosom, and cannot ever bear to lose sight of her.

Baby knows all manner of wise words, though few on earth can understand their meaning.
It is not for nothing that he never wants to speak.
The one thing he wants is to learn mother's words from mother's lips.
That is why he looks so innocent.

Baby had a heap of gold and pearls, yet he came like a beggar on to this earth.
It is not for nothing he came in such a disguise.
This dear little naked mendicant pretends to be utterly helpless, so that he may beg for mother's wealth of love.

Baby was so free from every tie in the land of the tiny crescent moon.
It was not for nothing he gave up his freedom.
He knows that there is room for endless joy in mother's little corner of a heart, and it is sweeter far than liberty to be caught and pressed in her dear arms.

Baby never knew how to cry. He dwelt in the land of perfect bliss.
It is not for nothing he has chosen to shed tears.
Though with the smile of his dear face he draws mother's yearning heart to him, yet his little cries over tiny troubles weave the double bond of pity and love.

不被注意的花饰

呵，谁给那件小外衫染上颜色的，我的孩子？谁使你的温软的肢体穿上那件红色小外衫的？

你在早晨就跑出来到天井里玩儿，你，跑着就像摇摇欲跌似的。

但是谁给那件小外衫染上颜色的，我的孩子？

什么事叫你大笑起来的，我的小小的命芽儿？

妈妈站在门边，微笑地望着你。

她拍着双手，她的手镯叮当地响着；你手里拿着你的竹竿儿在跳舞，活像一个小小的牧童儿。

但是什么事叫你大笑起来的，我的小小的命芽儿？

喔，乞丐，你双手攀搂住妈妈的头颈，要乞讨些什么？

喔，贪得无厌的心，要我把整个世界从天上摘下来，像摘一个果子似的，把它放在你的一双小小的玫瑰色的手掌上么？

喔，乞丐，你要乞讨些什么？

风高兴地带走了你踝铃的叮当。

太阳微笑着，望着你的打扮。

当你睡在你妈妈的臂弯里时，天空在上面望着你，而早晨蹑手蹑脚地走到你的床跟前，吻着你的双眼。

风高兴地带走了你踝铃的叮当。

仙乡里的梦婆飞过朦胧的天空，向你飞来。

在你妈妈的心头上，那世界母亲，正和你坐在一块儿。

他，向星星奏乐的人，正拿着他的横笛，站在你的窗边。

仙乡里的梦婆飞过朦胧的天空，向你飞来。

The Unheeded Pageant

Ah, who was it coloured that little frock, my child, and covered your sweet limbs with that little red tunic?
You have come out in the morning to play in the courtyard, tottering and tumbling as you run.
But who was it coloured that little frock, my child?

What is it makes you laugh, my little life-bud?
Mother smiles at you standing on the threshold.
She claps her hands and her bracelets jingle, and you dance with your bamboo stick in your hand like a tiny little shepherd.
But what is it makes you laugh, my little life-bud?

O beggar, what do you beg for, clinging to your mother's neck with both your hands?
O greedy heart, shall I pluck the world like a fruit from the sky to place it on your little rosy palm?
O beggar, what are you begging for?

The wind carries away in glee the tinkling of your anklet bells.
The sun smiles and watches your toilet.
The sky watches over you when you sleep in your mother's arms, and the morning comes tiptoe to your bed and kisses your eyes.
The wind carries away in glee the tinkling of your anklet bells.

The fairy mistress of dreams is coming towards you, flying through the twilight sky.
The world-mother keeps her seat by you in your mother's heart.
He who plays his music to the stars is standing at your window with his flute.
And the fairy mistress of dreams is coming towards you, flying through the twilight sky.

偷睡眠者

谁从孩子的眼里把睡眠偷了去呢？我一定要知道。

妈妈把她的水罐挟在腰间，走到近村汲水去了。

这是正午的时候。孩子们游戏的时间已经过去了；池中的鸭子沉默无声。

牧童躺在榕树的荫下睡着了。

白鹤庄重而安静地立在芒果树边的泥泽里。

就在这个时候，偷睡眠者跑来从孩子的两眼里捉住睡眠，便飞去了。

当妈妈回来时，她看见孩子四肢着地地在屋里爬着。

谁从孩子的眼里把睡眠偷了去呢？我一定要知道。我一定要找到她，把她锁起来。

我一定要向那个黑洞里张望。在这个洞里，有一道小泉从圆的和有皱纹的石上滴下来。

我一定要到醉花[1]林中的沉寂的树影里搜寻。在这林中鸽子在它们住的地方咕咕地叫着，仙女的脚环在繁星满天的静夜里叮当地响着。

我要在黄昏时，向静静的萧萧的竹林里窥望。在这林中，萤火虫闪闪地耗费它们的光明，只要遇见一个人，我便要问他："谁能告诉我偷睡眠者住在什么地方？"

谁从孩子的眼里把睡眠偷了去呢？我一定要知道。

只要我能捉住她，怕不会给她一顿好教训！

我要闯入她的巢穴，看她把所有偷来的睡眠藏在什么地方。

我要把它都夺了来，带回家去。

我要把她的双翼缚得紧紧的，把她放在河边，然后叫她拿一根芦苇，在灯心草和睡莲间钓鱼为戏。

当黄昏，街上已经收了市，村里的孩子们都坐在妈妈的膝上时，夜鸟便会讥笑地在她耳边说：

"你现在还想偷谁的睡眠呢？"

① 印度传说：美女口中吐出香液，此花始开。

Sleep-Stealer

Who stole sleep from baby's eyes? I must know.
Clasping her pitcher to her waist mother went to fetch water from the village near by.
It was noon. The children's playtime was over; the ducks in the pond were silent.
The shepherd boy lay asleep under the shadow of the banyan tree.
The crane stood grave and still in the swamp near the mango grove.
In the meanwhile the Sleep-stealer came and, snatching sleep from baby's eyes, flew away.
When mother came back she found baby travelling the room over on all fours.

Who stole sleep from our baby's eyes? I must know. I must find her and chain her up.

I must look into that dark cave, where, through boulders and scowling stones, trickles a tiny stream.
I must search in the drowsy shade of the bakula grove, where pigeons coo in their corner, and fairies' anklets tinkle in the stillness of starry nights.
In the evening I will peep into the whispering silence of the bamboo forest, where fireflies squander their light, and will ask every creature I meet, "Can anybody tell me where the Sleep-stealer lives?"

Who stole sleep from baby's eyes? I must know.
Shouldn't I give her a good lesson if I could only catch her!
I would raid her nest and see where she hoards all her stolen sleep.
I would plunder it all, and carry it home.
I would bind her two wings securely, set her on the bank of the river, and then let her play at fishing with a reed among the rushes and water-lilies.
When the marketing is over in the evening, and the village children sit in their mothers' laps, then the night birds will mockingly din her ears with:
"Whose sleep will you steal now?"

开始

“我是从哪儿来的？你，在哪儿把我捡起来的？”孩子问他的妈妈说。

她把孩子紧紧地搂在胸前，半哭半笑地答道——

“你曾被我当做心愿藏在我的心里，我的宝贝。

“你曾存在于我孩童时代玩的泥娃娃身上；每天早晨我用泥土塑造我的神像，那时我反复地塑了又捏碎了的就是你。

“你曾和我们的家庭守护神一同受到祀奉，我崇拜家神时也就崇拜了你。

“你曾活在我所有的希望和爱情里，活在我的生命里，我母亲的生命里。

“在主宰着我们家庭的不死的精灵的膝上，你已经被抚育了好多代了。

“当我做女孩子的时候，我的心的花瓣儿张开，你就像一股花香似的散发出来。

“你的软软的温柔，在我青春的肢体上开花了，像太阳出来之前的天空里的一片曙光。

“上天的第一宠儿，晨曦的孪生兄弟，你从世界的生命的溪流浮泛而下，终于停泊在我的心头。

“当我凝视你的脸蛋儿的时候，神秘之感湮没了我；你这属于一切人的，竟成了我的。

“为了怕失掉你，我把你紧紧地搂在胸前。是什么魔术把这世界的宝贝引到我这双纤小的手臂里来的呢？”

The Beginning

"Where have I come from, where did you pick me up?" the baby asked its mother.

She answered half crying, half laughing, and clasping the baby to her breast,—

"You were hidden in my heart as its desire, my darling.

"You were in the dolls of my childhood's games; and when with clay I made the image of my god every morning, I made and unmade you then.

"You were enshrined with our household deity, in his worship I worshipped you.

"In all my hopes and my loves, in my life, in the life of my mother you have lived.

"In the lap of the deathless Spirit who rules our home you have been nursed for ages.

"When in girlhood my heart was opening its petals, you hovered as a fragrance about it.

"Your tender softness bloomed in my youthful limbs, like a glow in the sky before the sunrise.

"Heaven's first darling, twin-born with the morning light, you have floated down the stream of the world's life, and at last you have stranded on my heart.

"As I gaze on your face, mystery overwhelms me; you who belong to all have become mine.

"For fear of losing you I hold you tight to my breast. What magic has snared the world's treasure in these slender arms of mine?"

孩子的世界

我愿我能在我孩子自己的世界的中心，占一角清净地。

我知道有星星同他说话，天空也在他面前垂下，用它呆呆的云朵和彩虹来娱悦他。

那些大家以为他是哑巴的人，那些看去像是永不会走动的人，都带了他们的故事，捧了满装着五颜六色的玩具的盘子，匍匐地来到他的窗前。

我愿我能在横过孩子心中的道路上游行，解脱了一切的束缚；

在那儿，使者奉了无所谓的使命奔走于无史的诸王的王国间；

在那儿，理智以它的法律造为纸鸢而飞放，真理也使事实从桎梏中自由了。

Baby's World

I wish I could take a quiet corner in the heart of
my baby's very own world.
I know it has stars that talk to him, and a sky that
stoops down to his face to amuse him with its
silly clouds and rainbows.
Those who make believe to be dumb, and look
as if they never could move, come creeping to
his window with their stories and with trays
crowded with bright toys.
I wish I could travel by the road that crosses
baby's mind, and out beyond all bounds;
Where messengers run errands for no cause
between the kingdoms of kings of no history;
Where Reason makes kites of her laws and flies
them, and Truth sets Fact free from its fetters.

时候与原因

当我给你五颜六色的玩具的时候，我的孩子，我明白了为什么云上水上是这样的色彩缤纷，为什么花朵上染上绚烂的颜色的原因了——当我给你五颜六色的玩具的时候，我的孩子。

当我唱着使你跳舞的时候，我真的知道了为什么树叶儿响着音乐，为什么波浪把它们的合唱的声音送进静听着的大地的心头的原因了——当我唱着使你跳舞的时候。

当我把糖果送到你贪得无厌的双手上的时候，我知道了为什么花萼里会有蜜，为什么水果里会秘密地充溢了甜汁的原因了——当我把糖果送到你贪得无厌的双手上的时候。

当我吻着你的脸蛋儿叫你微笑的时候，我的宝贝，我的确明白了在晨光里从天上流下来的是什么样的快乐，而夏天的微飔吹拂在我的身体上的又是什么样的爽快——当我吻着你的脸蛋儿叫你微笑的时候。

When and Why

When I bring you coloured toys, my child, I understand why there is such a play of colours on clouds, on water, and why flowers are painted in tints—when I give coloured toys to you, my child.

When I sing to make you dance, I truly know why there is music in leaves, and why waves send their chorus of voices to the heart of the listening earth—when I sing to make you dance.

When I bring sweet things to your greedy hands, I know why there is honey in the cup of the flower, and why fruits are secretly filled with sweet juice—when I bring sweet things to your greedy hands.

When I kiss your face to make you smile, my darling, I surely understand what pleasure streams from the sky in morning light, and what delight the summer breeze brings to my body—when I kiss you to make you smile.

责备

为什么你眼里有了眼泪，我的孩子？

他们真是可怕，常常无谓地责备你！

你写字时墨水玷污了你的手和脸——这就是他们所以骂你龌龊的原故么？

呵，呸！他们也敢因为圆圆的月儿用墨水涂了脸，便骂它龌龊么？

他们总要为了每一件小事去责备你，我的孩子。他们总是无谓地寻人错处。

你游戏时扯破了衣服——这就是他们说你不整洁的原故？

呵，呸！秋之晨从它的破碎的云衣中露出微笑，那末，他们要叫它什么呢？

他们对你说什么话，尽管可以不去理睬他，我的孩子。

他们把你做错的事长长地记了一笔账。

谁都知道你是十分喜欢糖果的——这就是他们所以称你贪婪的原故么？

呵，呸！我们是喜欢你的，那末他们要叫我们什么呢？

Defamation

Why are those tears in your eyes, my child?
How horrid of them to be always scolding you for nothing?
You have stained your fingers and face with ink while writing—is that why they call you dirty?
O, fie! Would they dare to call the full moon dirty because it has smudged its face with ink?

For every little trifle they blame you, my child. They are ready to find fault for nothing.
You tore your clothes while playing—is that why they call you untidy?
O, fie! What would they call an autumn morning that smiles through its ragged clouds?

Take no heed of what they say to you, my child.
They make a long list of your misdeeds.
Everybody knows how you love sweet things—is that why they call you greedy?
O, fie! What then would they call us who love you?

审判官

你想说他什么尽管说罢，但是我知道我孩子的短处。

我爱他并不因为他好，只是因为他是我的小小的孩子。

你如果把他的好处与坏处两两相权，你怎会知道他是如何的可爱呢？

当我必须责罚他的时候，他更成为我生命的一部分了。

当我使他的眼泪流出时，我的心也和他同哭了。

只有我才有权去骂他，去责备他；因为只有热爱人的人才可以惩戒人。

The Judge

Say of him what you please, but I know my child's failings.

I love him not because he is good, but because he is my little child.

How should you know how dear he can be when you try to weigh his merits against his faults?

When I must punish him he becomes all the more a part of my being.

When I cause his tears to come my heart weeps with him.

I alone have a right to blame and punish, for he only may chastise who loves.

玩具

孩子，你真是快活呀！一早晨坐在泥土里，耍着折下来的小树枝儿。

我微笑着看你在那里耍弄那根折下来的小树枝儿。

我正忙着算账，一小时一小时在那里加叠数字。

也许你在看我，心想："这种好没趣的游戏，竟把你一早晨的好时间浪费掉了！"

孩子，我忘了聚精会神玩耍树枝与泥饼的方法了。

我寻求贵重的玩具，收集金块与银块。

你呢，无论找到什么便去做你的快乐的游戏；我呢，却把我的时间与力气都浪费在那些我永不能得到的东西上。

我在我的脆薄的独木船里挣扎着，要航过欲望之海，竟忘了我也是在那里做游戏了。

Playthings

Child, how happy you are sitting in the dust, playing with a broken twig all the morning.

I smile at your play with that little bit of a broken twig.

I am busy with my accounts, adding up figures by the hour.

Perhaps you glance at me and think, "What a stupid game to spoil your morning with!"

Child, I have forgotten the art of being absorbed in sticks and mud-pies.

I seek out costly playthings, and gather lumps of gold and silver.

With whatever you find you create your glad games, I spend both my time and my strength over things I never can obtain.

In my frail canoe I struggle to cross the sea of desire, and forget that I too am playing a game.

天文家

我不过说:“当傍晚圆圆的满月挂在迦昙波①的枝头时，有人能去捉住它么?”

哥哥却对我笑道:“孩子呀，你真是我所见到的顶顶傻的孩子。月亮离我们这样远，谁能去捉住它呢?”

我说:“哥哥，你真傻！当妈妈向窗外探望，微笑着往下看我们游戏时，你也能说她远么?”

哥哥还是说:“你这个傻孩子！但是，孩子，你到哪里去找一个大得能逮住月亮的网呢?”

我说:“你自然可以用双手去捉住它呀。”

但哥哥还是笑着说:“你真是我所见到的顶顶傻的孩子！如果月亮走近了，你便知道它是多么大了。”

我说:“哥哥，你们学校里所教的，真是没有用呀！当妈妈低下脸儿跟我们亲嘴时，她的脸看来也是很大的么?”

但哥哥还是说:“你真是一个傻孩子。”

① 意译“白花”，即昙花。

The Astronomer

I only said, "When in the evening the round full moon gets entangled among the branches of that Kadam tree, couldn't somebody catch it?"
But dada [elder brother] laughed at me and said, "Baby, you are the silliest child I have ever known. The moon is ever so far from us, how could anybody catch it?"
I said, "Dada how foolish you are! When mother looks out of her window and smiles down at us playing, would you call her far away?"
Still said, "You are a stupid child! But, baby, where could you find a net big enough to catch the moon with?"
I said, "Surely you could catch it with your hands."
But dada laughed and said, "You are the silliest child I have known. If it came nearer, you would see how big the moon is."
I said, "Dada, what nonsense they teach at your school! When mother bends her face down to kiss us does her face look very big?"
But still dada says, "You are a stupid child."

云与波

妈妈，住在云端的人对我唤道——

“我们从醒的时候游戏到白日终止。

“我们与黄金色的曙光游戏，我们与银白色的月亮游戏。”

我问道：“但是，我怎么能够上你那里去呢？”

他们答道：“你到地球的边上来，举手向天，就可以被接到云端里来了。”

“我妈妈在家里等我呢，”我说，“我怎么能离开她而来呢？”

于是他们微笑着浮游而去。

但是我知道一件比这更好的游戏，妈妈。

我做云，你做月亮。

我用两只手遮盖你，我们的屋顶就是青碧的天空。

住在波浪上的人对我唤道——

“我们从早晨唱歌到晚上；我们前进又前进地旅行，也不知我们所经过的是什么地方。”

我问道：“但是，我怎么才能加入你们的队伍呢？”

他们告诉我说：“来到岸旁，站在那里，紧闭你的两眼，你就被带到波浪上来了。”

我说：“傍晚的时候，我妈妈常要我在家里——我怎么能离开她而去呢？”

于是他们微笑着，跳舞着奔流过去。

但是我知道一件比这更好的游戏。

我是波浪，你是陌生的岸。

我奔流而进，进，进，笑哈哈地撞碎在你的膝上。

世界上就没有一个人会知道我们俩在什么地方。

Clouds and Waves

Mother, the folk who live up in the clouds call out to me—
"We play from the time we wake till the day ends.
"We play with the golden dawn, we play with the silver moon."
I ask, "But, how am I to get up to you?"
They answer, "Come to the edge of the earth, lift up your hands to the sky, and you will be taken up into the clouds."
"My mother is waiting for me at home,"
I say. "How can I leave her and come?"
Then they smile and float away.
But I know a nicer game than that, mother.
I shall be the cloud and you the moon.
I shall cover you with both my hands, and our house-top will be the blue sky.

The folk who live in the waves call out to me—
"We sing from morning till night; on and on we travel and know not where we pass."
I ask, "But, how am I to join you?"
They tell me, "Come to the edge of the shore and stand with your eyes tight shut, and you will be carried out upon the waves."
I say, "My mother always wants me at home in the evening—how can I leave her and go?"
Then they smile, dance and pass by.
But I know a better game than that.
I will be the waves and you will be a strange shore.
I shall roll on and on and on, and break upon your lap with laughter.
And no one in the world will know where we both are.

金色花

假如我变了一朵金色花[①]，为了好玩，长在树的高枝上，笑嘻嘻地在空中摇摆，又在新叶上跳舞，妈妈，你会认识我么?

你要是叫道:“孩子，你在哪里呀?”我暗暗地在那里匿笑，却一声儿不响。

我要悄悄地开放花瓣儿，看着你工作。

当你沐浴后，湿发披在两肩，穿过金色花的林荫，走到做祷告的小庭院时，你会嗅到这花香，却不知道这香气是从我身上来的。

当你吃过午饭，坐在窗前读《罗摩衍那》[②]，那棵树的阴影落在你的头发与膝上时，我便要将我小小的影子投在你的书页上，正投在你所读的地方。

但是你会猜得出这就是你孩子的小小影子么?

当你黄昏时拿了灯到牛棚里去，我便要突然地再落到地上来，又成了你的孩子，求你讲故事给我听。

“你到哪里去了，你这坏孩子?”

“我不告诉你，妈妈。”这就是你同我那时所要说的话了。

---

① 印度圣树，木兰花属植物，开金黄色碎花。译名亦作“瞻波伽”或“占波”。

② 印度的一部叙事诗，相传系第五世纪 Valmiki 所作。全诗二万四千章，分为七卷。

The Champa Flower

Supposing I became a champa flower, just for fun, and grew on a branch high up that tree, and shook in the wind with laughter and danced upon the newly budded leaves, would you know me, mother?

You would call, "Baby, where are you?" and I should laugh to myself and keep quite quiet.

I should slyly open my petals and watch you at your work.

When after your bath, with wet hair spread on your shoulders, you walked through the shadow of the champa tree to the little court where you say your prayers, you would notice the scent of the flower, but not know that it came from me.

When after the midday meal you sat at the window reading Ramayana, and the tree's shadow fell over your hair and your lap, I should fling my wee little shadow on to the page of your book, just where you were reading.

But would you guess that it was the tiny shadow of your little child?

When in the evening you went to the cow-shed with the lighted lamp in your hand, I should suddenly drop on to the earth again and be your own baby once more, and beg you to tell me a story.

"Where have you been, you naughty child?"

"I won't tell you, mother." That's what you and I would say then.

仙人世界

如果人们知道了我的国王的宫殿在哪里，它就会消失在空气中的。

墙壁是白色的银，屋顶是耀眼的黄金。

皇后住在有七个庭院的宫苑里；她戴的一串珠宝，值得整整七个王国的全部财富。

不过，让我悄悄地告诉你，妈妈，我的国王的宫殿究竟在哪里。

它就在我们阳台的角上，在那栽着杜尔茜花的花盆放着的地方。

公主躺在远远的、隔着七个不可逾越的重洋的那一岸沉睡着。

除了我自己，世界上便没有人能够找到她。

她臂上有镯子，她耳上挂着珍珠，她的头发拖到地板上。

当我用我的魔杖点触她的时候，她就会醒过来；而当她微笑时，珠玉将会从她唇边落下来。

不过，让我在你的耳朵边悄悄地告诉你，妈妈，她就住在我们阳台的角上，在那栽着杜尔茜花的花盆放着的地方。

当你要到河里洗澡的时候，你走上屋顶的那座阳台来罢。

我就坐在墙的阴影所聚会的一个角落里。

我只让小猫儿跟我在一起，因为它知道那故事里的理发匠到底住在哪里。

不过，让我悄悄地告诉你，妈妈，故事里的理发匠到底住在哪里。

他住的地方，就在阳台的角上，在那栽着杜尔茜花的花盆放着的地方。

Fairyland

If people came to know where my king's palace is, it would vanish into the air.
The walls are of white silver and the roof of shining gold.
The queen lives in a palace with seven courtyards, and she wears a jewel that cost all the wealth of seven kingdoms.
But let me tell you, mother, in a whisper, where my king's palace is.
It is at the corner of our terrace where the pot of the tulsi plant stands.

The princess lies sleeping on the far-away shore of the seven impassable seas.
There is none in the world who can find her but myself.
She has bracelets on her arms and pearl drops in her ears; her hair sweeps down upon the floor.
She will wake when I touch her with my magic wand, and jewels will fall from her lips when she smiles.
But let me whisper in your ear, mother; she is there in the corner of our terrace where the pot of the tulsi plant stands.

When it is time for you to go to the river for your bath, step up to that terrace on the roof.
I sit in the corner where the shadows of the walls meet together.
Only puss is allowed to come with me, for she knows where the barber in the story lives.
But let me whisper, mother, in your ear where the barber in the story lives.
It is at the corner of the terrace where the pot of the tulsi plant stands.

流放的地方

妈妈，天空上的光成了灰色了；我不知道是什么时候了。

我玩得怪没劲儿的，所以到你这里来了。这是星期六，是我们的休息日。

放下你的活计，妈妈，坐在靠窗的一边，告诉我童话里的特潘塔沙漠在什么地方?

雨的影子遮掩了整个白天。

凶猛的电光用它的爪子抓着天空。

当乌云在轰轰地响着，天打着雷的时候，我总爱心里带着恐惧爬伏到你的身上。

当大雨倾泻在竹叶子上好几个钟头，而我们的窗户为狂风震得格格发响的时候，我就爱独自和你坐在屋里，妈妈，听你讲童话里的特潘塔沙漠的故事。

它在哪里，妈妈？在哪一个海洋的岸上？在哪些个山峰的脚下？在哪一个国王的国土里？

田地上没有此疆彼壤的界石，也没有村人在黄昏时走回家的或妇人在树林里捡拾枯枝而捆载到市场上去的道路。沙地上只有一小块一小块的黄色草地，只有一株树，就是那一对聪明的老鸟儿在那里做窝的，那个地方就是特潘塔沙漠。

我能够想象得到，就在这样一个乌云密布的日子，国王的年轻的儿子，怎样独自骑着一匹灰色马，走过这个沙漠，去寻找那被囚禁在不可知的重洋之外的巨人宫里的公主。

当雨雾在遥远的天空下降，电光像一阵突然发作的痛楚的痉挛似的闪射的时候，他可记得他的不幸的母亲，为国王所弃，正在打扫牛棚，眼里流着眼泪，当他骑马走过童话里的特潘塔沙漠的时候？

看，妈妈，一天还没有完，天色就差不多黑了，那边村庄的路上没有什么旅客了。

牧童早就从牧场上回家了，人们都已从田地里回来，坐在他们草屋檐下的草席上，眼望着阴沉的云块。

妈妈，我把我所有的书本都放在书架上了——不要叫我现在做功课。

当我长大了，大得像爸爸一样的时候，我将会学到必须学到的东西的。

但是，今天你可得告诉我，妈妈，童话里的特潘塔沙漠在什么地方？

The Land of the Exile

Mother, the light has grown grey in the sky; I do not know what the time is.

There is no fun in my play, so I have come to you. It is Saturday, our holiday.

Leave off your work, mother; sit here by the window and tell me where the desert of Tepantar in the fairy tale is?

The shadow of the rains has covered the day from end to end.

The fierce lightning is scratching the sky with its nails.

When the clouds rumble and it thunders, I love to be afraid in my heart and cling to you.

When the heavy rain patters for hours on the bamboo leaves, and our windows shake and rattle at the gusts of wind, I like to sit alone in the room, mother, with you, and hear you talk about the desert of Tepantar in the fairy tale.

Where is it, mother, on the shore of what sea, at the foot of what hills, in the kingdom of what king?

There are no hedges there to mark the fields, no footpath across it by which the villagers reach their village in the evening, or the woman who gathers dry sticks in the forest can bring her load to the market. With patches of yellow grass in the sand and only one tree where the pair of wise old birds have their nest, lies the desert of Tepantar.

I can imagine how, on just such a cloudy day, the young son of the king is riding alone on a grey horse through the desert, in search of the princess who lies imprisoned in the giant's palace across that unknown water.

When the haze of the rain comes down in the distant sky, and lightning starts up like a sudden fit of pain, does he remember his

unhappy mother, abandoned by the king, sweeping the cow-stall and wiping her eyes, while he rides through the desert of Tepantar in the fairy tale?

See, mother, it is almost dark before the day is over, and there are no travellers yonder on the village road.

The shepherd boy has gone home early from the pasture, and men have left their fields to sit on mats under the eaves of their huts, watching the scowling clouds.

Mother, I have left all my books on the shelf—do not ask me to do my lessons now.

When I grow up and am big like my father, I shall learn all that must be learnt.

But just for today, tell me, mother, where the desert of Tepantar in the fairy tale is?

雨天

乌云很快地集拢在森林的黝黑的边缘上。

孩子，不要出去呀！

湖边的一行棕树，向暝暗的天空撞着头；羽毛零乱的乌鸦，静悄悄地栖在罗望子树的枝上。河的东岸正被乌沉沉的暝色所侵袭。

我们的牛系在篱上，高声鸣叫。

孩子，在这里等着，等我先把牛牵进牛棚里去。

许多人都挤在池水泛溢的田间，捉那从泛溢的池中逃出来的鱼儿。雨水成了小河，流过狭衖，好像一个嬉笑的孩子从他妈妈那里跑开，故意要恼她一样。

听呀，有人在浅滩上喊船夫呢。

孩子，天色暝暗了，渡头的摆渡已经停了。

天空好像是在滂沱的雨上快跑着；河里的水喧叫而且暴躁；妇人们早已拿着汲满了水的水罐，从恒河畔匆匆地回家了。

夜里用的灯，一定要预备好。

孩子，不要出去呀！

到市场去的大道已没有人走，到河边去的小路又很滑。风在竹林里咆哮着，挣扎着，好像一只落在网中的野兽。

The Rainy Day

Sullen clouds are gathering fast over the black fringe of the forest.
O child, do not go out!
The palm trees in a row by the lake are smiting their heads against the dismal sky; the crows with their draggled wings are silent on the tamarind branches, and the eastern bank of the river is haunted by a deepening gloom.

Our cow is lowing loud, tied at the fence.
O child, wait here till I bring her into the stall.
Men have crowded into the flooded field to catch the fishes as they escape from the overflowing ponds; the rain water is running in rills through the narrow lanes like a laughing boy who has run away from his mother to tease her.

Listen, someone is shouting for the boatman at the ford.
O child, the daylight is dim, and the crossing at the ferry is closed.
The sky seems to ride fast upon the madly-rushing rain; the water in the river is loud and impatient; women have hastened home early from the Ganges with their filled pitchers.
The evening lamps must be made ready.
O child, do not go out!
The road to the market is desolate, the lane to the river is slippery. The wind is roaring and struggling among the bamboo branches like a wild beast tangled in a net.

纸船

我每天把纸船一个个放在急流的溪中。

我用大黑字把我的名字和我住的村名写在纸船上。

我希望住在异地的人会得到这纸船，知道我是谁。

我把园中长的秀利花载在我的小船上，希望这些黎明开的花能在夜里被平平安安地带到岸上。

我把我的纸船投到水里，仰望天空，看见小朵的云正张着满鼓着风的白帆。

我不知道天上有我的什么游伴把这些船放下来同我的船比赛！

夜来了，我的脸埋在手臂里，梦见我的纸船在子夜的星光下缓缓地浮泛向前。

睡仙坐在船里，带着满载着梦的篮子。

Paper Boats

Day by day I float my paper boats one by one down the running stream.
In big black letters I write my name on them and the name of the village where I live.
I hope that someone in some strange land will find them and know who I am.
I load my little boats with shiuli flowers from our garden, and hope that these blooms of the dawn will be carried safely to land in the night.
I launch my paper boats and look up into the sky and see the little clouds setting their white bulging sails.
I know not what playmate of mine in the sky sends them down the air to race with my boats!
When night comes I bury my face in my arms and dream that my paper boats float on and on under the midnight stars.
The fairies of sleep are sailing in them, and the lading is their baskets full of dreams.

水手

船夫曼特胡的船只停泊在拉琪根琪码头。

这只船无用地装载着黄麻，无所事事地停泊在那里已经好久了。

只要他肯把他的船借给我，我就给它安装一百只桨，扬起五个或六个或七个布帆来。

我决不把它驾驶到愚蠢的市场上去。

我将航行遍仙人世界里的七个大海和十三条河道。

但是，妈妈，你不会躲在角落里为我哭泣。

我不会像罗摩犍陀罗[①]似的，到森林中去，一去十四年才回来。

我将成为故事中的王子，把我的船装满了我所喜欢的东西。

我将带我的朋友阿细和我做伴。我们要快快乐乐地航行于仙人世界里的七个大海和十三条河道。

我将在绝早的晨光里张帆航行。

中午，你正在池塘里洗澡的时候，我们将在一个陌生的国王的国土上了。

我们将经过特浦尼浅滩，把特潘塔沙漠抛落在我们的后边。

当我们回来的时候，天色快黑了，我将告诉你我们所见到的一切。

我将越过仙人世界里的七个大海和十三条河道。

① 即罗摩。他是印度叙事诗《罗摩衍那》中的主角。为了尊重父亲的诺言和维持弟兄间的友爱，他抛弃了继承王位的权利，和妻子悉多在森林中被放逐了十四年。

The Sailor

The boat of the boatman Madhu is moored at the wharf of Rajgunj.
It is uselessly laden with jute, and has been lying there idle for ever so long.
If he would only lend me his boat, I should man her with a hundred oars, and hoist sails, five or six or seven.
I should never steer her to stupid markets. I should sail the seven seas and the thirteen rivers of fairyland.
But, mother, you won't weep for me in a corner.
I am not going into the forest like Ramachandra to come back only after fourteen years.
I shall becomc the prince of the story, and fill my boat with whatever I like.
I shall take my friend Ashu with me. We shall sail merrily across the seven seas and the thirteen rivers of fairyland.
We shall set sail in the early morning light.
When at noontide you are bathing at the pond, we shall be in the land of a strange king.
We shall pass the ford of Tirpurni, and leave behind us the desert of Tepantar.
When we come back it will be getting dark, and I shall tell you of all that we have seen.
I shall cross the seven seas and the thirteen rivers of fairyland.

对岸

我渴想到河的对岸去，

在那边，好些船只一行儿系在竹竿上；

人们在早晨乘船渡过那边去，肩上扛着犁头，去耕耘他们的远处的田；

在那边，牧人使他们鸣叫着的牛游泳到河旁的牧场去；

黄昏的时候，他们都回家了，只留下豺狼在这满长着野草的岛上哀叫。

妈妈，如果你不在意，我长大的时候，要做这渡船的船夫。

据说有好些古怪的池塘藏在这个高岸之后。

雨过去了，一群一群的野鹜飞到那里去。茂盛的芦苇在岸边四围生长，水鸟在那里生蛋；

竹鸡带着跳舞的尾巴，将它们细小的足印印在洁净的软泥上；

黄昏的时候，长草顶着白花，邀月光在长草的波浪上浮游。

妈妈，如果你不在意，我长大的时候，要做这渡船的船夫。

我要自此岸至彼岸，渡过来，渡过去，所有村中正在那儿沐浴的男孩女孩，都要诧异地望着我。

太阳升到中天，早晨变为正午了，我将跑到你那里去，说道："妈妈，我饿了！"

一天完了，影子俯伏在树底下，我便要在黄昏中回家来。

我将永不像爸爸那样，离开你到城里去做事。

妈妈，如果你不在意，我长大的时候，要做这渡船的船夫。

The Further Bank

I long to go over there to the further
bank of the river.
Where those boats are tied to the
bamboo poles in a line;
Where men cross over in their boats
in the morning with ploughs on their
shoulders to till their far-away fields;
Where the cowherds make their lowing
cattle swim across to the riverside
pasture;
Where they all come back home in the
evening, leaving the jackals to howl in
the island overgrown with weeds.
Mother, if you don't mind, I should like
to become the boatman of the ferryboat
when I am grown up.

They say there are strange pools hidden
behind that high bank,
Where flocks of wild ducks come when
the rains are over, and thick reeds grow
round the margins where waterbirds lay
their eggs;
Where snipes with their dancing tails
stamp their tiny footprints upon the
clean soft mud;
Where in the evening the tall grasses
crested with white flowers invite the
moonbeam to float upon their waves.
Mother, if you don't mind, I should like
to become the boatman of the ferryboat
when I am grown up.

I shall cross and cross back from bank
to bank, and all the boys and girls of the
village will wonder at me while they are
bathing.
When the sun climbs the mid sky and
morning wears on to noon, I shall come
running to you, saying, "Mother, I am
hungry!"
When the day is done and the shadows
cower under the trees, I shall come back
in the dusk.
I shall never go away from you into the
town to work like father.
Mother, if you don't mind, I should like
to become the boatman of the ferryboat
when I am grown up.

花的学校

当雷云在天上轰响，六月的阵雨落下的时候，

润湿的东风走过荒野，在竹林中吹着口笛。

于是一群一群的花从无人知道的地方突然跑出来，在绿草上狂欢地跳着舞。

妈妈，我真的觉得那群花朵是在地下的学校里上学。

它们关了门做功课。如果它们想在散学以前出来游戏，它们的老师是要罚它们站壁角的。

雨一来，它们便放假了。

树枝在林中互相碰触着，绿叶在狂风里萧萧地响，雷云拍着大手。这时花孩子们便穿了紫的、黄的、白的衣裳，冲了出来。

你可知道，妈妈，它们的家是在天上，在星星所住的地方。

你没有看见它们怎样地急着要到那儿去么？你不知道它们为什么那样急急忙忙么？

我自然能够猜得出它们是对谁扬起双臂来：它们也有它们的妈妈，就像我有我自己的妈妈一样。

The Flower-School

When storm clouds rumble in the sky
and June showers come down,
The moist east wind comes marching
over the heath to blow its bagpipes
among the bamboos.
Then crowds of flowers come out of a
sudden, from nobody knows where, and
dance upon the grass in wild glee.

Mother, I really think the flowers go to
school underground.
They do their lessons with doors shut,
and if they want to come out to play
before it is time, their master makes
them stand in a corner.

When the rains come they have their
holidays.
Branches clash together in the forest,
and the leaves rustle in the wild wind,
the thunder-clouds clap their giant
hands and the flower children rush out
in dresses of pink and yellow and white.

Do you know, mother, their home is in
the sky, where the stars are.
Haven't you seen how eager they are to
get there? Don't you know why they are
in such a hurry?
Of course, I can guess to whom they
raise their arms: they have their mother
as I have my own.

商人

妈妈，让我们想象，你待在家里，我到异邦去旅行。

再想象，我的船已经装得满满的，在码头上等候启碇了。

现在，妈妈，你想一想告诉我，回来时我要带些什么给你。

妈妈，你要一堆一堆的黄金么？

在金河的两岸，田野里全是金色的稻实。

在林荫的路上，金色花也一朵一朵地落在地上。

我要为你把它们全都收拾起来，放在好几百个篮子里。

妈妈，你要秋天的雨点一般大的珍珠么？

我要渡海到珍珠岛的岸上去。

那个地方，在清晨的曙光里，珠子在草地的野花上颤动，珠子落在绿草上，珠子被汹狂的海浪一大把一大把地撒在沙滩上。

我的哥哥呢，我要送他一对有翼的马，会在云端飞翔的。

爸爸呢，我要带一支有魔力的笔给他，他还没有感觉到，笔就写出字来了。

你呢，妈妈，我要把值七个王国的首饰箱和珠宝送给你。

The Merchant

Imagine, mother, that you are to stay at home and I am to travel into strange lands.
Imagine that my boat is ready at the landing fully laden.
Now think well, mother, before you say what I shall bring for you when I come back.

Mother, do you want heaps and heaps of gold?
There, by the banks of golden streams, fields are full of golden harvest.
And in the shade of the forest path the golden champa flowers drop on the ground.
I will gather them all for you in many hundred baskets.

Mother, do you want pearls big as the raindrops of autumn?
I shall cross to the pearl island shore.
There in the early morning light pearls tremble on the meadow flowers, pearls drop on the grass, and pearls are scattered on the sand in spray by the wild sea-waves.
My brother shall have a pair of horses with wings to fly among the clouds.
For father I shall bring a magic pen that, without his knowing, will write of itself.
For you, mother, I must have the casket and jewel that cost seven kings their kingdoms.

同情

如果我只是一只小狗，而不是你的小孩，亲爱的妈妈，当我想吃你盘里的东西时，你要向我说“不”么？

你要赶开我，对我说道，“滚开，你这淘气的小狗”么？

那末，走罢，妈妈，走罢！当你叫唤我的时候，我就永不到你那里去，也永不要你再喂我吃东西了。

如果我只是一只绿色的小鹦鹉，而不是你的小孩，亲爱的妈妈，你要把我紧紧地锁住，怕我飞走么？

你要对我指指点点地说道，“怎样的一只不知感恩的贱鸟呀！整日整夜地尽在咬它的链子”么？

那末，走罢，妈妈，走罢！我要跑到树林里去；我就永不再让你将我抱在你的臂里了。

Sympathy

If I were only a little puppy, not your baby, mother dear, would you say "No" to me if I tried to eat from your dish? Would you drive me off, saying to me, "Get away, you naughty little puppy?" Then go, mother, go! I will never come to you when you call me, and never let you feed me any more.

If I were only a little green parrot, and not your baby, mother dear, would you keep me chained lest I should fly away? Would you shake your finger at me and say, "What an ungrateful wretch of a bird! It is gnawing at its chain day and night?"
Then, go, mother, go! I will run away into the woods; I will never let you take me in your arms again.

职业

早晨，钟敲十下的时候，我沿着我们的小巷到学校去。

每天我都遇见那个小贩，他叫道："镯子呀，亮晶晶的镯子！"

他没有什么事情急着要做，他没有哪条街道一定要走，他没有什么地方一定要去，他没有什么规定的时间一定要回家。

我愿意我是一个小贩，在街上过日子，叫着："镯子呀，亮晶晶的镯子！"

下午四点钟，我从学校里回家。

从一家门口，我看见一个园丁在那里掘地。

他用他的锄子，要怎么掘，便怎么掘，他被尘土污了衣裳。如果他被太阳晒黑了或是身上被打湿了，都没有人骂他。

我愿意我是一个园丁，在花园里掘地，谁也不来阻止我。

天色刚黑，妈妈就送我上床。

从开着的窗口，我看见更夫走来走去。

小巷又黑又冷清，路灯立在那里，像一个头上生着一只红眼睛的巨人。

更夫摇着他的提灯，跟他身边的影子一起走着，他一生一次都没有上床去过。

我愿意我是一个更夫，整夜在街上走，提了灯去追逐影子。

Vocation

When the gong sounds ten in the morning and I walk to school by our lane,
Every day I meet the hawker crying, "Bangles, crystal bangles!"
There is nothing to hurry him on, there is no road he must take, no place he must go to, no time when he must come home.
I wish I were a hawker, spending my day in the road, crying, "Bangles, crystal bangles!"

When at four in the afternoon I come back from the school,
I can see through the gate of that house the gardener digging the ground.
He does what he likes with his spade, he soils his clothes with dust, nobody takes him to task if he gets baked in the sun or gets wet.
I wish I were a gardener digging away at the garden with nobody to stop me from digging.

Just as it gets dark in the evening and my mother sends me to bed,
I can see through my open window the watchman walking up and down.
The lane is dark and lonely, and the street-lamp stands like a giant with one red eye in its head.
The watchman swings his lantern and walks with his shadow at his side, and never once goes to bed in his life.
I wish I were a watchman walking the streets all night, chasing the shadows with my lantern.

长者

妈妈，你的孩子真傻！她是那末可笑地不懂事！

她不知道路灯和星星的区别。

当我们玩着把小石子当食物的游戏时，她便以为它们真是吃的东西，竟想放进嘴里去。

当我翻开一本书，放在她面前，要她读“a，b，c”时，她却用手把书页撕了，无端快活地叫起来；你的孩子就是这样做功课的。

当我生气地对她摇头，骂她，说她顽皮时，她却哈哈大笑，以为很有趣。

谁都知道爸爸不在家。但是，如果我在游戏时高叫一声“爸爸”，她便要高兴地四面张望，以为爸爸真是近在身边。

当我把洗衣人带来的运载衣服回去的驴子当做学生，并且警告她说，我是老师时，她却无缘无故地乱叫起我哥哥来。

你的孩子要捉月亮。她是这样的可笑；她把格尼许[1]唤作琪奴许。

妈妈，你的孩子真傻，她是那末可笑地不懂事！

① 是印度的一个普通名字。

Superior

Mother, your baby is silly! She is so absurdly childish!

She does not know the difference between the lights in the streets and the stars.

When we play at eating with pebbles, she thinks they are real food, and tries to put them into her mouth.

When I open a book before her and ask her to learn her a, b, c, she tears the leaves with her hands and roars for joy at nothing; this is your baby's way of doing her lesson.

When I shake my head at her in anger and scold her and call her naughty, she laughs and thinks it great fun.

Everybody knows that father is away, but if in play I call aloud "Father," she looks about her in excitement and thinks that father is near.

When I hold my class with the donkeys that our washerman brings to carry away the clothes and I warn her that I am the schoolmaster, she will scream for no reason and call me dada [elder brother].

Your baby wants to catch the moon. She is so funny; she calls Ganesh Ganush. [Ganesh, a common name in India.]

Mother, your baby is silly, she is so absurdly childish!

小大人

我人很小，因为我是一个小孩子。到了我像爸爸一样年纪时，便要变大了。

我的先生要是走来说道："时候晚了，把你的石板、你的书拿来。"

我便要告诉他道："你不知道我已经同爸爸一样大了么？我决不再学什么功课了。"

我的老师便将惊异地说道："他读书不读书可以随便，因为他是大人了。"

我将自己穿了衣裳，走到人群拥挤的市场里去。

我的叔叔要是跑过来说道："你要迷路了，我的孩子，让我抱着你罢。"

我便要回答道："你没有看见么，叔叔？我已经同爸爸一样大了。我决定要独自一人到市场里去。"

叔叔便将说道："是的，他随便到哪里去都可以，因为他是大人了。"

当我正拿钱给我保姆时，妈妈便要从浴室中出来，因为我是知道怎样用我的钥匙去开银箱的。

妈妈要是说道："你在做什么呀，顽皮的孩子？"

我便要告诉她道："妈妈，你不知道我已经同爸爸一样大了么？我必须拿钱给保姆。"

妈妈便将自言自语道："他可以随便把钱给他所喜欢的人，因为他是大人了。"

当十月里放假的时候，爸爸将要回家。他会以为我还是一个小孩子，为我从城里带了小鞋子和小绸衫来。

我便要说道："爸爸，把这些东西给哥哥罢，因为我已经同你一样大了。"

爸爸便将想一想，说道："他可以随便去买他自己穿的衣裳，因为他是大人了。"

The Little Big Man

I am small because I am a little child.
I shall be big when I am as old as my father is.
My teacher will come and say, "It is late, bring your slate and your books."
I shall tell him, "Do you not know I am as big as father? And I must not have lessons any more."
My master will wonder and say, "He can leave his books if he likes, for he is grown up."

I shall dress myself and walk to the fair where the crowd is thick.
My uncle will come rushing up to me and say, "You will get lost, my boy; let me carry you."
I shall answer, "Can't you see, uncle, I am as big as father. I must go to the fair alone."
Uncle will say, "Yes, he can go wherever he likes, for he is grown up."
Mother will come from her bath when I am giving money to my nurse, for I shall know how to open the box with my key.
Mother will say, "What are you about, naughty child?"
I shall tell her, "Mother, don't you know, I am as big as father, and I must give silver to my nurse."
Mother will say to herself, "He can give money to whom he likes, for he is grown up."

In the holiday time in October father will come home and, thinking that I am still a baby, will bring for me from the town little shoes and small silken frocks.
I shall say, "Father, give them to my dada [elder brother], for I am as big as you are."
Father will think and say, "He can buy his own clothes if he likes, for he is grown up."

十二点钟

妈妈，我真想现在不做功课了。我整个早晨都在念书呢。

你说，现在还不过是十二点钟。假定不会晚过十二点罢；难道你不能把不过是十二点钟想象成下午么？

我能够很容易地想象：现在太阳已经到了那片稻田的边缘上了，老态龙钟的渔婆正在池边采撷香草做她的晚餐。

我闭上了眼就能够想到，马塔尔树下的阴影是更深黑了，池塘里的水看来黑得发亮。

假如十二点钟能够在黑夜里来到，为什么黑夜不能在十二点钟的时候来到呢？

Twelve O'clock

Mother, I do want to leave off my lessons now. I have been at my book all the morning.
You say it is only twelve o'clock.
Suppose it isn't any later; can't you ever think it is afternoon when it is only twelve o'clock?
I can easily imagine now that the sun has reached the edge of that rice-field, and the old fisher-woman is gathering herbs for her supper by the side of the pond.
I can just shut my eyes and think that the shadows are growing darker under the madar tree, and the water in the pond looks shiny black.
If twelve o'clock can come in the night, why can't the night come when it is twelve o'clock?

著作家

你说爸爸写了许多书，但我却不懂得他所写的东西。

他整个黄昏读书给你听，但是你真懂得他的意思么？

妈妈，你给我们讲的故事，真是好听呀！我很奇怪，爸爸为什么不能写那样的书呢？

难道他从来没有从他自己的妈妈那里听见过巨人、神仙和公主的故事么？

还是已经完全忘记了？

他常常耽误了沐浴，你不得不走去叫他一百多次。

你总要等候着，把他的菜温着等他。但他忘了，还尽管写下去。

爸爸老是以著书为游戏。

如果我一走进爸爸房里去游戏。你就要走来叫道："真是一个顽皮的孩子！"

如果我稍为弄出一点声音，你就要说："你没有看见你爸爸正在工作么？"

老是写了又写，有什么趣味呢？

当我拿起爸爸的钢笔或铅笔，像他一模一样地在他的书上写着，——a，b，c，d，e，f，g，h，i，——那时，你为什么跟我生气呢，妈妈？

爸爸写时，你却从来不说一句话。

当我爸爸耗费了那末一大堆纸时，妈妈，你似乎全不在乎。

但是，如果我只取了一张纸去做一只船，你却要说："孩子，你真讨厌！"

你对于爸爸拿黑点子涂满了纸的两面，污损了许多许多张纸，心里以为怎样呢？

Authorship

You say that father writes a lot of books, but what he writes I don't understand.
He was reading to you all the evening, but could you really make out what he meant?
What nice stories, mother, you can tell us! Why can't father write like that, I wonder?
Did he never hear from his own mother stories of giants and fairies and princesses?
Has he forgotten them all?

Often when he gets late for his bath you have to go and call him an hundred times.
You wait and keep his dishes warm for him, but he goes on writing and forgets.
Father always plays at making books.
If ever I go to play in father's room, you come and call me, "what a naughty child!"
If I make the slightest noise, you say, "Don't you see that father's at his work?"
What's the fun of always writing and writing?

When I take up father's pen or pencil and write upon his book just as he does,—a, b, c, d, e, f, g, h, i,—why do you get cross with me, then, mother?
You never say a word when father writes.

When my father wastes such heaps of paper, mother, you don't seem to mind at all.
But if I take only one sheet to make a boat with, you say, "Child, how troublesome you are!"
What do you think of father's spoiling sheets and sheets of paper with black marks all over on both sides?

恶邮差

你为什么坐在那边地板上不言不动的？告诉我呀，亲爱的妈妈。

雨从开着的窗口打进来了，把你身上全打湿了，你却不管。

你听见钟已打了四下么？正是哥哥从学校里回家的时候了。

到底发生了什么事，你的神色这样不对？

你今天没有接到爸爸的信么？

我看见邮差在他的袋里带了许多信来，几乎镇里的每个人都分送到了。

只有爸爸的信，他留起来给他自己看。我确信这个邮差是个坏人。

但是不要因此不乐呀，亲爱的妈妈。

明天是邻村市集的日子。你叫女仆去买些笔和纸来。

我自己会写爸爸所写的一切信；使你找不出一点错处来。

我要从 A 字一直写到 K 字。

但是，妈妈，你为什么笑呢？

你不相信我能写得像爸爸一样好？

但是我将用心画格子，把所有的字母都写得又大又美。

当我写好了时，你以为我也像爸爸那样傻，把它投入可怕的邮差的袋中么？

我立刻就自己送来给你，而且一个字母一个字母地帮助你读。

我知道那邮差是不肯把真正的好信送给你的。

The Wicked Postman

Why do you sit there on the floor so quiet and silent, tell me, mother dear?

The rain is coming in through the open window, making you all wet, and you don't mind it.

Do you hear the gong striking four? It is time for my brother to come home from school.

What has happened to you that you look so strange?

Haven't you got a letter from father today?

I saw the postman bringing letters in his bag for almost everybody in the town.

Only, father's letters he keeps to read himself. I am sure the postman is a wicked man.

But don't be unhappy about that, mother dear.

Tomorrow is market day in the next village. You ask your maid to buy some pens and papers.

I myself will write all father's letters; you will not find a single mistake.

I shall write from A right up to K.

But, mother, why do you smile?

You don't believe that I can write as nicely as father does!

But I shall rule my paper carefully, and write all the letters beautifully big.

When I finish my writing, do you think I shall be so foolish as father and drop it into the horrid postman's bag?

I shall bring it to you myself without waiting, and letter by letter help you to read my writing.

I know the postman does not like to give you the really nice letters.

英雄

妈妈，让我们想象我们正在旅行，经过一个陌生而危险的国土。

你坐在一顶轿子里，我骑着一匹红马，在你旁边跑着。

是黄昏的时候，太阳已经下山了。约拉地希的荒地疲乏而灰暗地展开在我们面前。大地是凄凉而荒芜的。

你害怕了，想道——“我不知道我们到了什么地方了。”

我对你说道：“妈妈，不要害怕。”

草地上刺蓬蓬地长着针尖似的草，一条狭而崎岖的小道通过这块草地。

在这片广大的地面上看不见一只牛；它们已经回到它们村里的牛棚里去了。

天色黑了下来，大地和天空都显得朦朦胧胧的，而我们不能说出我们正走向什么所在。

突然间，你叫我，悄悄地问我道：“靠近河岸的是什么火光呀？”

正在那个时候，一阵可怕的呐喊声爆发了，好些人影子向我们跑过来。

你蹲坐在你的轿子里，嘴里反复地祷念着神的名字。

轿夫们，怕得发抖，躲藏在荆棘丛中。

我向你喊道：“不要害怕，妈妈，有我在这里。”

他们手里执着长棒，头发披散着，越走越近了。

我喊道：“要当心！你们这些坏蛋！再向前走一步，你们就要送命了。”

他们又发出一阵可怕的呐喊声，向前冲过来。

你抓住我的手，说道：“好孩子，看在上天面上，躲开他们罢。”

我说道："妈妈，你瞧我的。"

于是我刺策着我的马匹，猛奔过去，我的剑和盾彼此碰着作响。

这一场战斗是那末激烈，妈妈，如果你从轿子里看得见的话，你一定会发冷战的。

他们之中，许多人逃走了，还有好些人被砍杀了。

我知道你那时独自坐在那里，心里正在想着，你的孩子这时候一定已经死了。

但是我跑到你的跟前，浑身溅满了鲜血，说道："妈妈，现在战争已经结束了。"

你从轿子里走出来，吻着我，把我搂在你的心头，你自言自语地说道：

"如果没有我的孩子护送我，我简直不知道怎么办才好。"

一千件无聊的事天天在发生，为什么这样一件事不能够偶然实现呢？

这很像一本书里的一个故事。

我的哥哥要说道："这是可能的事么？我老是想，他是那末嫩弱呢！"

我们村里的人们都要惊讶地说道："这孩子正和他妈妈在一起，这不是很幸运么？"

The Hero

Mother, let us imagine we are travelling, and passing through a strange and dangerous country.
You are riding in a palanquin and I am trotting by you on a red horse.
It is evening and the sun goes down. The waste of Joradighi lies wan and grey before us. The land is desolate and barren.
You are frightened and thinking—"I know not where we have come to."
I say to you, "Mother, do not be afraid."

The meadow is prickly with spiky grass, and through it runs a narrow broken path.
There are no cattle to be seen in the wide field; they have gone to their village stalls.
It grows dark and dim on the land and sky, and we cannot tell where we are going.
Suddenly you call me and ask me in a whisper, "What light is that near the bank?"
Just then there bursts out a fearful yell, and figures come running towards us.
You sit crouched in your palanquin and repeat the names of the gods in prayer.
The bearers, shaking in terror, hide themselves in the thorny bush.
I shout to you, "Don't be afraid, mother. I am here."

With long sticks in their hands and hair all wild about their heads, they come nearer and nearer.

I shout, "Have a care! you villains! One step more and you are dead men."
They give another terrible yell and rush forward.
You clutch my hand and say, "Dear boy, for heaven's sake, keep away from them."
I say, "Mother, just you watch me."

Then I spur my horse for a wild gallop, and my sword and buckler clash against each other.
The fight becomes so fearful, mother, that it would give you a cold shudder could you see it from your palanquin.
Many of them fly, and a great number are cut to pieces.
I know you are thinking, sitting all by yourself, that your boy must be dead by this time.
But I come to you all stained with blood, and say, "Mother, the fight is over now."
You come out and kiss me, pressing me to your heart, and you say to yourself,
"I don't know what I should do if I hadn't my boy to escort me."
A thousand useless things happen day after day, and why couldn't such a thing come true by chance?
It would be like a story in a book.
My brother would say, "Is it possible? I always thought he was so delicate!"
Our village people would all say in amazement, "Was it not lucky that the boy was with his mother?"

告别

是我走的时候了，妈妈，我走了。

当清寂的黎明，你在暗中伸出双臂，要抱你睡在床上的孩子时，我要说道："孩子不在那里呀！"——妈妈，我走了。

我要变成一股清风抚摸着你；我要变成水中的涟漪，当你（沐）浴时，把你吻了又吻。

大风之夜，当雨点在树叶上淅沥时，你在床上会听见我的微语；当电光从开着的窗口闪进你的屋里时，我的笑声也偕了它一同闪进了。

如果你醒着躺在床上，想你的孩子直到深夜，我便要从星空向你唱道："睡呀！妈妈，睡呀。"

我要坐在各处游荡的月光上，偷偷地来到你的床上，乘你睡着时，躺在你的胸上。

我要变成一个梦儿，从你眼皮的微缝中钻到你的睡眠的深处。当你醒来吃惊地四望时，我便如闪耀的萤火似的，熠熠地向暗中飞去了。

当杜尔伽节[①]，邻家的孩子们来屋里游玩时，我便要融化在笛声里，整日价在你心头震荡。

亲爱的阿姨带了杜尔伽节礼物来，问道："我们的孩子在哪里，姊姊？"妈妈，你将要柔声地告诉她："他呀，他现在是在我的瞳仁里，他现在是在我的身体里，在我的灵魂里。"

① 即印度十月间的"难近母祭日"。

The End

It is time for me to go, mother; I am going.

When in the paling darkness of the lonely dawn you stretch out your arms for your baby in the bed, I shall say, "Baby is not there!"—mother, I am going.

I shall become a delicate draught of air and caress you; and I shall be ripples in the water when you bathe, and kiss you and kiss you again.

In the gusty night when the rain patters on the leaves you will hear my whisper in your bed, and my laughter will flash with the lightning through the open window into your room.

If you lie awake, thinking of your baby till late into the night, I shall sing to you from the stars, "Sleep mother, sleep."

On the straying moonbeams I shall steal over your bed, and lie upon your bosom while you sleep.

I shall become a dream, and through the little opening of your eyelids I shall slip into the depths of your sleep; and when you wake up and look round startled, like a twinkling firefly I shall flit out into the darkness.

When, on the great festival of puja, the neighbours' children come and play about the house, I shall melt into the music of the flute and throb in your heart all day.

Dear auntie will come with puja-presents and will ask, "Where is our baby, sister? Mother, you will tell her softly, "He is in the pupils of my eyes, he is in my body and in my soul.

召唤

她走的时候，夜间黑漆漆的，他们都睡了。

现在，夜间也是黑漆漆的，我唤她道："回来，我的宝贝；世界都在沉睡；当星星互相凝视的时候，你来一会儿是没有人知道的。"

她走的时候，树木正在萌芽，春光刚刚来到。

现在花已盛开，我唤道："回来，我的宝贝。孩子们漫不经心地在游戏，把花聚在一块儿，又把它们散开。你如果走来，拿一朵小花去，没有人会发觉的。"

那些常常在游戏的人，仍然还在那里游戏，生命总是如此的浪费。

我静听他们的空谈，便唤道："回来，我的宝贝，妈妈的心里充满着爱，你如果走来，仅仅从她那里接一个小小的吻，没有人会妒忌的。"

The Recall

The night was dark when she went away, and they slept.
The night is dark now, and I call for her, "Come back, my darling; the world is asleep; and no one would know, if you came for a moment while stars are gazing at stars."

She went away when the trees were in bud and the spring was young.
Now the flowers are in high bloom and I call, "Come back, my darling. The children gather and scatter flowers in reckless sport. And if you come and take one little blossom no one will miss it."

Those that used to play are playing still, so spendthrift is life.
I listen to their chatter and call, "Come back, my darling, for mother's heart is full to the brim with love, and if you come to snatch only one little kiss from her no one will grudge it."

第一次的茉莉

呵，这些茉莉花，这些白的茉莉花！

我仿佛记得我第一次双手满捧着这些茉莉花，这些白的茉莉花的时候。

我喜爱那日光，那天空，那绿色的大地；

我听见那河水淙淙的流声，在漆黑的午夜里传过来；

秋天的夕阳，在荒原上大路转角处迎我，如新妇揭起她的面纱迎接她的爱人。

但我想起孩提时第一次捧在手里的白茉莉，心里充满着甜蜜的回忆。

我生平看过许多快活的日子。在节日宴会的晚上，我曾跟着说笑话的人大笑。

在灰暗的雨天的早晨，我吟哦过许多飘逸的诗篇。

我颈上戴过爱人手织的醉花的花圈，作为晚装。

但我想起孩提时第一次捧在手里的白茉莉，心里充满着甜蜜的回忆。

The First Jasmines

Ah, these jasmines, these white jasmines!
I seem to remember the first day when I filled my hands with these jasmines, these white jasmines.
I have loved the sunlight, the sky and the green earth;
I have heard the liquid murmur of the river through the darkness of midnight;
Autumn sunsets have come to me at the bend of a road in the lonely waste, like a bride raising her veil to accept her lover.
Yet my memory is still sweet with the first white jasmines that I held in my hand when I was a child.

Many a glad day has come in my life, and I have laughed with merrymakers on festival nights.
On grey mornings of rain I have crooned many an idle song.
I have worn round my neck the evening wreath of bakulas woven by the hand of love.
Yet my heart is sweet with the memory of the first fresh jasmines that filled my hands when I was a child.

榕树

喂，你站在池边的蓬头榕树，你可曾忘记了那小小的孩子，就像那在你的枝上筑巢又离开了你的鸟儿似的孩子？

你不记得他怎样坐在窗内，诧异地望着你那深入地下的纠缠的树根么？

妇人们常到池边，汲了满罐的水去。你的大黑影便在水面上摇动，好像睡着的人挣扎着要醒来似的。

日光在微波上跳舞，好像不停不息的小梭在织着金色的花毡。

两只鸭子挨着芦苇，在芦苇影子上游来游去，孩子静静地坐在那里想着。

他想做风，吹过你萧萧的枝杈；想做你的影子，在水面上，随了日光而俱长；想做一只鸟儿，栖息在你的最高枝上；还想做那两只鸭，在芦苇与阴影中间游来游去。

The Banyan Tree

O you shaggy-headed banyan tree standing on the bank of the pond, have you forgotten the little child, like the birds that have nested in your branches and left you?

Do you not remember how he sat at the window and wondered at the tangle of your roots that plunged underground?

The women would come to fill their jars in the pond, and your huge black shadow would wriggle on the water like sleep struggling to wake up.

Sunlight danced on the ripples like restless tiny shuttles weaving golden tapestry.

Two ducks swam by the weedy margin above their shadows, and the child would sit still and think.

He longed to be the wind and blow through your rustling branches, to be your shadow and lengthen with the day on the water, to be a bird and perch on your top-most twig, and to float like those ducks among the weeds and shadows.

祝福

祝福这个小心灵，这个洁白的灵魂，他为我们的大地，赢得了天的接吻。

他爱日光，他爱见他妈妈的脸。

他没有学会厌恶尘土而渴求黄金。

紧紧把他抱在你心里，并且祝福他。

他已来到这个歧路百出的大地上了。

我不知道他怎么要从群众中选出你来，来到你的门前，抓住你的手问路。

他笑着，谈着，跟着你走，心里没有一点儿疑惑。

不要辜负他的信任，引导他到正路，并且祝福他。

把你的手按在他的头上，祈求着：底下的波涛虽然险恶，然而从上面来的风会鼓起他的船帆，送他到和平的港口的。

不要在忙碌中把他忘了，让他来到你的心里，并且祝福他。

Benediction

Bless this little heart, this white soul that has won the kiss of heaven for our earth.
He loves the light of the sun, he loves the sight of his mother's face.
He has not learned to despise the dust, and to hanker after gold.
Clasp him to your heart and bless him.

He has come into this land of an hundred cross-roads.
I know not how he chose you from the crowd, came to your door, and grasped your hand to ask his way.
He will follow you, laughing and talking, and not a doubt in his heart.
Keep his trust, lead him straight and bless him.
Lay your hand on his head, and pray that though the waves underneath grow threatening, yet the breath from above may come and fill his sails and waft him to the haven of peace.
Forget him not in your hurry, let him come to your heart and bless him.

赠品

我要送些东西给你，我的孩子，因为我们同是漂泊在世界的溪流中的。

我们的生命将被分开，我们的爱也将被忘记。

但我却没有那样傻，希望能用我的赠品来买你的心。

你的生命正是青青，你的道路也长着呢，你一口气饮尽了我们带给你的爱，便回身离开我们跑了。

你有你的游戏，有你的游伴。如果你没有时间同我们在一起，如果你想不到我们，那有什么害处呢？

我们呢，自然地，在老年时，会有许多闲暇的时间，去计算那过去的日子，把我们手里永久丢失了的东西，在心里爱抚着。

河流唱着歌很快地游去，冲破所有的堤防。但是山峰却留在那里，忆念着，满怀依依之情。

The Gift

I want to give you something, my child, for we are drifting in the stream of the world.

Our lives will be carried apart, and our love forgotten.

But I am not so foolish as to hope that I could buy your heart with my gifts.

Young is your life, your path long, and you drink the love we bring you at one draught and turn and run away from us.

You have your play and your playmates. What harm is there if you have no time or thought for us.

We, indeed, have leisure enough in old age to count the days that are past, to cherish in our hearts what our hands have lost for ever.

The river runs swift with a song, breaking through all barriers. But the mountain stays and remembers, and follows her with his love.

我的歌

我的孩子，我这一支歌将用它的乐声围绕你，好像那爱情的热恋的手臂一样。

我这一支歌将触着你的前额，好像那祝福的接吻一样。

当你只是一个人的时候，它将坐在你的身旁，在你耳边微语着；当你在人群中的时候，它将围住你，使你超然物外。

我的歌将成为你的梦的翼翅，它将把你的心移送到不可知的岸边。

当黑夜覆盖在你路上的时候，它又将成为那照临在你头上的忠实的星光。

我的歌又将坐在你眼睛的瞳仁里，将你的视线带入万物的心里。

当我的声音因死亡而沉寂时，我的歌仍将在你活泼泼的心中唱着。

My Song

This song of mine will wind its music around you, my child, like the fond arms of love.

This song of mine will touch your forehead like a kiss of blessing.

When you are alone it will sit by your side and whisper in your ear, when you are in the crowd it will fence you about with aloofness.

My song will be like a pair of wings to your dreams, it will transport your heart to the verge of the unknown.

It will be like the faithful star overhead when dark night is over your road.

My song will sit in the pupils of your eyes, and will carry your sight into the heart of things.

And when my voice is silent in death, my song will speak in your living heart.

孩子天使

他们喧哗争斗，他们怀疑失望，他们辩论而没有结果。

我的孩子，让你的生命到他们当中去，如一线镇定而纯洁之光，使他们愉悦而沉默。

他们的贪心和妒忌是残忍的；他们的话，好像暗藏的刀刃，渴欲饮血。

我的孩子，去，去站在他们愤懑的心中，把你的和善的眼光落在他们上面，好像那傍晚的宽宏大量的和平，覆盖着日间的骚扰一样。

我的孩子，让他们望着你的脸，因此能够知道一切事物的意义；让他们爱你，因此使他们也能相爱。

来，坐在无垠的胸膛上，我的孩子。在朝阳出来时，开放而且抬起你的心，像一朵盛开的花；在夕阳落下时，低下你的头，默默地做完这一天的礼拜。

The Child-Angel

They clamour and fight, they doubt and despair, they know no end to their wranglings.

Let your life come amongst them like a flame of light, my child, unflickering and pure, and delight them into silence.

They are cruel in their greed and their envy, their words are like hidden knives thirsting for blood.

Go and stand amidst their scowling hearts, my child, and let your gentle eyes fall upon them like the forgiving peace of the evening over the strife of the day.

Let them see your face, my child, and thus know the meaning of all things; let them love you and thus love each other.

Come and take your seat in the bosom of the limitless, my child. At sunrise open and raise your heart like a blossoming flower, and at sunset bend your head and in silence complete the worship of the day.

最后的买卖

早晨，我在石铺的路上走时，我叫道："谁来雇用我呀。"
皇帝坐着马车，手里拿着剑走来。
他拉着我的手，说道："我要用权力来雇用你。"
但是他的权力算不了什么，他坐着马车走了。

正午炎热的时候，家家户户的门都闭着。
我沿着屈曲的小巷走去。
一个老人带着一袋金钱走出来。
他斟酌了一下，说道："我要用金钱来雇用你。"
他一个一个地数着他的钱，但我却转身离去了。

黄昏了。花园的篱上满开着花。
美人走出来，说道："我要用微笑来雇用你。"
她的微笑黯淡了，化成泪容了，她孤寂地回身走进黑暗里去。

太阳照耀在沙地上，海波任性地浪花四溅。
一个小孩坐在那里玩贝壳。
他抬起头来，好像认识我似的，说道："我雇你不用什么东西。"
在这个小孩的游戏中做成的买卖，使我从此以后成了一个自由的人。

The Last Bargain

"Come and hire me," I cried, while in the morning I was walking on the stone-paved road.
Sword in hand, the King came in his chariot.
He held my hand and said, "I will hire you with my power."
But his power counted for nought, and he went away in his chariot.

In the heat of the midday the houses stood with shut doors.
I wandered along the crooked lane.
An old man came out with his bag of gold.
He pondered and said, "I will hire you with my money."
He weighed his coins one by one, but I turned away.

It was evening. The garden hedge was all a flower.
The fair maid came out and said, "I will hire you with a smile."
Her smile paled and melted into tears, and she went back alone into the dark.

The sun glistened on the sand, and the sea waves broke waywardly.
A child sat playing with shells.
He raised his head and seemed to know me, and said, "I hire you with nothing."
From thenceforward that bargain struck in child's play made me a free man.

飞鸟集

泰戈尔诗文彩图馆

译者自序

译诗是一件最不容易的工作。原诗音节的保留固然是绝不可能的事！就是原诗意义的完全移植，也有十分的困难。散文诗算是最容易译的，但有时也须费十分的力气。如惠德曼（Walt Whitman）的《草叶集》便是一个例子。这有两个原因：第一，有许多诗中特用的美丽文句，差不多是不能移动的。在一种文字里，这种字眼是“诗的”，是“美的”，如果把他移植在第二种文字中，不是找不到相当的好字，便是把原意丑化了，变成非“诗的”了。在泰戈尔的《人格论》中，曾讨论到这一层。他以为诗总是要选择那“有生气的”字眼，——就是那些不仅仅为报告用而能融化于我们心中，不因市井常用而损坏它的形式的字眼。譬如在英文里，“意识”（consciousness）这个字，带有多少科学的意义，所以诗中不常用它。印度文的同意字 chetana 则是一个“有生气”而常用于诗歌里的字。又如英文的“感情”（feeling）这个字是充满了生命的，但彭加利文[①]里的同意字 anubhuti 则诗中绝无用之者。在这些地方，译诗的人实在感到万分的困难。第二，诗歌的文句总是含蓄的，暗示的。他的句法的构造，多简短而含义丰富。有的时候，简直不能译。如直译，则不能达意。如稍加诠释，则又把原文的风韵与含蓄完全消灭，而使之不成一首诗了。

因此，我主张诗集的介绍，只应当在可能的范围选择，而不能——也不必——完全整册地搬运过来。

---

① 即孟加拉文。——编者注

大概诗歌的选译，有两个方便的地方：第一，选择可以适应译者的兴趣。在一个诗集中的许多诗，译者未必都十分喜欢它。如果不十分喜欢它，不十分感觉到它的美好，则他的译文必不能十分得神，至少也把这快乐的工作变成一种无意义的苦役。选译则可以减灭译者的这层痛苦。第二，便是减少上述的两层翻译上的困难。因为如此便可以把不能译的诗，不必译出来。译出来而丑化了或是为读者所看不懂，则反不如不译的好。

但我并不是在这里宣传选译主义。诗集的全选，是我所极端希望而且欢迎的。不过这种工作应当让给那些有全译能力的译者去做。我为自己的兴趣与能力所限制，实在不敢担任这种重大的工作。且为大多数的译者计，我也主张选译是较好的一种译诗方法。

现在我译泰戈尔的诗，便实行了这种选译的主张，以前我也有全译泰戈尔各诗集的野心。有好些友人也极力劝我把它们全译出来。我试了几次。但我的野心与被大家鼓起的勇气，终于给我的能力与兴趣打败了。

现在所译的泰戈尔各集的诗，都是我所最喜欢读的，而且是我的能力所比较的能够译得出的。

有许多诗，我自信是能够译得出的，但因为自己翻译它们的兴趣不大强烈，便不高兴去译它们。还有许多诗我是很喜欢读它们，而且是极愿意把它们译出来的。但因为自己能力的不允许，便也只好舍弃了它们。

即在这些译出的诗中，有许多也是自己觉得译得不好，心中很不满意的。但实在不忍再割舍它们了。只好请读者赏读它的原意，不必注意于粗陋的译文。

泰戈尔的诗集用英文出版的共有六部：

（一）《园丁集》　　（Gardener）

（二）《吉檀迦利》	（Jitanjali）
（三）《新月集》	（The Crescent Moon）
（四）《采果集》	（Fruit Cathering）
（五）《飞鸟集》	（Stray Birds）
（六）《爱者之贻与歧路》	（Lover's Gift And Crossing）

但据B.K.Roy的《泰戈尔与其诗》（R.Tagore：The Man And His Poetry）一书上所载，他用彭加利文写的重要诗集，却有下面的许多种：

Sandhva Sangit,	Kshanika,
Probhat Sangit,	Kanika,
Bhanusingher Padabali,	Kahini,
Chabi O Gan,	Sishn,
Kari O Komal,	Naibadya,
Prakritir Pratisodh,	Utsharga,
Sonartari,	Kheya,
Chaitali,	Gitanzali,
Kalpana,	Gitimalya,
Katha.	

我的这几本诗选，是根据那六部用英文写的诗集译下来的。因为我不懂梵文。

在这几部诗集中，间有重出的诗篇，如《海边》一诗，已见于《新月集》中，而又列入《吉檀迦利》，排为第六十首。《飞鸟集》的第九十八首，也与同集中的第二百六十三首相同。像这一类的诗篇，都照先见之例，把他列入最初见的地方。

我的译文自信是很忠实的。误解的地方，却也保不定完全没有。如读者偶有发现，肯公开地指教我，那是我所异常欢迎的。

郑振铎

再版自序

《飞鸟集》曾经全译出来一次，因为我自己的不满意，所以又把它删节为现在的选译本①。以前，我曾看见有人把这诗集选译过，但似乎错得太多，因此我译时不曾拿它来参考。

近来小诗十分发达。他们的作者大半都是直接或间接受泰戈尔此集的影响的。此集的介绍，对于没有机会得读原文的，至少总有些贡献。

这诗集的一部分译稿是积了许多时候的，但大部分却都是在西湖俞楼译的。

我在此谢谢叶圣陶、徐玉诺二君。他们替我很仔细地校读过这部译文，并且供给了许多重要的意见给我。

郑振铎

① 本书中的《飞鸟集》为全译本。——编者注

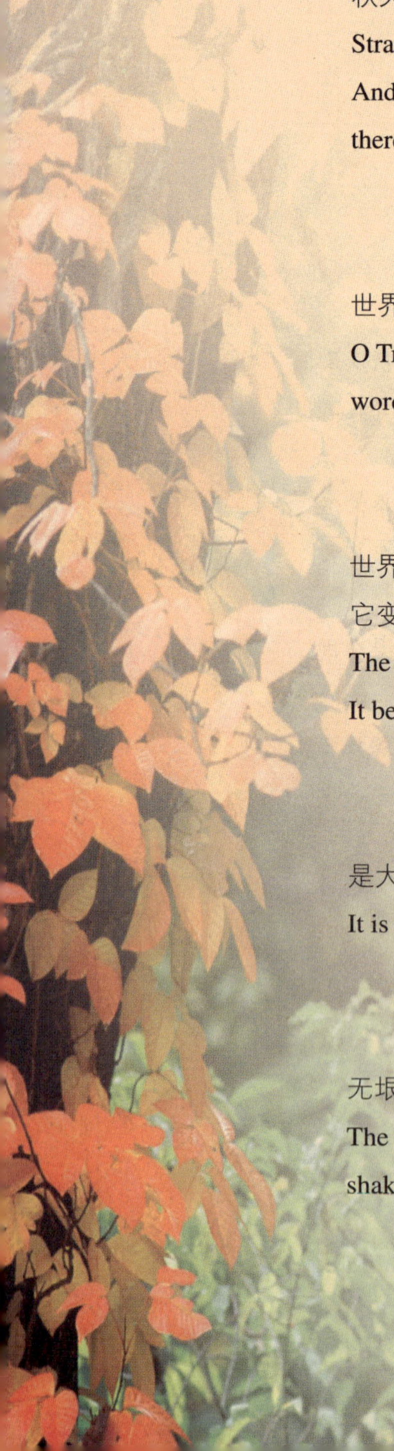

1

夏天的飞鸟，飞到我窗前唱歌，又飞去了。
秋天的黄叶，它们没有什么可唱，只叹息一声，飞落在那里。
Stray birds of summer come to my window to sing and fly away.
And yellow leaves of autumn,which have no songs, flutter and fall there with a sign.

2

世界上的一队小小的漂泊者呀，请留下你们的足印在我的文字里。
O Troupe of little vagrants of the world,leave your footprints in my words.

3

世界对着它的爱人，把它浩瀚的面具揭下了。
它变小了，小如一首歌，小如一回永恒的接吻。
The world puts off its mask of vastness to its lover.
It becomes small as one song,as one kiss of the eternal.

4

是大地的泪点，使她的微笑保持着青春不谢。
It is the tears of the earth that keep here smiles in bloom.

5

无垠的沙漠热烈追求一叶绿草的爱，她摇摇头笑着飞开了。
The mighty desert is burning for the love of a bladeof grass who shakes her head and laughs and flies away.

6

如果你因失去了太阳而流泪，那末你也将失去群星了。

If you shed tears when you miss the sun,you also miss the stars.

7

跳舞着的流水呀，在你途中的泥沙，要求你的歌声，你的流动呢。你肯挟跛足的泥沙而俱下么?

The sands in your way beg for your song and your movement, dancing water. Will you carry the burden of their lameness?

8

她的热切的脸，如夜雨似的，搅扰着我的梦魂。

Her wishful face haunts my dreams like the rain at night.

9

有一次，我们梦见大家都是不相识的。

我们醒了，却知道我们原是相亲相爱的。

Once we dreamt that we were strangers.

We wake up to find that we were dear to each other.

10

忧思在我的心里平静下去，正如暮色降临在寂静的山林中。

Sorrow is hushed into peace in my heart like the evening among the silent trees.

11

有些看不见的手指，如懒懒的微飔似的，正在我的心上奏着潺湲的乐声。

Some unseen fingers,like an idle breeze,are playing upon my heart the music of the ripples.

12

“海水呀，你说的是什么？”

“是永恒的疑问。”

“天空呀，你回答的话是什么？”

“是永恒的沉默。”

What language is thine,O sea?

The language of eternal question.

What language is thy answer,O sky?

The language of eternal silence.

13

静静地听，我的心呀，听那世界的低语，这是它对你求爱的表示呀。

Listen,my heart,to the whispers of the world with which it makes love to you.

14

创造的神秘，有如夜间的黑暗——是伟大的。而知识的幻影却不过如晨间之雾。

The mystery of creation is like the darkness of night—it is great.Delusions of knowledge are like the fog of the morning.

15

不要因为峭壁是高的，便让你的爱情坐在峭壁上。

Do not seat your love upon a precipice because it is high.

16

我今晨坐在窗前，世界如一个过路人似的，停留了一会儿，向我点点头又走过去了。

I sit at my window this morning where the world like a passer-by stops for a moment, nods to me and goes.

17

这些微飔，是绿叶的簌簌之声呀；它们在我的心里欢悦地微语着。

There little thoughts are the rustle of leaves; they have their whisper of joy in my mind.

18

你看不见你自己，你所看见的只是你的影子。

What you are you do not see, what you see is your shadow.

19

神呀，我的那些愿望真是愚傻呀，它们杂在你的歌声中喧叫着呢。让我只是静听着吧。

My wishes are fools, they shout across thy song, my Master.
Let me but listen.

20

我不能选择那最好的。

是那最好的选择我。

I cannot choose the best.

The best chooses me.

21

那些把灯背在背上的人，把他们的影子投到了自己前面。

They throw their shadows before them who carry their lantern on their back.

22

我的存在，对我是一个永久的神奇，这就是生活。

That I exist is a perpetual surprise which is life.

23

“我们萧萧的树叶都有声响回答那风和雨。你是谁呢，那样的沉默着？”

“我不过是一朵花。”

We, the rustling leaves, have a voice that answers the storms,but who are you so silent?

I am a mere flower.

24

休息与工作的关系，正如眼睑与眼睛的关系。

Rest belongs to the work as the eyelids to the eyes.

25

人是一个初生的孩子，他的力量，就是生长的力量。

Man is a born child, his power is the power of growth.

26

神希望我们酬答他，在于他送给我们的花朵，而不在于太阳和土地。

God expects answers for the flowers he sends us, not for the sun the earth.

27

光明如一个裸体的孩子，快快活活地在绿叶当中游戏，它不知道人是会欺诈的。

The light that plays, like a naked child, among the green leaves happily knows not that man can lie.

28

啊，美呀，在爱中找你自己吧，不要到你镜子的谄谀中去找寻。

O Beauty, find thyself in love, not in the flattery of thy mirror.

29

我的心把她的波浪在世界的海岸上冲激着，以热泪在上边写着她的题记："我爱你。"

My heart beats her waves at the shore of the world and writes upon,it her signature in tears with the words, "I love thee."

30

"月儿呀，你在等候什么呢？"

"向我将让位给他的太阳致敬。"

Moon, for what do you wait?

To salute the sun for whom I must make way.

31

绿树长到了我的窗前，仿佛是喑哑的大地发出的渴望的声音。

The trees come up to my window like the yearning voice of the dumb earth.

32

神自己的清晨，在他自己看来也是新奇的。

His own mornings are new surprises to God.

33

生命从世界得到资产，爱情使它得到价值。

Life finds its wealth by the claims of the world, and its worth by the claims of love.

34

枯竭的河床，并不感谢它的过去。

The dry river-bed finds no thanks for its past.

35

鸟儿愿为一朵云。

云儿愿为一只鸟。

The bird wishes it were a cloud.

The cloud wishes it were a bird.

36

瀑布歌唱道：“我得到自由时便有歌声了。”

The waterfall sing, “I find my song, when I find my freedom.”

37

我说不出这心为什么那样默默地颓丧着。

是为了它那不曾要求、不曾知道、不曾记得的小小的需要。

I cannot tell why this heart languishes in silence.

It is for small needs it never asks, or knows or remembers.

38

妇人，你在料理家事的时候，你的手足歌唱着，正如山间的溪水歌唱着在小石中流过。

Woman, when you move about in your household service your limbs sing like a hill stream among its pebbles.

39

当太阳横过西方的海面时，对着东方留下他最后的敬礼。

The sun goes to cross the Western sea, leaving its last salutation to the East.

40

不要因为你自己没有胃口而去责备你的食物。

Do not blame your food because you have no appetite.

41

群树如表示大地的愿望似的，踮起脚来向天空窥望。

The trees, like the longings of the earth, stand atiptoe to peep at the heaven.

42

你微微地笑着，不同我说什么话。而我觉得，为了这个，我已等待得久了。

You smiled and talked to me of nothing and I felt that for this I had been waiting long.

43

水里的游鱼是沉默的，陆地上的兽类是喧闹的，空中的飞鸟是歌唱着的。
但是，人类却兼有海里的沉默、地上的喧闹与空中的音乐。

The fish in the water is silent, the animal on the earth is noisy, the bird in the air is singing.
But Man has in him the silence of the sea, the noise of the earth and the music of the air.

44

世界在踌躇之心的琴弦上跑过去，奏出忧郁的乐声。

The world rushes on over the strings of the lingering heart making the music of sadness.

45

他把他的刀剑当做他的上帝。
当他的刀剑胜利时他自己却失败了。

He has made his weapons his gods.
When his weapons win he is defeated himself.

46

神从创造中找到他自己。

God finds himself by creating.

47

阴影戴上她的面幕，秘密地，温顺地，用她的沉默的爱的脚步，跟在“光”后边。

Shadow, with her veil drawn, follows Light in secret meekness,with her silent steps of love.

48

群星不怕显得像萤火那样。

The stars are not afraid to appear like fireflies.

49

谢谢神，我不是一个权力的轮子，而是被压在这轮下的活人之一。

I thank thee that I am none of the wheels of power but I am one with the living creatures that are crushed by it.

50

心是尖锐的，不是宽博的，它执着在每一点上，却并不活动。

The mind, sharp but not broad, sticks at every point but does not move.

51

你的偶像委散在尘土中了，这可证明神的尘土比你的偶像还伟大。

You idol is shattered in the dust to prove that God's dust is greater than your idol.

52

人不能在他的历史中表现出他自己，他在历史中奋斗着露出头角。

Man does not reveal himself in his history, he struggles up through it.

53

玻璃灯因为瓦灯叫它做表兄而责备瓦灯。但当明月出来时，玻璃灯却温和地微笑着，叫明月为——“我亲爱的，亲爱的姊姊。”

While the glass lamp rebukes the earthen for calling it cousin the moon rises, and the glass lamp, with a bland smile, calls her, —My dear, dear sister.

54

我们如海鸥之与波涛相遇似的，遇见了，走近了。海鸥飞去，波涛滚滚地流开，我们也分别了。

Like the meeting of the seagulls and the waves we meet and come near.

The seagulls fly off, the waves roll away and we depart.

55

我的白昼已经完了，我像一只泊在海滩上的小船，谛听着晚潮跳舞的乐声。

My day is done, and I am like a boat drawn on the beach, listening to the dance-music of the tide in the evening.

56

我们的生命是天赋的，我们惟有献出生命，才能得到生命。

Life is given to us, we earn it by giving it.

57

当我们是大为谦卑的时候，便是我们最近于伟大的时候。

We come nearest to the great when we are great in humility.

58

麻雀看见孔雀负担着它的翎尾，替它担忧。

The sparrow is sorry for the peacock at the burden of its tail.

59

决不要害怕刹那——永恒之声这样唱着。

Never be afraid of the moments—thus sings the voice of the everlasting.

60

飓风于无路之中寻求最短之路，又突然地在“无何有之国”终止了它的寻求。

The hurricane seeks the shortest road by the no-road, and suddenly ends its search in the Nowhere.

61

在我自己的杯中，饮了我的酒吧，朋友。
一倒在别人的杯里，这酒的腾跳的泡沫便要消失了。
Take my wine in my own cup, friend.
It loses its wreath of foam when poured into that of others.

62

“完全”为了对“不全”的爱，把自己装饰得美丽。
The perfect decks itself in beauty for the love of the Imperfect.

63

神对人说道：“我医治你所以伤害你，爱你所以惩罚你。”
God says to man, “I heal you therefore I hurt, love you therefore punish.”

64

谢谢火焰给你光明，但是不要忘了那执灯的人，他是坚忍地站在黑暗当中呢。
Thank the flame for its light, but do not forget the lampholder standing in the shade with constancy of patience.

65

小草呀，你的足步虽小，但是你拥有你足下的土地。
Tiny grass, your steps are small, but you possess the earth under your tread.

66

幼花的蓓蕾开放了，它叫道：“亲爱的世界呀，请不要萎谢了。”
The infant flower opens its bud and cries,“Dear World, please do not fade.”

67

神对于那些大帝国会感到厌恶，却决不会厌恶那些小小的花朵。
God grows weary of great kingdoms, but never of little flowers.

68

错误经不起失败，但是真理却不怕失败。

Wrong cannot afford defeat but Right can.

69

瀑布歌唱道:“虽然渴者只要少许的水便够了，我却很快活地给予了我全部的水。”

“I give my whole water in joy,”sings the waterfall,“though it is enough for the thirsty.”

70

把那些花朵抛掷上去的那一阵子无休无止的狂欢大喜的劲儿，其源泉是在哪里呢？

Where is the fountain that throws up these flowers in a ceaseless outbreak of ecstasy?

71

樵夫的斧头，问树要斧柄。

树便给了他。

The woodcutter’s axe begged for its handle from the tree.

The tree gave it.

72

这寡独的黄昏，幕着雾与雨，我在我心的孤寂里，感觉到它的叹息。

In my solitude of heart I feel the sigh of this widowed evening veiled with mist and rain.

73

贞操是从丰富的爱情中生出来的财富。

Chastity is a wealth that comes from abundance of love.

74

雾，像爱情一样，在山峰的心上游戏，生出种种美丽的变幻。

The mist, like love, plays upon the heart of the hills and bring out surprises of beauty.

75

我们把世界看错了，反说它欺骗我们。

We read the world wrong and say that it deceives us.

76

诗人——飙风，正出经海洋和森林，追求它自己的歌声。

The poet wind is out over the sea and the forest to seek his own voice.

77

每一个孩子出生时都带来信息说：神对人并未灰心失望。
Every child comes with the message that God is not yet discouraged of man.

78

绿草求她地上的伴侣。
树木求他天空的寂寞。
The grass seeks her crowd in the earth.
The tree seeks his solitude of the sky.

79

人对他自己建筑起堤防来。
Man barricades against himself.

80

我的朋友，你的语声飘荡在我的心里，像那海水的低吟声缭绕在静听着的松林之间。
Your voice, my friend, wanders in my heart, like the muffled sound of the sea among these listening pines.

81

这个不可见的黑暗之火焰，以繁星为其火花的，到底是什么呢？
What is this unseen flame of darkness whose sparks are the stars?

82

使生如夏花之绚烂，死如秋叶之静美。
Let life be beautiful like summer flowers and death like autumn leaves.

83

那想做好人的，在门外敲着门；那爱人的，看见门敞开着。

He who wants to do good knocks at the gate; he who loves finds the gate open.

84

在死的时候，众多合而为一；在生的时候，一化为众多。

神死了的时候，宗教便将合而为一。

In death the many becomes one; in life the one becomes many.

Religion will be one when God is dead.

85

艺术家是自然的情人，所以他是自然的奴隶，也是自然的主人。

The artist is the lover of Nature, therefore he is her slave and her master.

86

“你离我有多远呢，果实呀？”

“我藏在你心里呢，花呀。”

How far are you from me, O Fruit?

I am hidden in your heart, O Flower.

87

这个渴望是为了那个在黑夜里感觉得到、在大白天里却看不见的人。

This longing is for the one who is felt in the dark, but not seen in the day.

88

露珠对湖水说道：“你是在荷叶下面的大露珠，我是在荷叶上面的较小的露珠。”

“You are the big drop of dew under the lotus leaf, I am the smaller one on its upper side.” said the dewdrop to the lake.

89

刀鞘保护刀的锋利，它自己则满足于它的迟钝。

The scabbard is content to be dull when it protects the keenness of the sword.

90

在黑暗中，“一”视若一体；在光亮中，“一”便视若众多。

In darkness the One appears as uniform; in the light the One appears as manifold.

91

大地借助于绿草，显出她自己的殷勤好客。

The great earth makes herself hospitable with the help of the grass.

92

绿叶的生与死乃是旋风的急骤的旋转，它的更广大的旋转的圈子乃是在天上繁星之间徐缓的转动。

The birth and death of the leaves are the rapid whirls of the eddy whose wider circles move slowly among stars.

93

权势对世界说道：“你是我的。”
世界便把权势囚禁在她的宝座下面。
爱情对世界说道：“我是你的。”
世界便给予爱情以在她屋内来往的自由。

Power said to the world, “You are mine.”
The world kept it prisoner on her throne.
Love said to the world, “I am thine.”
The world gave it the freedom of her house.

94

浓雾仿佛是大地的愿望。
它藏起了太阳，而太阳原是她所呼求的。

The mist is like the earth's desire.
It hides the sun for whom she cries.

95

安静些吧，我的心，这些大树都是祈祷者呀。

Be still, my heart, these great trees are prayers.

96

瞬刻的喧声，讥笑着永恒的音乐。

The noise of the moment scoffs at the music of the Eternal.

97

我想起了浮泛在生与爱与死的川流上的许多别的时代，以及这些时代之被遗忘，我便感觉到离开尘世的自由了。

I think of other ages that floated upon the stream of life and love and death and are forgotten, and I feel the freedom of passing away.

98

我灵魂里的忧郁就是她的新婚的面纱。
这面纱等候着在夜间卸去。

The sadness of my soul is her bride's veil.
It waits to be lifted in the night.

99

死之印记给生的钱币以价值，使它能够用生命来购买那真正的宝物。

Death's stamp gives value to the coin of life; making it possible to buy with life what is truly precious.

100

白云谦逊地站在天之一隅。
晨光给它戴上了霞彩。

The cloud stood humbly in a corner of the sky.
The morning crowned it with splendour.

101

尘土受到损辱，却以她的花朵来报答。

The dust receives insult and in return offers her flowers.

102

只管走过去，不必逗留着采了花朵来保存，因为一路上花朵自会继续开放的。

Do not linger to gather flowers to keep them, but walk on, for flowers will keep themselves blooming all your way.

103

根是地下的枝。

枝是空中的根。

Roots are the branches down in the earth.

Branches are roots in the air.

104

远远去了的夏之音乐，翱翔于秋间，寻求它的旧垒。

The music of the far-away summer flutters around the Autumn seeking its former nest.

105

不要从你自己的袋里掏出勋绩借给你的朋友，这是污辱他的。

Do not insult your friend by lending him merits from your own pocket.

106

无名的日子的感触，攀缘在我的心上，正像那绿色的苔藓，攀缘在老树的周身。

The touch of the nameless days clings to my heart like mosses round the old tree.

107

回声嘲笑着她的原声，以证明她是原声。

The echo mocks her origin to prove she is the original.

108

当富贵利达的人夸说他得到神的特别恩惠时，上帝却羞了。

God is ashamed when the prosperous boasts of His special favour.

109

我投射我自己的影子在我的路上，因为我有一盏还没有燃点起来的明灯。

I cast my own shadow upon my path, because I have a lamp that has not been lighted.

110

人走进喧哗的群众里去，为的是要淹没他自己的沉默的呼号。

Man goes into the noisy crowed to drown his own clamour of silence.

111

终止于衰竭的是“死亡”，但“圆满”却终止于无穷。

That which ends in exhaustion is death, but the perfect ending is in the endless.

112

太阳只穿一件朴素的光衣，白云却披了灿烂的裙裾。

The sun has his simple rode of light. The clouds are decked with gorgeousness.

113

山峰如群儿之喧嚷，举起他们的双臂，想去捉天上的星星。

The hills are like shouts of children who raise their arms, trying to catch stars.

114

道路虽然拥挤，却是寂寞的，因为它是不被爱的。

The road is lonely in its crowd for it is not loved.

115

权势以它的恶行自夸，落下的黄叶与浮游的云片却在笑它。

The power that boasts of its mischiefs is laughed at by the yellow leaves that fall, and clouds that pass by.

116

今天大地在太阳光里向我营营哼鸣，像一个织着布的妇人，用一种已经被忘却的语言，哼着一些古代的歌曲。

The earth hums to me today in the sun, like a woman at her spinning, some ballad of the ancient time in a forgotten tongue.

117

绿草是无愧于它所生长的伟大世界的。

The grass-blade is worthy of the great world where it grows.

118

梦是一个一定要谈话的妻子，

睡眠是一个默默地忍受的丈夫。

Dream is a wife who must talk,

Sleep is a husband who silently suffers.

119

夜与逝去的日子接吻，轻轻地在他耳旁说道：“我是死，是你的母亲。我就要给你以新的生命。”

The night kisses the fading day whispering to his ear, “I am death,your mother. I am to give you fresh birth. ”

120

黑夜呀，我感觉到你的美了。你的美如一个可爱的妇人，当她把灯灭了的时候。

I feel thy beauty, dark night, like that of the loved woman when she has put out the lamp.

121

我把在那些已逝去的世界上的繁荣带到我的世界上来。

I carry in my world that flourishes the worlds that have failed.

122

亲爱的朋友呀，当我静听着海涛时，我好几次在暮色深沉的黄昏里，在这个海岸上，感到你的伟大思想的沉默了。

Dear friend, I feel the silence of your great thoughts of many a deepening eventide on this beach when I listen to these waves.

123

鸟以为把鱼举在空中是一种慈善的举动。

The bird thinks it is an act of kindness to give the fish a life in the air.

124

夜对太阳说道：“在月亮中，你送了你的情书给我。

“我已在绿草上留下我的流着泪点的回答了。”

“In the moon thou sendest thy love letters to me, ”said the night to the sun,“I leave my answers in tears upon the grass. ”

125

伟人是一个天生的孩子，当他死时，他把他的伟大的孩提时代给了世界。

The great is a born child; when he dies he gives his great childhood to the world.

126

不是槌的打击，乃是水的载歌载舞，使鹅卵石臻于完美。

Not hammer-strokes, but dance of the water sings the pebbles into perfection.

127

蜜蜂从花中啜蜜，离开时营营地道谢。

浮华的蝴蝶却相信花是应该向它道谢的。

Bees sip honey from flowers and hum their thanks when they leave.

The gaudy butterfly is sure that the flowers owe thanks to him.

128

如果你不等待着要说出完全的真理，那末把真话说出来是很容易的。

To be outspoken is easy when you do not wait to speak the complete truth.

129

“可能”问“不可能”道：

“你住在什么地方呢？”

它回答道：“在那无能为力者的梦境里。”

Asks the Possible to the Impossible,

“Where is your dwelling-place?”

“In the dreams of the impotent,” comes the answer.

130

闲暇在动作时便是工作。

静止的海水荡动时便成波涛。

Leisure in its activity is work.

The stillness of the sea stirs in waves.

131

绿叶恋爱时便成了花。

花崇拜时便成了果实。

The leaf becomes flower when it loves.

The flower becomes fruit when it worships.

132

如果你把所有的错误都关在门外时，真理也要被关在外面了。

If you shut your door to all errors truth will be shut out.

133

我听见有些东西在我心的忧闷后面萧萧作响，——我不能看见它们。

I hear some rustle of things behind my sadness of heart, —I cannot see them.

134

埋在地下的树根使树枝产生果实，却不要求什么报酬。

The roots below the earth claim no rewards for making the branches fruitful.

135

阴雨的黄昏，风无休止地吹着。

我看着摇曳的树枝，想念着万物的伟大。

This rainy evening the wind is restless.

I look at the swaying branches and ponder over the greatness of all things.

136

子夜的风雨，如一个巨大的孩子，在不合时宜的黑夜里醒来，开始游戏和喧闹。

Storm of midnight, like a giant child awakened in the untimely dark, has begun to play and shout.

137

文字对工作说道：“我惭愧我的空虚。”

工作对文字说道：“当我看见你时，我便知道我是怎样的贫乏了。”

“I am ashamed of my emptiness, ”said the Word to the Work.

“I know how poor I am when I see you,” said the Work to the Word.

138

海呀，你这暴风雨的孤寂的新妇呀，你虽掀起波浪追随你的情人，但是无用呀。

Thou raisest thy waves vainly to follow thy lover, O sea, thou lonely bride of the storm.

139

时间是变化的财富。时钟模仿它，却只有变化而无财富。

Time is the wealth of change, but the clock in its parody makes it mere change and no wealth.

140

真理穿了衣裳，觉得事实太拘束了。
在想象中，她却转动得很舒畅。

Truth in her dress finds facts too tight.
In fiction she moves with ease.

141

当我到这里那里旅行着时，路呀，我厌倦你了；但是现在，当你引导我到各处去时，我便爱上你，与你结婚了。

When I travelled to here and to there, I was tired of thee, O Road, but now when thou leadest me to everywhere I am wedded to thee in love.

142

让我设想，在群星之中，有一颗星是指导着我的生命通过不可知的黑暗的。

Let me think that there is one among those stars that guides my life through the dark unknown.

143

妇人，你用了你美丽的手指，触着我的什物，
秩序便如音乐似的生出来了。
Woman, with the grace of your fingers you touched my things and order came out like music.

144

一个忧郁的声音，筑巢于逝水似的年华中。
它在夜里向我唱道："我爱你。"
One sad voice has its nest among the ruins of the years.
It sings to me in the night, —I loved you.

145

燃着的火，以它熊熊的光焰警告我不要走近它。
把我从潜藏在灰中的余烬里救出来吧。
The flaming fire warns me off by its own glow.
Save me from the dying embers hidden under ashes.

146

我有群星在天上，
但是，唉，我屋里的小灯却没有点亮。
I have my stars in the sky.
But oh for my little lamp unlit in my house.

147

死文字的尘土沾着你。
用沉默去洗净你的灵魂吧。
The dust of the dead words clings to thee.
Wash thy soul with silence.

148

生命里留了许多罅隙，从中送来了死之忧郁的音乐。

Gaps are left in life through which comes the sad music of death.

149

世界已在早晨敞开了它的光明之心。

出来吧，我的心，带着你的爱去与它相会。

The world has opened its heart of light in the morning.

Come out, my heart, with thy love to meet it.

150

我的思想随着这些闪耀的绿叶而闪耀；我的心灵因了这日光的抚触而歌唱；我的生命因为偕了万物一同浮泛在空间的蔚蓝、时间的墨黑中而感到欢快。

My thoughts shimmer with these shimmering leaves and my heart sings with the touch of this sunlight; my life is glad to be floating with all things into the blue of space, into the dark of time.

152

在梦中，一切事都散漫着，都压着我，但这不过是一个梦呀。当我醒来时，我便将觉得这些事都已聚集在你那里，我也便将自由了。

This is a dream in which things are all loose and they oppress.

I shall find them gathered in thee when I awake and shall be free.

151

神的巨大的威权是在柔和的微飔里，而不在狂风暴雨之中。

God’s great power is in the gentle breeze, not in the storm.

153

落日问道：“有谁继续我的职务呢？”

瓦灯说道：“我要尽我所能地做去，我的主人。”

“Who is there to take up my duties?” asked the setting sun.

“I shall do what I can, my Master,” said the earthen lamp.

154

采着花瓣时，得不到花的美丽。

By plucking her petals you do not gather the beauty of the flower.

155

沉默蕴蓄着语声，正如鸟巢拥围着睡鸟。

Silence will carry your voice like the nest that holds the sleeping birds.

156

大的不怕与小的同游。

居中的却远而避之。

The Great walks with the Small without fear.

The Middling keeps aloof.

157

雨点吻着大地，微语道：“我们是你的思家的孩子，母亲，现在从天上回到你这里来了。”

The raindrops kissed the earth and whispered, —We are thy homesick children, mother, come back to thee from the heaven.

367Art.com

158

夜秘密地把花开放了，却让那白日去领受谢词。

The night opens the flowers in secret and allows the day to get thanks.

159

权势认为牺牲者的痛苦是忘恩负义。

Power takes as ingratitude the writhings of its victims.

160

当我们以我们的充实为乐时，那末，我们便能很快乐地跟我们的果实分手了。

When we rejoice in our fulness, then we can part with our fruits with joy.

161

蛛网好像要捉露点，却捉住了苍蝇。

The cobweb pretends to catch dewdrops and catches flies.

162

爱情呀，当你手里拿着点亮了的痛苦之灯走来时，我能够看见你的脸，而且以你为幸福。

Love! When you come with the burning lamp of pain in your hand, I can see your face and know you as bliss.

163

在黄昏的微光里，有那清晨的鸟儿来到了我的沉默的鸟巢里。

In the dusk of the evening the bird of some early dawn comes to the nest of my silence.

164

沟洫总喜欢想：河流的存在，是专为它供给水流的。

The canal loves to think that rivers exist solely to supply it with water.

165

萤火对天上的星说道：“学者说你的光明总有一天会消灭的。”

天上的星不回答它。

“The leaned say that your lights will one day be no more,” said the firefly to the stars.

The stars made no answer.

166

思想掠过我的心上，如一群野鸭飞过天空。

我听见它们鼓翼之声了。

Thoughts pass in my mind like flocks of lucks in the sky.

I hear the voice of their wings.

167

世界以它的痛苦同我接吻，而要求歌声作报酬。

The world has kissed my soul with its pain, asking for its return in songs.

168

压迫着我的，到底是我的想要外出的灵魂呢，还是那世界的灵魂，敲着我心的门，想要进来呢？

That which oppresses me, is it my soul trying to come out in the open, or the soul of the world knocking at my heart for its entrance?

169

思想以它自己的言语喂养它自己而成长起来。

Thought feeds itself with its own words and grows.

170

我把我的心之碗轻轻浸入这沉默之时刻中，它盛满了爱了。

I have dipped the vessel of my heart into this silent hour; it has filled with love.

171

或者你在工作，或者你没有。

当你不得不说“让我们做些事吧”时，那末就要开始胡闹了。

Either you have work or you have not.

When you have to say, “Let us do something”, then begins mischief.

172

向日葵羞于把无名的花朵看做它的同胞。

太阳升上来了，向它微笑，说道：“你好么，我的宝贝儿？”

The sunflower blushed to own the nameless flower as her kin.

The sun rose and smiled on it, saying, “Are you well, my darling?”

173

“谁如命运似的推着我向前走呢？”

“那是我自己，在身背后大跨步走着。”

Who drives me forward like fate?

The Myself striding on my back.

174

云把水倒在河的水杯里，它们自己却藏在远山之中。

The clouds fill the watercups of the river, hiding themselves in the distant hills.

175

我一路走去，从我的水瓶中漏出水来。

只剩下极少极少的水供我回家使用了。

I spill water from my water jar as I walk on my way, very little remains for my home.

176

杯中的水是光辉的；海中的水却是黑色的。

小理可以用文字来说清楚；大理却只有沉默。

The water in a vessel is sparkling; the water in the sea is dark.

The small truth has words that are clear; the great truth has great silence.

177

你的微笑是你自己田园里的花，你的谈吐是你自己山上的松林的萧萧；但是你的心呀，却是那个女人，那个我们全都认识的女人。

Your smile was the flowers of your own fields, your talk was the rustle of your own mountain pines, but your heart was the woman that we all know.

178

我把小小的礼物留给我所爱的人，——大的礼物却留给一切的人。

It is the little things that I leave behind for my loved ones, —great things are for everyone.

179

妇人呀，你用泪海包绕着世界的心，正如大海包绕着大地。

Woman, thou hast encircled the world’s heart with the depth of thy tears as the sea has the earth.

180

太阳以微笑向我问候。

雨，他的忧闷的姊姊，向我的心谈话。

The sunshine greets me with a smile.

The rain, his sad sister, talks to my heart.

181

我的昼间之花，落下它那被遗忘的花瓣。

在黄昏中，这花成熟为一颗记忆的金果。

My flower of the day dropped its petals forgotten.

In the evening it ripens into a golden fruit of memory.

182

我像那夜间之路，正静悄悄地谛听着记忆的足音。

I am like the road in the night listening to the footfalls of its memories in silence.

183

黄昏的天空，在我看来，像一扇窗户，一盏灯火，灯火背后的一次等待。

The evening sky to me is like a window, and a lighted lamp, and a waiting behind it.

184

太急于做好事的人，反而找不到时间去做好人。

He who is too busy doing good finds no time to be good.

185

我是秋云，空空地不载着雨水，但在成熟的稻田中，可以看见我的充实。

I am the autumn cloud, empty of rain, see my fulness in the field of ripened rice.

186

他们嫉妒，他们残杀，人反而称赞他们。

然而上帝却害了羞，匆匆地把他的记忆埋藏在绿草下面。

They hated and killed and men praised them.

But God in shame hastens to hide its memory under the green grass.

187

脚趾乃是舍弃了其过去的手指。

Toes are the fingers that have forsaken their past.

188

黑暗向光明旅行，但是盲者却向死亡旅行。

Darkness travels towards light, but blindness towards death.

189

小狗疑心大宇宙阴谋篡夺它的位置。

The pet dog suspects the universe for scheming to take its place.

190

静静地坐着吧，我的心，不要扬起你的尘土。
让世界自己寻路向你走来。

Sit still, my heart, do not raise your dust.
Let the world find its way to you.

191

弓在箭要射出之前，低声对箭说道：“你的自由就是我的自由。”

The bow whispers to the arrow before it speeds forth—your freedom is mine.

192

妇人，在你的笑声里有着生命之泉的音乐。

Woman, in your laughter you have the music of the fountain of life.

193

全是理智的心，恰如一柄全是锋刃的刀。

它叫使用它的人手上流血。

A mind all logic is like a knife all blade.

It makes the hand bleed that uses it.

194

神爱人间的灯光甚于他自己的大星。

God loves man's lamp lights better than his own great stars.

195

这世界乃是为美之音乐所驯服了的狂风骤雨的世界。

This world is the world of wild storms kept tame with the music of beauty.

196

晚霞向太阳说道：“我的心经了你的接吻，便似金的宝箱了。”

“My heart is like the golden casket of thy kiss,” cloud to the sun.

197

接触着，你许会杀害；远离着，你许会占有。

By touching you may kill, by keeping away you may possess.

198

蟋蟀的唧唧，夜雨的淅沥，从黑暗中传到我的耳边，好似我已逝的少年时代沙沙地来到我梦境中。

The cricket's chirp and the patter of rain come to me through the dark, like the rustle of dreams from my past youth.

199

花朵向星辰落尽了的曙天叫道："我的露点全失落了。"

"I have lost my dewdrop,"cries the flower to the morning sky that has lost all its stars.

200

燃烧着的木块，熊熊地生出火光，叫道："这是我的花朵，我的死亡。"

The burning log bursts in flame and cries, —"This is my flower, my death."

201

黄蜂认为邻蜂储蜜之巢太小。

他的邻人要他去建筑一个更小的。

The wasp thinks that the honeyhive of the neighbouring bees is too small.

His neighbours ask him to build one still smaller.

202

河岸向河流说道："我不能留住你的波浪。

"让我保存你的足印在我心里吧。"

"I cannot keep your waves," says the bank to the river,

"Let me keep your footprints in my heart. "

203

白日以这小小地球的喧扰，淹没了整个宇宙的沉默。

The day, with the noise of this little earth, drowns the silence of all worlds.

204

歌声在空中感到无限，图画在地上感到无限，诗呢，无论在空中、在地上都是如此。

因为诗的词句含有能走动的意义与能飞翔的音乐。

The song feels the infinite in the air, the picture in the earth, the poem in the air and the earth;For its words have meaning that walks and music that soars.

205

太阳在西方落下时，他的早晨的东方已静悄悄地站在他面前。

When the sun goes down to the West, the East of his morning stands before him in silence.

206

让我不要错误地把自己放在我的世界里而使它反对我。

Let me not put myself wrongly to my world and set it against me.

207

荣誉使我感到惭愧，因为我暗地里求着它。

Praise shames me, for I secretly beg for it.

208

当我没有什么事做时，便让我不做什么事、不受骚扰地沉入安静深处吧，一如那海水沉默时海边的暮色。

Let my doing nothing when I have nothing to do become untroubled in its depth of peace like the evening in the seashore when the water is silent.

209

少女呀，你的纯朴，如湖水之碧，表现出你的真理之深邃。

Maiden, your simplicity, like the blueness of the lake, reveals your depth of truth.

210

最好的东西不是独来的，
它伴了所有的东西同来。

The best does not come alone.
It comes with the company of the all.

211

神的右手是慈爱的，但是他的左手却可怕。

God's right hand is gentle, but terrible is his left hand.

212

我的晚色从陌生的树木中走来，它用我的晓星所不懂得的语言说话。

My evening came among the alien trees and spoke in a language which my morning stars did not know.

213

夜之黑暗是一只口袋，迸出黎明的金光。

Night's darkness is a bag that bursts with the gold of the dawn.

214

我们的欲望把彩虹的颜色借给那只不过是云雾的人生。

Our desire lends the colours of the rainbow to the mere mists and vapours of life.

215

神等待着，要从人的手上把他自己的花朵作为礼物赢回去。

God waits to win back his own flowers as gifts from man's hands.

216

我的忧思缠扰着我，要问我它们自己的名字。

My sad thoughts tease me asking me their own names.

217

果实的事业是尊贵的，花的事业是甜美的；但是让我做叶的事业吧，叶是谦逊地、专心地垂着绿荫的。

The service of the fruit is precious, the service of the flower is sweet, but let my service be the service of the leaves in its shade of humble devotion.

218

我的心向着阑珊的风张了帆，要到无论何处的荫凉之岛去。

My heart has spread its sails to the idle winds for the shadowy island of Anywhere.

219

独夫们是凶暴的，但人民是善良的。

Men are cruel, but Man is kind.

220

把我当做你的杯吧，让我为了你，而且为了你的人而盛满水吧。

Make me thy cup and let my fulness be for thee and for thine.

221

狂风暴雨像是在痛苦中的某个天神的哭声，因为他的爱情被大地所拒绝。

The storm is like the cry of some god in pain whose love the earth refuses.

222

世界不会流失，因为死亡并不是一个罅隙。

The world does not leak because death is not a crack.

223

生命因为付出了的爱情而更为富足。

Life has become richer by the love that has been lost.

224

我的朋友，你伟大的心闪射出东方朝阳的光芒，正如黎明中一个积雪的孤峰。

My friend, your great heart shone with the sunrise of the East like the snowy summit of a lonely hill in the dawn.

225

那些有一切东西而没有您的人，我的上帝，在讥笑着那些没有别的东西而只有您的人呢。

Those who have everything but thee, my God, laugh at those who have nothing but thyself.

226

死之流泉，使生的止水跳跃。

The fountain of death makes the still water of life play.

227

生命的运动在它自己的音乐里得到它的休息。

The movement of life has its rest in its own music.

228

踢足只能从地上扬起灰尘而不能得到收获。

Kicks only raise dust and not crops from the earth.

229

我们的名字，便是夜里海波上发出的光，痕迹也不留就泯灭了。

Our names are the light that glows on the sea waves at night and then dies without leaving its signature.

230

让睁眼看着玫瑰花的人也看看它的刺。

Let him only see the thorns who has eyes to see the rose.

231

鸟翼上系上了黄金，这鸟便永不能再在天上翱翔了。

Set the bird's wings with gold and it will never again soar in the sky.

232

我们地方的荷花又在这陌生的水上开了花，放出同样的清香，只是名字换了。

The same lotus of our clime blooms here in the alien water with the same sweetness, under another name.

233

在心的远景里，那相隔的距离显得更广阔了。

In heart’s perspective the distance looms large.

234

月儿把她的光明遍照在天上，却留着她的黑斑给她自己。

The moon has her light all over the sky, her dark spots to herself.

235

不要说“这是早晨”，别用一个“昨天”的名词把它打发掉。你第一次看到它，把它当做还没有名字的新生孩子吧。

Do not say, “It is morning,” and dismiss it with a mane of yesterday.

See it for the first time as a new-born child that has no name.

236

雨点向茉莉花微语道：“把我永久地留在你的心里吧。”

茉莉花叹息了一声，落在地上了。

The raindrop whispered to the jasmine, “Keep me in your heart for ever.”

The jasmine sighed, “Alas,” and dropped to the ground.

237

青烟对天空夸口，灰烬对大地夸口，都以为它们是火的兄弟。

Smoke boasts to the sky, and Ashes to the earth, that they are brothers to the fire.

238

胆怯的思想呀，不要怕我。

我是一个诗人。

Timid thoughts, do not be afraid of me.

I am a poet.

239

我的心在朦胧的沉默里，似乎充满了蟋蟀的鸣声——声音的灰暗的暮色。

The dim silence of my mind seems filled with crickets' chirp—the grey twilight of sound.

240

爆竹呀，你对于群星的侮蔑，又跟着你自己回到地上来了。

Rockets, your insult to the stars follows yourself back to the earth.

241

您曾经带领着我，穿过我的白天的拥挤不堪的旅程，而到达了我的黄昏的孤寂之境。

在通宵的寂静里，我等待着它的意义。

Thou hast led me through my crowded travels of the day to my evening's loneliness.

I wait for its meaning through the stillness of the night.

242

我们的生命就似渡过一个大海，我们都相聚在这个狭小的舟中。
死时，我们便到了岸，各往各的世界去了。

This life is the crossing of a sea, where we meet in the same narrow ship.
In death we reach the shore and go to our different worlds.

243

真理之川从它的错误之沟渠中流过。

The stream of truth flows through its channels of mistakes.

244

今天我的心是在想家了，在想着那跨过时间之海的那一个甜蜜的时候。

My heart is homesick today for the one sweet hour across the sea of time.

245

鸟的歌声是曙光从大地反响过去的回声。

The bird-song is the echo of the morning light back from the earth.

246

晨光问毛茛道：“你是骄傲得不肯和我接吻么？”

“Are you too proud to kiss me?” the morning light asks the buttercup.

247

小花问道：“我要怎样地对你唱，怎样地崇拜你呢，太阳呀？”

太阳答道：“只要用你的纯洁的素朴的沉默。”

“How may I sing to thee and worship, O Sun?” asked the little flower.

“By the simple silence of thy purity,” answered the sun.

248

当人是兽时，他比兽还坏。

Man is worse than an animal when he is an animal.

249

黑云受光的接吻时便变成天上的花朵。

Dark clouds become heaven’s flowers when kissed by light.

250

不要让刀锋讥笑它柄子的拙钝。

Let not the sword-blade mock its handle for being blunt.

251

死像大海的无限的歌声，日夜冲击着生命的光明岛的四周。

Around the sunny island of Life swells day and night death’s limitless song of the sea.

252

夜的沉默，如一个深深的灯盏，银河便是它燃着的灯光。

The night's silence, like a deep lamp, is burning with the light of its milky way.

253

花瓣似的山峰在饮着日光，这山岂不像一朵花吗？

Is not this mountain like a flower, with its petals of hill, drinking the sunlight?

254

“真实”的含义被误解，轻重被倒置，那就成了“不真实”。

The real with its meaning read wrong and emphasis misplaced is the unreal.

255

我的心呀，从世界的流动中找你的美吧，正如那小船得到风与水的优美似的。

Find your beauty, my heart, from the world's movement, like the boat that has the grace of the wind and the water.

256

眼不以能视来骄人，却以它们的眼镜来骄人。

The eyes are not proud of their sight but of their eyeglasses.

257

我住在我的这个小小世界里，生怕使它再缩小一丁点儿。把我抬举到您的世界里去吧，让我有高高兴兴地失去我的一切的自由。

I live in this little world of mine and am afraid to make it the least less. Life me into thy world and let me have the freedom gladly to lose my all.

258

虚伪永远不能凭借它生长在权力中而变成真实。

The false can never grow into truth by growing in power.

259

我的心，同着它的歌的拍拍舐岸的波浪，渴望着要抚爱这个阳光熙和的绿色世界。

My heart, with its lapping waves of song, longs to caress this green world of the sunny day.

260

道旁的草，爱那天上的星吧，你的梦境便可在花朵里实现了。

Wayside grass, love the star, then your dreams will come out in flowers.

261

让你的音乐如一柄利刃，直刺入市井喧扰的心中吧。

Let your music, like a sword, pierce the noise of the market to its heart.

262

这树的颤动之叶，触动着我的心，像一个婴儿的手指。

The trembling leaves of this tree touch my heart like the fingers of an infant child.

263

小花睡在尘土里。

它寻求蛱蝶走的道路。

The little flower lies in the dust.

It sought the path of the butterfly.

264

我是在道路纵横的世界上。

夜来了。打开您的门吧，家之世界呵！

I am in the world of the roads.

The night comes. Open thy gate, thou world of the home.

265

我已经唱过了您的白天的歌。

在黄昏时候，让我拿着您的灯走过风雨飘摇的道路吧。

I have sung the songs of thy day.

In the evening let me carry thy lamp through the stormy path.

266

我不要求你进我的屋里。

你到我无量的孤寂里来吧，我的爱人！

I do not ask thee into the house.

Come into my infinite loneliness, my lover.

267

死亡隶属于生命，正与生一样。

举足是走路，正如落足也是走路。

Death belongs to life as birth does.

The walk is in the raising of the foot as in the laying of it down.

268

我已经学会了你在花与阳光里微语的意义。——再教我明白你在苦与死中所说的话吧。

I have learnt the simple meaning of thy whispers in flowers and sunshine—teach me to know thy words in pain and death.

269

夜的花朵来晚了，当早晨吻着她时，她战栗着，叹息了一声，萎落在地上了。

The night's flower was late when the morning kissed her, she shivered and sighed and dropped to the ground.

270

从万物的愁苦中，我听见了“永恒母亲”的呻吟。

Through the sadness of all things I hear the crooning of the Eternal Mother.

271

大地呀，我到你岸上时是一个陌生人，住在你屋内时是一个宾客，离开你的门时是一个朋友。

I came to your shore as a stranger, I lived in your house as a guest,
I leave your door as a friend, my earth.

272

当我去时，让我的思想到你那里来，如那夕阳的余光，映在沉默的星天的边上。

Let my thoughts come to you, when I am gone, like the after glow of sunset at the margin of starry silence.

273

在我的心头燃点起那休憩的黄昏星吧，然后让黑夜向我微语着爱情。

Light in my heart the evening star of rest and then let the night whisper to me of love.

274

我是一个在黑暗中的孩子。

我从夜的被单里向您伸出我的双手，母亲。

I am a child in the dark.

I stretch my hands through the coverlet of night for thee, Mother.

275

白天的工作完了。把我的脸掩藏在您的臂间吧，母亲。

让我入梦吧。

The day of work is done. Hide my face in your arms, Mother.

Let me dream.

276

集会时的灯光，点了很久，会散时，灯便立刻灭了。

The lamp of meeting burns long; it goes out in a moment at the parting.

277

当我死时，世界呀，请在你的沉默中，替我留着“我已经爱过了”这句话吧。

One word keep for me in thy silence, O World, when I am dead, I have loved.

278

我们在热爱世界时便生活在这世界上。

We live in this world when we love it.

279

我看见你，像那半醒的婴孩在黎明的微光里看见他的母亲，于是微笑而又睡去了。

I have seen thee as the half-awakened child sees his mother in the dusk of the dawn and then smiles and sleeps again.

280

让死者有那不朽的名，但让生者有那不朽的爱。

Let the dead have the immortality of fame, but the living the immortality of love.

281

我将死了又死，以明白生是无穷无尽的。

I shall die again and again to know that life is inexhaustible.

282

当我和拥挤的人群一同在路上走过时，我看见您从阳台上送过来的微笑，我歌唱着，忘却了所有的喧哗。

While I was passing with the crowd in the road I saw thy smile from the balcony and I sang and forgot all noise.

283

爱就是充实了的生命，正如盛满了酒的酒杯。

Love is life in its fulness like the cup with its wine.

284

他们点了他们自己的灯，在他们的寺院内，吟唱他们自己的话语。

但是小鸟们却在你的晨光中，唱着你的名字，——因为你的名字便是快乐。

They light their own lamps and sing their own words in their temples.

But the birds sing thy name in thine own morning light,—for thy name is joy.

285

让那些选择了他们自己的焰火嗞嗞的世界的，就生活在那里吧。

我的心渴望着您的繁星，我的上帝。

Let them live who choose in their own hissing world of fireworks.

My heart longs for thy stars, my God.

286

领我到您的沉寂的中心，使我的心充满了歌吧。

Lead me in the centre of thy silence to fill my heart with songs.

287

爱的痛苦环绕着我的一生，像汹涌的大海似的唱着；而爱的快乐却像鸟儿们在花林里似的唱着。

Love's pain sang round my life like the unplumbed sea, and love's joy sang like birds in its flowering groves.

288

假如您愿意，您就熄了灯吧。

我将明白您的黑暗，而且将喜爱它。

Put out the lamp when thou wishest.

I shall know thy darkness and shall love it.

289

当我在那日子的终了，站在您的面前时，您将看见我的伤疤，而知道我有我的许多创伤，但也有我的医治的法儿。

When I stand before thee at the day's end thou shalt see my scars and know that I had my wounds and also my healing.

290

总有一天，我要在别的世界的晨光里对你唱道："我以前在地球的光里，在人的爱里，已经见过你了。"

Some day I shall sing to thee in the sunrise of some other world, "I have seen thee before in the light of the earth, in the love of man."

291

从别的日子里飘浮到我的生命里的云，不再落下雨点或引起风暴了，却只给予我的夕阳的天空以色彩。

Clouds come floating into my life from other days no longer to shed rain or usher storm but to give colour to my sunset sky.

292

真理引起了反对它自己的狂风骤雨，那场风雨吹散了真理的广播的种子。

Truth raises against itself the storm that scatters its seeds broadcast.

293

昨夜的风雨给今日的早晨戴上了金色的和平。

The storm of the last night has crowned this morning with golden peace.

294

真理仿佛带了它的结论而来，而那结论却产生了它的第二个。

Truth seems to come with its final word; and the final word gives birth to its next.

295

他是有福的，因为他的名望并没有比他的真实更光亮。

Blessed is he whose fame does not outshine his truth.

296

您的名字的甜蜜充溢着我的心，而我忘掉了我自己的——就像您的早晨的太阳升起时，那大雾便消失了。

Sweetness of thy name fills my heart when I forget mine—like thy morning sun when the mist is melted.

297

静悄悄的黑夜具有母亲的美丽，而吵闹的白天具有孩子的美。

The silent night has the beauty of the mother and the clamorous day of the child.

298

当人微笑时，世界爱了他；当他大笑时，世界便怕他了。

The world loved man when he smiled. The world became afraid of him when he laughed.

299

神等待着人在智慧中重新获得童年。

God waits for man to regain his childhood in wisdom.

300

让我感到这个世界乃是您的爱的成形吧，那末，我的爱也将帮助着它。

Let me feel this world as thy love taking form, then my love will help it.

301

您的阳光对着我的心头的冬天微笑着，从来不怀疑它的春天的花朵。

Thy sunshine smiles upon the winter days of my heart, never doubting of its spring flowers.

302

神在他的爱里吻着“有涯”，而人却吻着“无涯”。

God kisses the finite in his love and man the infinite.

303

您越过不毛之地的沙漠而到达了圆满的时刻。

Thou crossest desert lands of barren years to reach the moment of fulfilment.

304

神的静默使人的思想成熟而为语言。

God’s silence ripens man’s thoughts into speech.

305

“永恒的旅客”呀，你可以在我的歌中找到你的足迹。

Thou will find, Eternal Traveller, marks of thy footsteps across my songs.

306

让我不至羞辱您吧，父亲，您在您的孩子们身上显现出您的光荣。

Let me not shame thee, Father, who displayest thy glory in thy children.

307

这一天是不快活的。光在蹙额的云下，如一个被责打的儿童，灰白的脸上留着泪痕；风又叫号着，似一个受伤的世界的哭声。但是我知道，我正跋涉着去会我的朋友。

Cheerless is the day, the light under frowning clouds is like a punished child with traces of tears on its pale cheeks, and the cry of the wind is like the cry of a wounded world. But I know I am travelling to meet my Friend.

308

今天晚上棕榈叶在嚓嚓地作响，海上有大浪，满月呵，就像世界在心脉悸跳。从什么不可知的天空，您在您的沉默里带来了爱的痛苦的秘密?

Tonight there is a stir among the palm leaves, a swell in the sea, Full Moon, like the heart throb of the world. From what unknown sky hast thou carried in thy silence the aching secret of love?

309

我梦见一颗星，一个光明岛屿，我将在那里出生。在它快速的闲暇深处，我的生命将成熟它的事业，像秋天阳光下的稻田。

I dream of a star, an island of light, where I shall be born and in the depth of its quickening leisure my life will ripen its works like the rice-field in the autumn sun.

310

雨中的湿土的气息，就像从渺小的无声的群众那里来的一阵巨大的赞美歌声。

The smell of the wet earth in the rain rises like a great chant of praise from the voiceless multitude of the insignificant.

311

说爱情会失去的那句话，乃是我们不能够当做真理来接受的一个事实。

That love can ever lose is a fact that we cannot accept as truth.

312

我们将有一天会明白，死永远不能够夺去我们的灵魂所获得的东西。因为她所获得的，和她自己是一体。

We shall know some day that death can never rob us of that which our soul has gained, for her gains are one with herself.

313

神在我的黄昏的微光中，带着花到我这里来。这些花都是我过去的，在他的花篮中还保存得很新鲜。

God comes to me in the dusk of my evening with the flowers from my past kept fresh in his basket.

314

主呀，当我的生之琴弦都已调得谐和时，你的手的一弹一奏，都可以发出爱的乐声来。

When all the strings of my life will be tuned, my Master, then at every touch of thine will come out the music of love.

315

让我真真实实地活着吧，我的上帝。这样，死对于我也就成了真实的了。

Let me live truly, my Lord, so that death to me become true.

316

人类的历史在很忍耐地等待着被侮辱者的胜利。

Man's history is waiting in patience for the triumph of the insulted man.

317

我这一刻感到你的眼光正落在我的心上，像那早晨阳光中的沉默落在已收获的孤寂的田野上一样。

I feel thy gaze upon my heart this moment like the sunny silence of the morning upon the lonely field whose harvest is over.

318

在这喧哗的波涛起伏的海中，我渴望着咏歌之岛。

I long for the Island of Songs across this heaving Sea of Shouts.

319

夜的序曲是开始于夕阳西下的音乐，开始于它对难以形容的黑暗所作的庄严的赞歌。

The prelude of the night is commenced in the music of the sunset, in its solemn hymn to the ineffable dark.

320

我攀登上高峰，发现在名誉的荒芜不毛的高处，简直找不到一个遮身之地。我的引导者呵，领导着我在光明逝去之前，进到沉静的山谷里去吧。在那里，一生的收获将会成熟为黄金的智慧。

I have scaled the peak and found no shelter in fame's bleak and barren height. Lead me, my Guide, before the light fades, into the valley of quiet where life's harvest mellows into golden wisdom.

321

在这个黄昏的朦胧里，好些东西看来都仿佛是幻象一般——尖塔的底层在黑暗里消失了，树顶像是墨水的模糊的斑点似的。我将等待着黎明，而当我醒来的时候，就会看到在光明里的您的城市。

Things look phantasmic in this dimness of the dusk—the spires whose bases are lost in the dark and tree tops like blots of ink. I shall wait for the morning and wake up to see thy city in the light.

322

我曾经受过苦，曾经失望过，曾经体会过“死亡”，于是我以我在这伟大的世界里为乐。

I have suffered and despaired and known death and I am glad that I am in this great world.

323

在我的一生里，也有贫乏和沉默的地域。它们是我忙碌的日子得到日光与空气的几片空旷之地。

There are tracts in my life that are bare and silent. They are the open spaces where my busy days had their light and air.

324

我的未完成的过去，从后边缠绕到我身上，使我难于死去。请从它那里释放了我吧。

Release me from my unfulfilled past clinging to me from behind making death difficult.

325

“我相信你的爱。”让这句话作我的最后的话。

Let this be my last word, that I trust thy love.

故事诗集

泰戈尔诗文彩图馆

无上布施

“世尊之名，请你布施。
啊！世人，谁已清醒？”
给孤独长者庄严而低沉的声音在呼唤。

彼时，舍卫城承接苍天的宫阙上，
初升旭日睁开了尚有朦胧睡意的艳红笑眼。

神灵的颂唱着尚沉睡梦乡，
祝福的晨歌未曾弹唱。
杜鹃因对黎明天色的怀疑，
它的啼声轻缓迟疑。

比丘僧高声呼唤：“酣睡的城市，理应清醒！给我布施。”

这声音使梦中的男女竟然不寒而栗。

“世人！六月云霞愿牺牲自身而洒落甘霖，
大千世界的诸般宗教，布施最为第一。”

佛子声音仿若湿婆天的音乐，
从凯拉萨深山处远远传来，
震撼了红尘十丈中欢醉的男女。

帝王心内的空虚非是江山财富能填满，
家务的繁琐致使忙碌的家主为之叹息，
青春靓丽的姑娘们毫无因由滚落泪滴。

沉醉于爱欲欢乐中的男女，
忆起了于作业逝去的柔情蜜意，
仿佛散碎花环上一朵干枯的茉莉。

世人推开各自门窗，
眨动着带有朦胧睡意的双眼，
好奇地伸头凝望着晦暗中的街路。

“苏醒吧，向佛施舍”的呼声传入沉睡的万家，
世尊的门徒独自从空旷街心走来。

珠宝商的娇妻与爱女将珍宝捧捧抛向街心，

她摘下项链，他则奉献头上的摩尼。

富有者的盘盘黄金未曾被比丘理睬，任由它们被抛弃当场，
他仍在高呼“为了佛陀，我向你们乞讨。”

尘埃上铺满锦绣，
无价之宝在晨光中绽放光彩，
给孤独长者手中的钵盂仍旧空空。

“世人啊，请你们明白。我的世尊赐福保佑众生，
请将你们财富中最美好的布施给他。”

帝王起驾回宫，珠宝商也回转家中，
没有什么献礼可以作为敬佛的供养，
偌大的舍卫国的繁华都城低下羞惭的头。

朝阳在东方天际升起，

城市的人也不再休息，
比丘顺着大街缓缓步入城边的林里。

一位贫穷的妇女躺在林中，
身体唯有一件褴褛的衣衫，
她跪倒比丘莲花足前双手顶礼。

妇人随后将身形隐藏在林里，
脱掉那褴褛的破衣，
伸出手，毫不怜惜地将它抛出林地。

比丘高举双臂欢呼：
“给你祝福，可敬的母亲，你的一念成就了佛陀的心意。”

比丘欢悦地离开城市，
头上顶着那件褴褛的破衣，
将要将它奉献在世尊光辉的足底。

代理人

这一日的清晨，希瓦吉在塞达拉堡的门前见到
他的师傅，拉姆达斯，
正如一个可怜的穷人挨家乞讨。

他为眼前的情景心生疑惑。
这是怎么回事?
师傅竟然用钵盂沿街乞讨。
他拥有一切，家境绝不贫寒，
匍匐于他脚前的国王都无法填满他的欲望。
就好像不断将水倒在残破的碗中来消灭干渴，
一切都是白费气力。

希瓦吉想："倒要看看究竟如何才能将行乞的钵盂装满。"
他拿起笔写下什么东西，将这事吩咐给大臣巴拉吉：
"如果我敬爱的师傅行乞到城堡之前，就将此信奉献于他的脚底。"

师傅边走边歌唱，

无数行人车马在他面前走过。

“啊，商羯罗，啊！湿婆，你赐予众生家园，却令我走遍天涯。

安那普尔纳女神，负有哺育宇宙的责任，使众生皆大欢喜；

啊，毗卡利！永恒的使者！却将我从女神处抢走，成为你的奴隶。”

曲终之后，经过中午的沐浴，

师傅走到了城堡的宫门外——

巴拉吉恭敬地行礼，将书信摆放在他的脚前。

师傅好奇地将书信从地上捡起，仔细地阅读书简。

希瓦吉，他的弟子，

献上了自己的国土和王冠，拜伏在他莲花般的脚底。

第二天，师傅来到国王的面前，说：

“孩子，回答我，既然你将国土献给我，那如此聪明能干的你将何去何从？”

希瓦吉顶礼师傅说：

“我将我的生命也奉献给你，我将愉快地成为你的奴隶。”

师傅说：“好，背上这条口袋与我同去行乞。”

希瓦吉陪伴着师傅，手捧钵盂挨家挨户乞求供养的食物。

孩子们惊惧地跑回家，喊叫他们的爹娘围观行乞的国王。

拥有无尽的财富，却愿意沿街行乞，好像石头漂浮在水面之上。

人们畏怯地赠与食物，他们的手还在簌簌发抖，心中想的是：这莫不是大人物的玩笑？

随着碉楼上午炮响起，人们停下了生活的繁忙，进入午睡的梦乡。

拉姆达斯则虔诚地高颂神曲，泪水中闪烁着欢欣。

“啊！三界的主宰，你的心思我无法猜中，一切理应归你所有。

你却向人们的内心深处伸出乞讨的手，我的主，你想要求得财富中的财富。”

天色已晚，师徒们在城外堤岸边的河水中沐浴之后，
煮熟了乞讨来的粥糜。
师傅将一些分给了徒弟，自己愉快地享用晚餐。
希瓦吉笑着说：
“你曾将国王的骄傲抹杀，使他变成乞讨的乞丐；
我永远是你的奴隶，宁愿受尽苦辛也愿满足师傅的愿望。”

师傅说：“那么且听我说，
你既然作出如此誓言坚定不移，
可以换个行为将责任担起。

我如此向你嘱托，收回曾献给我的国土。
我任命你为乞丐的代理——国王本就是卑微的托钵人。
你须牢记国王的职责，亦是完成对我的职务。
身为国王，你却要谨记自己是没有国土的平民。”

“孩子，拿走我赭色的衣服带走我的祝福，
苦行者的破衣也可称为神圣的国旗，让它插在你的国土飘扬。”

国王，弟子静坐在河边沉默无语，
眉头凝结着深深的忧虑。
牧童儿的笛声停止，牛羊结队归去，太阳渐渐消失在西山之后。

师傅拉姆达斯编唱着黄昏的歌曲——
“让我留在尘世装扮成国王，你却隐藏身份暗中逃避？
啊，我心中的国王，我宁愿坐在踏脚凳上，宝座之上供奉着你的旧履。
黄昏已经到来，还要我再等待多久，你为何还不返回自己的国土？”

婆罗门

黄昏的太阳落入到萨拉斯瓦蒂河边苍茫的森林中，
隐士的徒弟们顶着柴捆回到静谧的静修林，
眨着深沉的眼睛，疲惫的神牛踱进牛栏。
弟子们洗过晚澡后纷纷环坐在师傅——圣者乔达摩的足前。

茅屋天井中的祭坛上燃烧火光熊熊，
无垠的天空里陈列着点点繁星，对圣者的弟子们好奇地观瞧。
圣者说："喂！孩子们。我现在将要开始讲解《吠陀》。"
圣者的声音解除了静修林的寂寞。

此时一个年轻的孩子走进林中，手捧着奉献的礼物，
他将鲜花蔬果献上，虔诚地向圣者礼拜说：
"师傅，我住在拘尸凯德罗，我的名字叫做苏陀珈摩，前来拜见您学习《吠陀》。"
孩子的声音如黄雀般清脆，如甘露般甜蜜。

圣者和蔼地点头，微笑着说："可爱的孩子，我给予你祝福。你属于什么种姓？
你可知道？唯有婆罗门才有权诵读圣典《吠陀》。"
孩子的声音微弱："师傅，我不知自己的种姓为何，请允我归家问询母亲，再来向您汇说。"

孩子辞别圣者，独自在浓重的黑暗中穿过林间道路，渡过了清澈的萨拉斯瓦蒂河，返回家中。
村庄在河滩上沉睡静卧，母亲的破茅屋就在村庄的尽头。
灯光仍旧照亮着门外的道路，遮婆罗在门外凝望着儿子回来的道路。

苏陀珈摩走进母亲的身边，遮婆罗将他抱在怀中，亲吻着他的头发，轻声送给他祝福。

孩子说：

“母亲，告诉我，谁是我的父亲？我出自什么样的家庭？

我曾拜访圣者，他说只有婆罗门才有权诵读《吠陀》。

母亲，我的种姓是什么？”

母亲的头无声地下，许久后才轻轻回答：

“妈妈的青春满是穷苦，我曾是不少男人的奴隶。

你的母亲并没有丈夫，妈妈不知道你的种姓是什么。”

第二天，曙光洒脱地照耀着静修林的树梢，

师傅乔达摩的弟子们全都早早起床，

他们的容光焕发，仿佛曙光中晶莹的露珠，

虔诚一如祈祷时留下的泪滴。

晨浴的肌肤泛出红润的光泽，湿漉漉的发髻挽在头顶之上。

弟子们围绕着圣者乔达摩环坐在榕树的树荫之下。

百鸟齐声合唱欢快的晨歌，

蜜蜂长久地嗡嗡做乐，

潺潺的溪水轻打着节拍，

与弟子们稚嫩嗓音的《吠陀》赞歌相和。

就在这时，苏陀珈摩来到了圣者身旁，

恭敬地向他致敬摸足。

“祝福你，俊雅善良的孩子，”

圣者继续昨日的提问：“你的种姓是什么？”

孩子高昂起头说：“师傅，我不知道我的种姓为何。

我曾询问我的母亲，母亲对我说：‘你生在没有丈夫的遮婆罗的怀中，妈妈曾经侍奉过许多男人，不知道你的父亲是哪个。’”

苏陀珈摩的话音刚落，

圣者的弟子有如受惊的蜂群般惊慌失措，

仿佛飞舞的蜂群嗡嗡不休地议论闲扯。

有人讥笑，有人则为他羞愧，有人则叫骂：

“无耻的非亚利安贱种！”

圣者却伸出双臂离开了他的坐席，

只因为孩子的真诚令他感动。

“孩子！”

圣者将苏陀珈摩抱在怀中：

“你不是一个非婆罗门，你就是再生种姓中最高的一种，

从不欺骗的婆罗门家庭生育了你。”

卖头

乔萨罗的国王无人可比，
他享有大千世界中的一致赞扬。
他庇护弱者，犹如穷苦百姓的爹娘。
迦尸国王被无上的赞扬激怒气愤的火焰，
“我的百姓，迦尸的人民竟将他位于我之上！
弹丸小国的卑微君主怎可能比我广泛济世。
这些信仰、好施、慈悲统统虚伪，这是他对我的挑衅和嫉妒！”

迦尸王传下他的王命：
“将军们！拔出你的剑，集合大军立刻出征！
乔萨罗王实在太过狂妄，竟妄图将威望凌驾我之上！”

披着战袍的迦尸王步入战场，乔萨罗王成为亡国君上。
乔萨罗王羞愧地离开国土，逃亡到远处的森林中隐居生活。
迦尸王坐在宝座之上，微笑着向臣僚宣称：
“手握权柄才能保有金银珠宝，这样的君王才能慷慨地无限施舍。”

百姓哭泣着怨恨：
“罗睺是如此残暴，竟一口吞噬空中的明月。幸运的女神拉克什米啊，你竟漠视品德，也去趋炎附势。”

四面八方响起哭声一片。
“我们失去了父亲，我们痛恨与我们所爱君王为敌之人！”
迦尸听后雷霆震怒：

"我的都城为何愁云惨淡？我在这里，人民是为了谁而哭泣不止？

威赫神武的我征服了帝国，却仿佛我成了亡国之君。

法典之上字字鲜明：'斩草除根，岂能轻放敌人。'

曼特里，即可传旨四方——有人能生擒乔萨罗王，将首赐君王的黄金百两。"

国王的使者逐一传达君王旨令，无论日夜也不敢怠慢停留。

百姓气愤地捂住双耳，眼睛因为惊惧而无奈闭上。

王国的乔萨罗王独自在森林中徘徊，伴随他的只有脏烂的破衣。

一日，迷途的旅人来到他的身旁，含着眼泪请求指引方向：

"隐士啊，这森林可有边际，我如何才能走到乔萨罗去？"

乔萨罗王听后回答：

"那是一个不幸的国家，你为什么要前去那方？"

旅人说："我是一名商人，货船遭遇风浪打沉在海底。

我如今苟延残喘沿途行乞。乔萨罗王是慈悲的海洋，他的名声响彻四方。

无依靠的人可得到他的庇护，贫穷者能够在他的宫殿获取怜悯。"

乔萨罗王的脸上微笑掠过，已有泪水模糊他的目光。

沉思片刻，乔萨罗王叹息回答：

"我将给你指引一条道路，可以使你到达渴望的目标。

来自远方的受难客人，你能从那里得到心满意足。”

迦尸王的朝堂之上，走进了蓬头垢面的隐士。

迦尸微笑询问：

“隐士，是什么让你登上我的朝堂？”

“我是乔萨罗王，本在森林中逃亡。”

林中的隐士从容作答。

“请赐予我的同伴黄金百两，作为他将我生擒的犒赏。”

大臣们无不吃惊，朝堂之上一片宁静，手持甲仗的侍卫竟已满眼泪光。

迦尸沉默半晌，忽然大笑回应：

“你的计策如此上上！我却要让你希望丢光。

就在今日的战场上，胜利依旧属于我的荣光。

你的疆土今日还你，我的心也想你拜服。”

衣衫褴褛的乔萨罗王被扶上宝座，

由迦尸王将王冠戴上，

百姓们则放声欢呼。

供养女

频婆娑罗王跪倒在佛陀坐下，
求得了一片趾甲供养。
一座敬信庄严的大理石宝塔为了供奉而建立在御苑深处。

每到黄昏，皇后和公主们便更换上朴素整洁的衣裳，
手捧敬佛的金盘，
将鲜花献于塔下，
亲手将金盘中的行行黄金灯盏点亮。

阿阇世王坐上了父王的宝座，
他用无边的鲜血冲洗掉父王的佞佛，
将佛祖释迦牟尼的经文献于阿那罗的火焰。

阿阇世王召集所有宫廷女侍，警告她们：
“除了敬信《吠陀》、婆罗门与国王，
宇宙间绝不许你们有第二信仰。
这王命须切记在心，
如有违背，定遭祸殃。”

一个秋后的晚上，
宫女师利摩蒂在净水沐浴后，
捧着礼佛的金盘，
静静来到太后座前，
无言地看着她的脚尖。
太后恐惧申斥：
“你竟违抗国王的申令，

敬信佛塔之人，就只有死于矛尖或者远方流放。”

宫女默默走向皇后阿弥达的房间，
皇后正梳起拖地的长发，
对着宝镜专心地将朱砂点染在发缝中央。

瞥见了师利摩蒂，
因为气愤而手指发抖，
皇后竟然描弯了发缝里的朱砂。
“蠢货，竟然如此大胆。
竟把敬佛的鲜花携带！
被人看见不堪设想。”

公主苏格萝独自坐在窗边，
借着落日的余光诵读故事诗篇，
听到门外的脚环声响，
从书本上移开目光。

她将动人的诗篇掷于地上，
急忙跑到宫女身旁，
忧心忡忡在她耳边把话言讲：
“国王的命令无人不知，
你如此不计后果，
只怕死于祸殃。”

师利摩蒂在宫中走遍四方。
“姐妹们，礼佛时间已到，
我们要对佛恭敬。”
害怕，诅咒，人们这样想。

白天最后的阳光从城楼褪尽，
闹市声音转为微弱，
路上人踪尽灭，
国王的古老钟祠传出声声祈祷钟响。

秋天清澈的暗夜中，
空中闪烁无数繁星。
宫门外吹响号角，
囚徒齐声歌唱。
“诸位大臣的议事已完。”
持刃的侍卫齐声高喊。

就在这刹那，皇宫的卫士们见到：
国王幽暗的花园中，宝塔阴阴的石阶前，
一行行明灯忽然亮起，仿佛金灿灿的黄金花蔓。

卫士们拔出宝剑，
疾奔上前查看。
“你是何人？
竟然冒死供奉佛陀！”
传来甜美的声音：
“我名为师利摩蒂，佛陀的奴隶！”

这一日，白石做成的塔阶上留下鲜血的记述。
这日悲秋夜晚中，寂寥的御苑深处，
塔下熄灭了最后的供奉灯烛。

密约

往昔一日，尊者邬波笈多正酣睡在秣菟罗的城根，
此时街灯已经在风中熄灭，
城里百姓也关闭了家的门户，
深夜的天空偶有几颗星星，
在雨季的乌云中闪烁。

纤足轻轻踏在尊者的身上，上面带有叮当的脚镯。
尊者吃惊翻身坐起，睡意在朦胧中飘然散去，
他的目光被一片闪闪的灯光刺痛。

城中的舞姬春情荡漾，
急切要在深夜中去会情郎，
天青色衣衫披在身上，
上嵌着环佩叮咚作响。
一脚踏在尊者身上，瓦萨婆达多无比惊慌，忙停下匆匆的脚步。

手持着纱灯仔细打量，
年轻的尊者如此俊朗，
温柔的笑容浮在红润唇上，

明亮的眼中包含慈祥光芒，
白皙的额头闪耀着如月光的宁静与安详。

羞涩涌入眼内，
女子放声温柔情动：
“少年，我请你原谅。
可否随我归家？
这冰冷生硬的湿地，怎能做你的睡床。”

尊者报以温柔的回应：
“啊！貌美多情的姑娘！
今日并非你我相约的时机，
你先去你原本的地方，
若是一日机缘来到，
我自会走入你的闺房。”

猛然间暴雨从雷电中张开狰狞大口，
瓦萨婆达多在恐惧中瑟瑟发抖，
足以灭世的狂风在空中呼啸，
空中震动的雷霆，
大声地发出嘲弄世人的狂笑。

距这日的相见时隔未到一岁，
又到了四月的傍晚，
春风蜕变得更加风情迷人，
路旁枝叶点缀着满是花蕾，
茉莉与素馨盛开在皇宫御苑。

清风从远方慢慢吹来，
携带着迷人婉转的短笛之声，
城中的男女们齐聚到秣菟罗林中欢度春宵。

明月在空中微笑，
凝视着沉静的一座空城。

月光下行人稀少，
尊者独自漫步在林间小道。
杜鹃啼鸣在头顶的绿叶枝条中，
难道说今夜真是个幽会情人的良宵？

别离城市，
尊者走入城外的林道，
他停止在护城河边不再前行。
那女人是谁？
孤独地躺在芒果林下的影中，
就处于尊者的脚边。

鼠疫无情地肆虐蔓延，
瓦萨婆达多也未曾幸免，
如雪的肌肤布满漆黑斑点，
被城中的居民丢弃在护城河边。

尊者将昏迷的情人轻轻放在膝头，
用清水滋润她干裂的双唇，
为女子轻颂着经咒，
亲手为她全身涂抹清凉的檀香油。

月夜散落盛开的花瓣，
杜鹃在枝头低声悲鸣。
女人轻轻地询问：
“你是谁？如此慈悲。”
尊者回答说：“瓦萨婆达多，
今夜，邬波笈多特地来与你欢会。”

报答

“竟有人敢偷到国库？立刻将匪徒带到我的眼前，
否则就让你们身首异处，守城官！”
守城官尊奉国王旨令，四处搜寻盗宝的贼人。
城外破庙中蜷卧着瓦季勒森——一名商人，德克西拉的百姓。
贩马来到迦尸城，却被强盗打劫，失望地想要返回家乡。
巡逻的卫士捉住了他，诬陷他是窃贼，
给他戴上了枷锁，要将他投入大牢。

恰好，夏玛——迦尸的美女，
正坐在窗前向外闲望，
旁观着如梦般的人群在街上熙熙攘攘。
她忽然吃惊呼叫：
“啊，这因陀罗般的花样少年，为何给他戴上适合强盗的沉重枷锁？
快，亲爱的侍女，以我的名义告诉巡逻的守城官——
就说夏玛邀请他，邀请他光临寒舍，要他将囚犯带到我的面前。”
夏玛的名字如同一道魔咒，
受宠若惊的守城官得知邀请后，

欣喜若狂，连毫毛都发抖。

他迅速走进房间，身后押着囚犯瓦季勒森——因为羞愧而两颊泛红，愤恨地低着头。

守城官微笑着说：

“这真不巧，竟在此时得到您的召唤。但现在我必须回复王命。

漂亮的姑娘，我希望得到你的允许。”

瓦季勒森突然抬起他的头说：

“你，女人，你在耍什么手段。

将我从大街上带到你的家中，

嘲笑我这个无辜受辱的异乡人来满足你残忍无情的好奇心！”

“嘲笑你？”夏玛高呼：

“我宁愿用全身的珠宝换取你身戴的枷锁。

远方的青年，羞辱你就等于是在羞辱我自己。”

说出这番话，夏玛的睫毛上挂着泪珠，她的眼睛凝视着年青人，

仿佛要用泪水洗刷他受到的侮辱。

夏玛转身向守城官哀求：

“带走我的一切，换取这囚徒的自由。”

守城官拒绝说：

“漂亮的姑娘，我必须拒绝你的要求。

国库被盗窃的耻辱，需要罪人的生命才能平息国王的雷霆之怒。”

夏玛握住守城官的双手低声说：

“我请求你对他的死刑延缓两日。”

守城官会心地微笑点头：

“我会将你的嘱托铭记心田。”

第二天晚上的午夜时分，狱卒悄悄打开了监狱大门。

手持纱灯，夏玛走进了监狱，

明日将被处决的瓦季勒森正低诵着神名祈祷。
夏玛的目光一闪暗示，狱卒即可打开了囚犯的镣铐。
瓦季勒森无比惊讶地呆望着女人莲花般的美丽容颜。

他低声哽咽：
“是谁为我带来光明，好像黎明带来了深夜噩梦之后的晨星。
你是谁？啊，你是自由的化身，是残忍的迦尸城中慈悲的女人。”
“慈悲的女人？”夏玛于惊讶中发出狂笑，更添了阴森监牢中的恐怖纷扰。

狂笑之后紧跟着哭泣，夏玛的声音呜咽：
“夏玛的心坚硬过迦尸城中的岩石，比无情夏玛胜过所有的人。”
女人紧握着囚徒的手臂，
将瓦季勒森带出了阴森的牢狱。

黎明的光辉闪耀在瓦鲁纳的河岸。
小船在渡口，姑娘在船头。
“上船吧，相逢不识的青年。
我请你将我的话记在心头。
挣脱所有束缚，我亲爱的，
我和你同在这河流上泛舟。”

松开系船的绳索，小舟轻轻地飘荡，
林中的鸟儿唱起欢快歌声。

将夏玛拥在怀中，瓦季勒森说：
“亲爱的异乡女友，告诉我，
你用多少钱财换取了我的自由。”
同样紧拥着他，夏玛悄声说：
“不要说话。现在还不是说的时候。”

小舟在炽热的风中顺流飘荡，
午时的空中高悬酷热的太阳。
午浴过后村中妇女穿着湿衣，顶着汲水的铜罐走回家中。
市集散场后，已经没有了人声鼎沸，
只有寂静的村中小路无声闪耀在阳光中。

榕树荫凉下面有青石砌成的渡口，
饥渴的水手将小舟在那里停靠。
此时，鸟儿躲藏在树荫中午睡，
慵懒的蜜蜂在令人疲倦的白日里飞舞。

热风吹过，吹下了夏玛的面纱，
瓦季勒森心情澎湃，声音发涩地在她耳边说：
“亲爱的，你可知否？
就在你打开我身上枷锁的一瞬，
你也将爱的镣铐永恒带在我身。
你是如何排除万难将我解救，
亲爱的，你一定要告诉我其中经过。
你为我做到一切，我发誓用生命为报。”
夏玛戴上面纱，轻轻地回答：

“现在先不要去谈这些。”

白昼中带着光的小舟竖起了金色风帆，
缓缓地行驶向远方的太阳落下的港湾。
附近岸上长着一片森林的河边，
夏玛的小船在晚风中停靠。
无波的河面上闪烁着初四的弯弯月影，
树根下的昏暗中蟋蟀在唱着好像琴声的歌。

夏玛熄灭了灯光，无声坐在窗口，
将头依靠在青年的肩膀。
她散发异香的蓬松长发掩盖在青年的胸口，
如波浪般柔滑，如睡眠的丝网般漆黑。
她低声说：
“我为你做的事情异常艰难，但要对你讲，
我最亲爱的人，确实更为不易。
你听后，一定要立刻将它从心中忘记。
一个单恋我如狂的少年乌蒂耶，
在我的嘱咐下代替你承担了犯下的案件，
他将生命当作了爱情的奉献。
担负这样的罪恶，我的知己，
我这样做，只因我爱你。”

月钩西沉，森林在鸟儿的睡眠中稳稳矗立。
环抱着爱人腰肢的双臂慢慢松开，
残酷的分离无声竖立在两人之间。
瓦季勒森沉默无语如冰冷石像，
夏玛则一如折断的藤蔓瘫倒地上。

忽然，夏玛抱紧了青年的膝盖，
跪在他的脚边哭泣哀求：

“这罪恶的无边惩罚，留待上帝手中给予处罚。
亲爱的你，请原谅我！”
移开了自己的脚，瓦季勒森大声呼喝：
“用你罪恶的代价换取我的生命，这生命理应承受无边诅咒。
无耻的女人！可耻生命的债主！
你让我生命中的每次呼吸都带着耻辱。”
他跳下船登上岸边，走入丛林。

黑暗中的枯叶在他脚下不停作响，
腐败的草木散发扑鼻的发霉气息，
老树的枝桠伸向四面八方，形成了诡怪的黑影。
他漫步不断向前，直到道路的尽头。
整个森林用纠缠的乱腾化成手臂，
在黑暗中阻挠了他继续前行。

他疲倦地坐在地上休息，一个幽灵一样的人站在他的背后。
她一声不响，默默跟踪来到此间，
血淋淋的足迹留在黑夜的路上。
蓬松的长发，异香的一群，
急促的呼吸和雨一般的亲吻，
如洪水般淹没了他的身体。
夏玛哭泣着说：
“我不能离开你，不，我不离开你。
为你我犯下罪恶，惩罚我吧，我的主人。
如果你愿意，杀了我，用你的双手结束我的罪恶。”

突然，黑夜都在星辰看不透的森林中颤抖，
地面弯曲的树根因恐惧而战栗。
窒息中透出一声绝望叹息，
之后，有谁跌落在地上枯叶之中。

瓦季勒森从林中走出的时候，

第一道晨曦正照射在远方的湿婆庙顶。

整个早晨他像疯子般茫然失措，在河边的沙滩上徘徊行走。

正午燃烧的日光，化成鞭子拷打他的全身。

他口中饥渴，却不知喝一口眼前的河水。

他漠视汲水的村女的怜悯呼唤：

“远方的客人，请到我的家中休息。”

晚上，疲惫的瓦季勒森奔回小船，

像飞蛾一样怀着满心希望扑向灯火。

啊！小船上躺着一只玲珑的脚镯！

他一次次将它紧贴于胸口，

镯上的金玲细响如箭一样一下下刺入他的心脏。

船角上放着一件蓝色细纱，

他扑上去将脸埋在褶皱之中。

丝纱的柔软，看不见的想起，使他不由自主想起可爱动人的身材记忆。

晶莹的初五的月牙，慢慢躲藏在七叶树的身后，
瓦季勒森向着森林深处伸出双手呼唤：
“回来吧，亲爱的！”
森林中浓浓的黑暗中出现了人影，
幽灵一样独立在沙滩。
“亲爱的！我已经回来。”
夏玛扑倒在他的脚边说：
“原谅我，最亲爱的，你慈悲的手未曾杀死我，看来我命不该绝。”
瓦季勒森凝望着她的脸，
用双手紧拥她在怀中，
忽然他一阵战栗，
又猛然将她远远推出。
他惊叫着：
“为什么，为什么你又回来？”
他的眼睛闭上，脸向一旁转开，轻声说：
“不要跟着我。”
女人沉默片刻，
跪下向青年摸足行礼，
随后向岸边走去，
如梦一样逐渐消失在森里的黑暗之中。

轻微的损害

腊月中，寒风将瓦鲁纳河水吹荡起清澈的涟漪。

远离城镇的村庄里，宁静的芭蕉林中，石砌的堤坝上走来了迦尸的皇后格鲁娜，

一百名宫女拥着她前去沐浴。

国王下了禁令，清晨的河堤上看不到人影，
住在附近茅屋中的人们早已回避，
河边一片寂静，只有树林中听到鸟儿的轻声啼叫。

瓦鲁纳河水在呼啸北风中浪花滚滚，
金色阳光闪耀在水面之上，
欢乐地在波浪上跳跃，
好像狂舞不休的舞女将装饰宝石的舞裙飘荡。

女子的甜蜜声音使浪花的话语都变得羞愧，
莲藕一样美丽的手臂使河水充满融融缠绵情意，
苍天不安地看着欢声响起的宫女。

沐浴过后，女子们登上堤坝。
皇后说：
“啊，真冷！
我的身体都在发抖，
点燃火堆吧，朋友，
让火焰驱除寒冷。”

宫女们走进树林采集柴火准备生火，
她们快乐地争抢着树枝玩乐，
忽然皇后对所有人惊喜地说：
“你们快看呀！
看那边，有茅屋就在眼前。
你们可以用它来生火，
让我的手脚感受温暖。”
皇后兴奋地笑着说，就如同蜂蜜的甜美。

宫女玛乐蒂温温柔劝告：
“皇后！这是无理的玩笑。
怎能放火将房屋烧毁，
是谁修建了这座茅屋？
穷人、异乡过客，或是修道的隐士。”

皇后说：
“将你的廉价同情抛到一旁！”
无法抑制的好奇，
疯狂主宰的狂妄，
残忍的年轻女子将茅屋布满火光。

浓烟旋转着四散蔓延，
刹那间，浓烟中射出闪光的火焰，

烈火变成贪婪的舌头席卷上青天。
像一群愤怒的火蛇从地狱中逃窜，
舞动着头颅直上青天，
发出嘶嘶的咆哮，
在女人们的耳边疯狂地奏出毁灭的燃烧曲。

鸟儿们惊恐地停止了快乐的歌唱，
一群群乌鸦呱呱地鸣叫，
北风吹动的力道加倍，
茅屋连着茅屋都被熊熊大火吞并。

毁灭的火焰将河边的村庄蚕食干净，
冷清的路上，腊月的清晨中，
欢乐的疲倦，带着百名宫女，
皇后回到皇宫，手中拿着青莲，身上穿着红纱。

法庭中的审判宝座之上，
端坐迦尸的君王。
无家可归的人们逐一走来，
带着恐慌匍匐在他的脚前，
战抖中结结巴巴说出他们的苦痛。

君王的头颅低下，
羞愤使他的脸颊通红，
离开法庭，他回到后宫，
质问他的皇后：
“你做了什么好事！
竟然烧毁百姓的房屋！
说！这是谁给你的权力？”

皇后冷笑着回答：
“难道那些也算是房屋？
烧掉了几间残破草房，
会给他们带来多少损伤？
皇后的刹那欢乐值得多少金银珠宝？”

君王怒声斥责，
愤怒之火填满心窝。
“只要你仍是我的妻子，
我知道你的无知理不清房屋被烧给穷人带来的损失，
然而，我会让你清楚你的罪责。”

君王令女侍脱去皇后华贵的衣衫，
无情去剥下深红耀眼的华衫，
将女丐才穿的破衣披在她的身上。

君王将皇后拉到路旁：
“去当一个讨饭的乞丐，
直到你可以重建烧毁的几间茅屋
——只为了你片刻欢悦的补偿。”

“我给你一年的期限，
期满你再回到这里，
恭敬地来到法庭中央，
当众宣布，
损坏破旧的茅屋对穷人而言是多大的伤害。”

价格的添增

腊月的夜晚格外寒冷，
一片残荷的枯干败叶在寒霜的无情中飘荡，
卖花人善奴的池塘中确有一朵白莲盛开在水中央。

卖花人摘下白莲，
来到宫殿外，
他要求见国王，
将它待价而沽。

这时，一位长者见到莲花，
心中着实喜悦。
他问："你要卖多少钱?
我想要买下你这朵迟开的白莲。
今日佛陀将在城中说法，
我要将花献于他的座前。"
善奴说："一两黄金，我可以将它卖出。"

长者正要付钱，忽然眼前气象庄严，
侍从们捧着檀香花蔓，
波斯匿王高颂梵语赞歌，
为了拜见佛陀而出现在清晨的宫门之前。

这朵迟开的白莲吸引了波斯匿王的视线。
他问："你卖多少钱? 我要将它献于佛陀座前。"

卖花人回答："啊，国王陛下。

一两金子的价格，这位长者已经将它买下。”
“十两黄金我要将它买下。”
国王陛下吩咐说。
长者说：“二十两黄金我要买它。”
二人谁也不愿让步，同声说：“我要买它。”
白莲的价格逐步增加。

卖花人暗自琢磨：
“为了谁他们如此争吵？
我若将花卖给那人，
岂不是更有利可图？”

卖花人合掌恳求说：
“请二位谅解，
这朵花我不再卖出。”
善奴向林中跑去，
那里佛陀常驻，
园中佛光普照。

佛陀端坐于莲座之上，
显露出愉悦的宝相庄严。
他目光如清泉般宁静，
慈悲的微笑绽放在唇边。
卖花人凝望着佛陀庄严妙相，
目不转睛哑口无言。
忽然他五体投地，
将迟开的白莲奉献在佛陀莲花般的脚前。

佛陀笑着慈祥询问：
“善男子！讲出你的所愿。”
卖花人无措回答：
“世尊！我愿乞请您脚上的灰尘一点。”

比丘尼

昔日，大灾荒爆发在
室罗伐系底城中，
四处都是灾民嗷嗷待哺的悲声。
佛陀向弟子一一询问：
“你们中谁愿担负救济灾民的责任？”

珠宝商人悉多合什敬礼佛陀，
他沉思半晌方才低声道：
“全城都被极寒笼罩，
世尊，我哪有如此大的救济能力。”

将军胜军接着说：
“为了满足你命令，
赴汤蹈火在所不辞，
哪怕要剖开胸膛流出滚烫的鲜血。
只是在我的家中，
实是没有一粒粮食。”

大地主法护站了出来，
他对佛陀无奈叹息：
“赶上这种灾年，
我那黄金的庄园都只有一片荒芜。
我已变得穷苦，无法交上皇家税赋。”

你看我，我瞅你，
佛陀的弟子默然无语。

世尊佛殿中静寂一片，
望向受难的灾城，
佛陀睁开他黄昏星辰般慈悲的明亮双眼。

给孤独长者的女儿羞红的脸颊低垂，
眼中含有痛苦的泪珠，
匍匐拜倒在释迦足前，
谦卑恭敬却心志坚决地低声说出自己的心愿。

“无能的善爱比丘尼愿意完成世尊的心愿。
那些哭号的黎民全都是我的儿女，
从今日起，我负责给灾民提供救济的粮食。”

这些话令所有人惊诧。
“你这个比丘的女儿比丘尼，
如此狂妄，自不量力。
揽下这样艰难的责任妄图出人头地。
那么你的粮食在哪里？”

她向众人合掌礼敬说：
“我唯有乞讨的钵盂。
身为一个卑微女子，
比谁都无能的比丘尼，
如果要完成世尊的使命，
只能依靠你们慈悲的施舍。”

“我那丰盈的谷仓就设在你们每个人的家里，
你们的慷慨将会装满我取之不尽的钵盂，
沿街乞讨化来的粮食，
将会养活这片饥饿的大地。”

不忠实的丈夫

圣者克比尔虔诚的名声传遍了全国各地，
他的茅屋里面汇集了来自四方的善男信女。
有人说："世间真有神在吗？请你做证。"
有人说："请为我诵经，驱除我的疾病。"
有人说："请你显示超凡的法力。"
不孕的妇女哭着请求："请让我能够生育。"

克比尔含泪合十向大神柯利祈祷：
"你使我降生于卑贱的家庭，
我以为无人会来到我的身边，
只有你慈悲地与我同在，
你如今在玩弄什么！捉弄人的大神！
你将世人领到我的家里，难道你要弃我而去？"

城里所有的婆罗门气愤地商量：

“真是滑稽，人们竟然崇拜异教徒的织布匠！
看来充满罪恶的世界末日已经来临，
不能够力挽狂澜，是我们婆罗门放弃了责任。”
于是，婆罗门命妓女设下诡计，
密令她接受指示和金币。

一天，圣者克比尔来到市集卖布，
忽然从人丛走出女子扯住他哭泣。
“啊，狡猾的骗子，真是没良心，
为什么如此暗中欺骗善良的女人？
抛弃了无辜的我，假冒伪善的僧侣！
忍饥挨饿，我容颜憔悴，肤色变黑。”

一旁的一群婆罗门装作愤怒难忍：
“好一个玷污宗教、欺世盗名的僧侣！
你接受供养，却将尘土撒在诚实人的眼里，
令这个弱女子衣食无着四处行乞。”
克比尔说：“我承受罪业，你来我的家中吧。
我有粮食，女人，为什么会让你挨饿。”

克比尔恭敬地将妓女带回家中，
温柔地对她说：“是柯利大神派遣你来。”
此时，女人羞愧悔恨地留下泪滴：
“贪心让我犯下罪行，我将会在你的诅咒中死去。”
克比尔说：“尊敬的母亲，别怕我会由此怨恨，
你带给我的诽谤，将会成为我头上最好的装饰。”

唤醒了妓女的觉悟，驱除了她心中的恶念，
克比尔教她用甜美的声音诵读梵赞。
消息传遍四方，伪善的克比尔，虚假的虔诚僧。
克比尔听了说：“是的，谁都比我值得尊敬。

如果能够渡往彼岸，身后的荣名何足眷恋？
神啊，你高高在上，我愿比任何人都低贱。”

国王听到了圣者的赞歌，派出了使者。
克比尔拒绝前往，摇头对使者说：
“我愿远离一切可敬之人，在侮辱中隐居，
像我这样的无能者，不配成为宫中的装饰。”
使者说：“圣者如不肯去，我等将大难临头，
你的声誉使国王见你的心情无比渴望。”

殿堂之上端坐国王，侍从站在两旁，
女人紧跟在身后，圣者克比尔走入宫廷。
有人窃笑，有人皱眉，有人厌恶地低头。
国王心想：真是无耻，竟带着女人跟在身后。
他目光闪动，侍卫们将圣者赶出殿堂，
克比尔恭敬地带着女人回到自己的家园。

沿途看到尽情欢笑的婆罗门，
他们将难堪的咒骂送给虔诚僧，
此时，女人哭泣着拜倒在圣者脚旁：
“为什么你要将我拯救出罪恶的泥潭？
为什么甘受诽谤，留罪人在你的家门之中？”
克比尔说：“母亲，只因你是柯利的恩赐。”

丈夫的重获

有一天杜尔西达斯在恒河岸边荒凉的火葬场中，
在黄昏时候独自徘徊，
沉迷于自己编唱的歌曲。
忽然，他抬头看见一位萨蒂端坐在亡人的脚边，
下了决心要和她的丈夫一同逝于火中。

女伴们欢呼不断，用来鼓励她征服死亡的胜利，
婆罗门祭司围绕在四周朗诵着赞美她高贵品行的诗篇。

女人忽然看到杜尔西来到面前。
她慌忙行礼，恭敬地说：
“神啊，愿你的金口给我指点迷津。”
杜尔西问道：“母亲，你要到哪里去，如此的庄严气象。”
女人回答：“和丈夫一同升入天堂，这是我的愿望。”
“为什么要舍弃尘世，前往天堂？”杜尔西微笑问道。
“喂，母亲，难道天堂属于神，凡间就不归他的掌握？”

听不懂他的话，女人显得茫然失措和惊讶。
她合掌乞求："如果能够得到丈夫，天堂我也不在乎。"
杜尔西微笑说："请回到你的家中，我这样对你承诺。
从今天算起的一个月后，你将会获得心爱的丈夫。"
女人怀着希望离开火葬场返回家中，
杜尔西沉思在恒河岸边宁静的深夜中。

女人虔诚地独自在冷清的房屋中等候，
杜尔西每天来把潜修的经典传授。
到达了一个月的期限，邻居们汇聚在她的门口，
问："得到了丈夫？"
女人说："嗯，那是自然。"
邻居们连忙又问："赶快告诉我们，他在哪个房间居住？"
女人微笑着说："我的丈夫住在我心灵的深处。"

点金石

瓦林达般的耶摩纳河边，
萨拿坦正在虔诚地诵读梵赞，
一个身穿褴褛衣衫的婆罗门蹒跚地走来跪倒在他的身前。
萨拿坦问：
“你来自何方，婆罗门，你叫什么名字？”
婆罗门回答说：
“我不知从何说起，为了前来参拜你，我来自遥远的小城市，
我是莫纳加尔镇的吉班，
小镇从属于巴尔特曼县。
世界上再也找不到如我一样不幸和可怜的人，
我有几亩田地，收入却无法糊口，
贫困使我在人前难以抬头。
从前我曾以布施和奉献而成名，

如今我只有空空两手，一无所有。
为了能够变贫困变为富有，
我向湿婆大神祈祷求福。
一天黎明前，我在梦中听到了湿婆大神的吩咐：
‘我将使你的愿望满足。前往耶摩纳河边，叩拜苦行者萨拿坦的双足，
如父亲般尊敬他，
他的手中拥有使你致富的道路。’”

萨拿坦听了他的话忧心忡忡。
“出家人一无所有。
昔日的一切我早已抛弃，
只剩下乞食的钵盂。”
忽然间一事涌上心头，
苦行者说：“嗯，是的，
有一天我曾在这河边捡到一块点金石。

我将它埋在那边的沙滩中，
曾想将它用来作为布施。
婆罗门，将它带走，
你的不幸将会消失。”

婆罗门连忙跑过去扒开沙土，
找到了一块点金石。
他试以辟邪锁两只，
铁锁立刻变成黄灿灿的金子。
婆罗门惊诧地坐倒于沙滩，
困惑地独自冥思苦想。

耶摩纳河水的波涛滚滚，
内含深意在他耳边歌唱。
河对岸铺开了一张朱红色画图，
西方落下了黄昏中疲倦的太阳。
婆罗门忽然双膝跪倒，哭泣着将额头贴紧在萨拿坦的脚上：
“师傅！恳求您，
传授我不屑珍宝，轻视黄金的秘诀。”
婆罗门说着将点金石扔到了耶摩纳河水之中。

被俘的英雄

五河环绕的英雄之邦，
辫子盘在头上的锡克响应古鲁的号召站了起来。
不屈不挠，勇敢坚强。
“古鲁琪万岁”的欢呼回荡在旁遮普的四面八方，
新觉醒的锡克不眨眼地凝望着清晨里升起的太阳。

“阿拉克·尼郎姜！”
一声欢呼扯断了奴隶脚下的铁枷与绳索。
腰间的宝剑仿佛也在欢快中铿锵跳跃。
旁遮普到处震响着：
“阿拉克·尼郎姜！”

这一天终于来到，
千万人的心中再不会被恐惧缠绕，
也不用牵挂未偿的债务，
生与死不过是脚下奴隶，
精神中再也没有苦痛烦恼。

在旁遮普五条河的十个岸畔，
终于等来了这样的一天。

德里的皇宫中，
巴德沙贾达的睡眠一再从眼中飞去，
什么人的欢呼惊动天地，撕裂了黑夜的宁静？
什么人的熊熊火炬染红了远方的天际。

英雄们的鲜血洒落在五河的岸边，
战士们的生命如鸟儿归巢般离开了成千上万被利刃穿过的胸膛。
母亲——祖国的眉心里有颗鲜红色的圣痣辉煌，
英雄们的鲜血洒遍五河的岸边。

面对死亡的拥抱，
莫卧儿和锡克交锋。
战场上进行着生与死的搏杀，
互相掐紧对方的咽喉，
好像巨蟒与负伤的苍鹰搏斗。
在连天的激战中响起厮杀叫喊，
低吼着“古鲁琪万岁”的是锡克族的英雄，
在血泊中高呼着“胜利”的是疯狂的莫卧儿士兵。

在这场战争中，
锡克的领袖般达成了莫卧儿的俘虏，
像雄狮被带上枷锁捆绑着押往通向德里的大路。
啊！般达在这次战争中成为了莫卧儿的俘虏。

前面走的是莫卧儿的士卒，
扬起地上的尘土，
枪尖上挑着被割下的锡克英雄的头颅，

后面带着七百个铁锁叮当的锡克俘虏，
大街上无人行走，
家家开着窗户。
不畏死的锡克俘虏高呼：
“万岁，古鲁！”
锡克的英雄和莫卧儿的士兵，
今天扬起了德里大街上的尘土。

俘虏们一个个高呼：
“古鲁琪万岁！”
从容就死于刽子手的刀下。
一日一夜，
百名英雄丢掉了百个头颅。

七日夜刀下亡魂七百个，
最后，审判官带上被捆缚双手的般达之子，
将他带到般达的身旁。
“杀了他，用你自己的双手结束他的生命。”

未发一语，
般达慢慢将孩子拉到胸前，
将右手放在他的头顶为他祝福，
将亲吻送给他红色头巾的边缘。

匕首握在手中，
般达凝望着孩子的脸。
他悄声在孩子的耳边说：
“高呼一声‘古鲁琪万岁！’，
我的好儿子，若害怕便不配做锡克的英雄。”
勇敢无畏的光辉闪耀在孩子稚嫩的脸上，
口中高呼：
“古鲁琪万岁！”
法庭中回荡孩子的高呼，
孩子望向般达的面孔。

般达用左臂抱住孩子的头颅，
用力将右手的匕首刺进他的心口，
尸身倒在大地之上，
口中兀自高呼：“胜利，古鲁琪。”

法庭中静寂无比。
刽子手用烧红的火箸撕裂开般达的身体。
英雄站立着迎来死亡，
未曾发出一声痛苦叹息。
旁观者全都闭上双眼，
法庭唯独有宁静一片。

不屈的人

昔日，奥朗则布蚕食着印度的锦绣河山。
一天，马鲁瓦的君王佳苏般特前来拜见：
“陛下，在一个漆黑夜晚，
侍卫埋伏在阿遮勒堡壕沟里面，
悄悄捉住了希鲁西王苏洛坦，
他如今已成为我的阶下之囚。
我的主人，听您的吩咐，该对他如何处理？”

奥朗则布听后说：
“真是个惊喜的消息！
耗费时光捉住了这惊人的霹雳。
他率领数百健儿驰骋于高山丛林，
这位拉其普特的豪杰一向行踪飘忽，
犹如沙漠中的耀眼彩虹。
我要召见他，派人将他带到这来。”

马鲁瓦国王佳苏般特合掌请求：
“囚禁在我庭院中的是一只刹帝利种姓的幼狮，
陛下召见他，请先恩准我的乞求。
不要给予这位年轻勇士侮辱和蔑视，
得到您的允诺，
我将亲自带他来此。”

奥朗则布微笑着回答：
“你怎能如此说话，
睿智的英雄，马鲁瓦的国王！
我内心略感羞惭，
它竟出自你口。
无人可损伤自尊英雄的尊严。
答应你，无须担忧，
尽管带他走入我的宫廷。”

希鲁西王来到朝廷之上，
陪同他的是马鲁瓦的国王。
他昂然抬起头颅，
平视前方的眼睛炯炯发光。
侍从们大喝：
“跪下！不懂历法的贼人。”
头依靠在佳苏般特的肩膀，
苏罗坦安然回复：
“除了父母的双脚，我不向他人叩首。”

奥朗则布的侍从瞪起气愤的红眼望向苏罗坦：
“我来教导你礼仪，我会按下你的头颅。”
希鲁西王微笑作答：
“妄想如此，斜坡岂能令我低头，

我从不知惧怕是为何物。"
英雄苏罗坦傲立在宫殿，手抚着腰间长剑。

奥朗则布拉着苏罗坦，
让他坐在自己身旁，说：
"英雄，五印度中，
哪里最适合你的心愿？"
苏罗坦回答：
"阿遮勒堡，世间唯有此间好！"
肃穆的朝堂上响起断续的低声嘲笑，
奥朗则布笑着说："我允你永驻阿遮勒堡。"

更多的给予

帕坦的士兵们绑来了一群被俘的锡克人，
舒里特干基的地面已经被鲜血染红。
那瓦布说："喂，特鲁辛格，我要给你特赦。"
特鲁辛格反问说："你岂能对我如此轻视？"
那瓦布说："只因你是大英雄，我不能对你无礼。
割下你的发辫，你即可离开。
我只有这条要求。"
特鲁辛格说："你的慈悲我永怀感激。
你索取的太少，我将给与更多——
发辫加上我的头颅。"

王的审判

婆罗门说：
“我的妻子在屋子内，
贼人却在半夜闯入要行无礼。
我将他拿下，现在告诉我，贼人应承受何种惩罚？”
“死！”
罗陀罗奥王只吐出一字。

飞奔而来的使者说：
“贼人就是太子，
婆罗门在夜晚将他捉住，
在清晨将将他杀死。
我捉住了他，要给婆罗门什么惩罚？”
“释放他！”
罗陀罗奥王只回一句话。

戈宾德·辛格

“朋友，你们全部回去吧，现在仍时机未到。”
天光拂晓，耶摩纳河边，
山岭逶迤的幽暗森林中，
锡克的宗师戈宾德嘱咐他的门徒。

走吧，拉姆达斯；走吧，莱哈里，
你也回去吧，萨胡。
不要诱惑我，不要呼唤我跃入战斗的海洋，
权且让我停留在这远离人世的舞台。

我已背过脸去，堵上耳朵，
躲藏在森林中。
远方无边的人海还在咆哮，
掀起了巨浪哀嚎。
在这里，我只是一个独自沉入自己隐秘事业的人。

从喧嚣的人境中，似乎人类的灵魂向我召唤。
静寂的深夜中，我从梦中惊醒，
大声呼唤：“我已到来，我即将到来。”
我是如此的渴望——将身、心、灵魂投入到伟大的人群浪潮之中。

看到你们，我的灵魂震荡，
我的心疯狂驰骋。
我的血沸腾燃烧，仿佛千百条火蛇舞动。
似乎在嘲笑着我，剑鞘中的宝剑在龙吟作响。

那是怎样的欢快！
离开这森林，手持胜利的号角。
冲入汇聚的人群，
将暴君推翻，重整河山。
将侵略者的胸膛用利剑刺穿。

有如野马般难以驾驭的命运，
我曾将它驯服。
亲自套上了缰绳，
鞭驾它越过一切障碍，
不辞千辛与苦，踏上自己的路。

哪个敢阻挡我的去路？
有人躲开，有人滚落尘埃，
妄想抵抗的皆化齑粉，
后面只留下我的脚印。
在可毁灭一切的烈火浓烟中，
青天也睁大了恐惧的眼。

我曾经无数次跃过死亡深渊，
登上人生的彼岸。
昔日的天边有不眨眼的星星，
为人们在黑夜中指明方向。
人群的洪流在两岸四周怒吼着回旋激荡。

哪管它黑暗的午夜，亦或是炎热的白天；
哪管它空中乌云密布，雷声隆隆；
哪管它狂风肆虐，笼罩当头。

“来！来！”我向众人呼唤，

他们飞奔着汇聚在我的身边。
打开了房门，
抛弃了家园，
将快乐、幸福和爱情的牵绊统统无情扯断。

就像印度五河之水汇入海洋，
听到我的呼唤，谁肯裹足不前。
信徒们与我的心结成一片，
旁遮普四处响起了“万岁！万岁”的胜利呼唤。

“你要去哪里？懦夫！”
我的声音遍布山岭、丛林、隐秘的角落。
清晨中听到了呼唤——来呀，来呀！
劳动的人停止了辛劳。
深夜中听到了呼唤——来呀，你们来呀！
人们便忘记睡眠。

我在前行，四周人群涌动，
阻塞了道路，挤满了渡口，
忘记了种姓和门第的差距，
轻易将自己的生命献出，
尊贵的、卑贱的、婆罗门和锡克团结在一起。

算了，朋友，不要再做这样的梦！
现在仍时机未到。
如今我须独自渡过漫长的荷叶，
仍须要不眠地铭记分秒的时间，
仍须目不转睛地凝视东方的天机，
等待旭日初升的黎明现身。

我如今只在虚幻的世界中纵横驰骋，
森林是我的王城。
今日，我只能宁静地思索，
唯可无奈的独自修炼。
无论白昼和黑夜，只能够静坐着倾听自己的心声。

于是我独自来到耶摩纳河边的崎岖坎坷的山岭之中。
旁遮普高原将我养育到壮年，
我的歌声和耶摩纳河的飞溅浪花融入一起。
为了未来的事业培养能力，我需要暗中辛苦锻炼。

如此渡过了二十年的漫长光阴，
还要等待多少时光蔓延。
我从周围不朽的灵魂中吸取了一点一滴的营养，
何时我才能说我已经功成圆满？

什么时候我才能够宣布：
时机已到！
起来吧，朋友们，跟随我，
你们的师傅呼唤你们全部，
起来，朋友们。
从我的生命中你们将获取新的生命力。

再也不存恐惧和怀疑，
再也没有犹疑动摇和重重顾虑。
我已经找到了方向，掌握了真理。
打破了世界的束缚，傲然站立。
在我的眼中无生亦无死，
虚无、虚无，尽归虚无。

我的心仿佛听到天上的召唤
“从我的光耀中站起来！
看，从远方因你而来的人何止千万？”

听，这是波涛的汹涌之声，
心灵的河流在奔腾。
坚决地站起！
你要如一座灯塔般警觉，
在这黑夜中，你如沉睡，他们就会重返家中。

你们看，在遥远天边，张开了漆黑的夜幕。
狂风带着死亡即将到来，
我的心中点燃了明灯，
即是狂风中也不会熄灭，
它将永远给大家照亮前路。

走吧，萨胡；走吧，拉姆达斯，
回去吧，我劝你们重返故乡。
在你们全都回去之后，
来，高呼一声“古鲁万岁！”
举起双臂，高呼：“万岁，万岁，万岁，阿拉克·尼郎姜。”

最后的一课

有一天，锡克教的宗师戈宾德孤独地在原野中回忆自己经历的一生，
那些曾在青春中谱写光芒万丈的雄心壮志如今在何方?
主神前的誓师，矢志不渝的宏愿，
曾使婆罗多的一统得以实现。
但是，祖国啊，如今它风雨飘摇，
弱小无力，任人宰割，支离破碎。
这是谁的责任?
生命难道白白虚度?
无比的疑惑，疲惫的身体，痛苦的心灵，
戈宾德在思考中渡过朦胧的傍晚。
这时，来个一个帕坦人，对他说:
“我要返回故乡，把你拖欠我的马钱给我。”
戈宾德回答:“锡克琪，我向你致意。
明天我将会把钱还你，请您今天暂时回去。”
帕坦人怒骂着:“钱，是必须在今天归还。”
边说边用力抓住他的手，污蔑他是一个强盗、骗子，要将他带走。
戈宾德听了，闪电般抽出宝剑，
转瞬间砍下了帕坦人的头，鲜血在地上流淌。
看到自己的所作所为，古鲁摇头说:
“看来我的生命应该完结。
这把不杀无辜者的宝剑竟违背我的本心，
鲁莽地使无罪之人流出鲜血。
信心已经从我的手臂中永远消失，
我发誓要洗去这罪孽和耻辱。
从今天起，我将做完最后一件事。”

帕坦人有一个儿子，还很年幼。
戈宾德将他找来抚养在身边，
日日夜夜，如同亲生子般教他背诵经典、学习兵法和剑术。

年迈的英雄，锡克的古鲁琪，
和孩子一样在清晨和黄昏里陪着帕坦人的儿子一起玩耍。
他的信徒们看到这些，走来对他说：
“师傅啊，你这是干什么？我们感到恐惧。
如此爱惜一只虎崽，难道你想要改变他天性？
一旦他长大成人，爪牙势必将会长出，危险啊。
敬爱的师傅，人是会被锐爪所伤。”
戈宾德笑着说：“我正希望这样。
一只虎崽如果不使他变为猛虎，
我又何须如此费尽心机。”

孩子在戈宾德的怀中逐渐长大，
孩子如影随行跟在他的左右，
孩子侍奉他如同亲生子女，
戈宾德爱他如同自己的生命，

戈宾德爱他如同自己的右手，
戈宾德的儿子全在战场上失去生命。
如今，帕坦人的儿子填补了年迈的古鲁心中的寂寞。
古老榕树的树洞中来了一粒被风送来的种子，
逐渐生根发芽，慢慢地绿色葱葱遮盖了垂老的枝条。

这一日，孩子跪在古鲁脚前说：
“感谢您亲自教导，我已经熟悉武技，
如果得到师傅的允许，凭着我这超人能力足以参加国王的军队。”
戈宾德轻抚他的脊背：
“你还有最后一课需要学习。”
第二天的傍晚，古鲁戈宾德独自走出房门，对孩子说：
“带上你的武器跟我来！”

二人无语地走向河边的树林中。
露出石子的河岸边上，有雨季的山洪将血红色沙土冲破的蜿蜒痕迹。
四周都是一颗颗高大的婆罗树，树根旁丛生着密集的灌木。
及膝的河水如水晶般清澈。
渡过河后，古鲁向孩子使了一个眼色，孩子停下脚步。
火红的晚霞仿佛蝙蝠的翅膀一样展开长长的影子，
在肃穆的空中向着西方缓缓飞去。
戈宾德对孩子说：
“马穆德，来这里，挖掘开这块土地。”
孩子挖开了沙土，露出一块青石，
上面还沾有血染的痕迹。
古鲁说：“石上的红，是你父亲的血痕。
我没有还他的债，也没容他动手，就是在这儿，我砍下了他的头。
今天正是时候，啊，帕坦！
如果你是你父亲的好儿子，
就拔出宝剑，杀掉害死你父亲的仇人。
用他的鲜血来祭奠饥渴的亡魂。”

一声如猛虎咆哮的怒吼，双眼血红的帕坦跳起扑在戈宾德的身上，
古鲁如同木偶般呆立原地。
帕坦扔下武器，在他的脚边下跪：
“师傅！请不要和魔鬼开这样可怕的玩笑！
父亲的冤仇，从情理上我应该遗忘。
在漫长的岁月中，我将你当成为父亲、师傅和朋友。
愿这深厚的情感充溢我的心中，压制下仇恨的想法。
师傅，我向您致敬。”
说完这些，帕坦飞一样逃出树林，一下没有回头，一步没有停留。
戈宾德的眼中滚下泪珠。

帕坦自从那天从树林中归来，
就总是远远地避开戈宾德。
黎明，他不再到宁静的卧室唤醒师傅，
夜晚，他不再手持武器守卫在师傅门前。
他不再独自一人陪着师傅到对岸打猎，
也不会在无人时听从师傅的呼唤来到他的身前。

这一天，戈宾德和帕坦在下棋消遣，
没有注意到天色已晚。
屡次的失败激怒了帕坦。
黄昏后，黑夜降临。
弟子们全都归家，夜已经渐深。
全神贯注地低头，帕坦在思考着下一步棋子从何着手。
这时，戈宾德忽然用棋子狠狠打中帕坦的头，狂笑着说：
“与杀父仇人一同对弈，这样的胆怯鬼，还妄想获取胜利？”
帕坦立刻从腰间拔出匕首，闪电般刺入戈宾德的胸口。
戈宾德微笑着说：
“你似乎才明白该如何向不义之人复仇，最后的一课我已经教导传授。
孩子，我已心满意足，让我来给你最后一次的祝福。”

仿造的布迪堡

“绝不饮水，绝不进食！”
奇多尔王发誓：
“只要布迪堡还有一日存于地上。”
大臣们说：“陛下，这是什么样的誓言！
此事非人力所能及，岂能让它实现？”
奇多尔王说：“不成功，则成仁。”
布尔迪堡距离奇多尔有五十里的路程，
那里的哈拉族人全是勇敢的英雄。
那是哈姆王的领地，在那里无人理会恐惧。
布迪堡的大名，奇多尔王的誓言就是证明。
布迪堡距离奇多尔只有五十里的路程。

大臣们暗中设计：
“今夜不去休息，
用泥土建成仿照布迪堡的虚假城堡。
陛下将亲自来将它变成地面上的一堆泥沙。
否则为了一句大话，他的生命将会迎来毁灭。”
于是在奇多尔的中心，建成了假的城堡。

贡波是奇多尔王的仆人，哈拉族的英雄。
射鹿归来的他，肩上背着硬弓和利箭。
他听到消息后说：“凭你是谁！
想把伪造的布迪堡摧毁，想让哈拉族在拉其普他纳没脸见人？
我是哈拉族的豪杰，要保卫仿造的布迪堡。”

奇多尔王前来摧毁伪造的布迪堡。
“滚开！”贡波高欢，声如霹雷。
“妄图拿布迪堡之名戏耍？我绝不能容对它的侮辱和践踏。
建成堡垒的任何泥沙，一粒都不能被破坏。”
“滚开！”贡波高欢，声如霹雷。

双手拉弓，单膝跪在地面，
贡波独自守卫着伪造的布迪堡。
奇多尔带来的士兵高举着宝刀向他围攻，
贡波的头转眼间滚落在城堡门外的一角。
他的鲜血使伪造的布迪堡增添荣耀。

洒红节

普那戈国王的皇后从凯杜那里送给帕坦的凯撒尔·卡一封书信：

“你认为可以用战争获得友谊?

春天会从面前姗姗离去，

来吧，将军，带着你的帕坦军队和我们拉其普特的女人欢迎新春。”

战败后丢失了很多城镇，从凯杜那里皇后送去了书信。

凯撒尔·卡心中狂喜，笑眯眯捋着唇上的胡髯。

眼皮染着黑色的黛黑，

头巾选择了绛红颜色，

手中的罗帕香气袭人，千百次在嘴唇上来回擦拭。

皇后要和帕坦人洒红游戏，

凯撒尔·卡笑眯眯捋着唇上的胡髯。

馨香的花丛中吹拂三月中的醉人威风。

芒果林散发出沁人的芳香，

不听话的蜜蜂自由自在，随心所以地嗡嗡歌唱，在芒果林中四处回转飞翔。

凯杜那城中今天迎来了一队队过洒红节的帕坦士兵。

凯杜那城国王的御苑之中，布满了落日血红的颜色。

爬塔的士兵来到花园中，乐队的笛声唱着黄昏歌曲。

来了一百个皇后的宫女，要陪伴帕坦人欢度洒红节日。

此时正是落日时分，金乌喷出愤怒的血红之色。

长裙拖到脚面，春风中飘荡着披肩，
左手端着装红粉的金盘，
喷红的小筒挂在腰间。
右手挽着装满玫瑰水的铜罐，
一队队宫女来到花园。
一步步飘曳着长裙，春风中飘荡着披肩。

狡黠的微笑闪动在眼角，
凯撒尔·卡向女人敬礼：
“百战劫余，我侥幸不死，
看来今天要魂飞魄散。”
猛然间响起一阵狂笑，笑倒了皇后的一百个宫女。
歪戴着红色头巾，凯撒尔·卡笑嘻嘻向女人敬礼。

开始了洒红游戏，
红粉飘荡，染红了黄昏的天空。
素馨花换成了新的颜色，
树根下洒满红色的水痕，
鸟儿忘记啼叫，惊呆在拉其普特女人的狂笑中。
啊，是哪里飘来了红雾，染红了黄昏的天空。

为什么我没有目醉心迷，
凯撒尔·卡暗自思忖。
胸膛竟不是丰满突起？
女人脚镯上的金铃为何如此嘈杂不合韵律，
手镯的叮当声也欠缺文雅。
唉，为什么我没有目醉心迷，
凯撒尔·卡暗自思忖。

帕坦士兵心想：拉其普特的女人身上没有半点柔媚风情。
一双手臂不像莲藕，
声音使天上的雷霆都感到羞臊，
好像沙漠中僵硬枯萎的无花枯藤。
帕坦士兵心想：拉其普特的女人身上没有半点柔媚风情。

“伊曼”曲中的笛声急促威严。
胸前悬着珍珠项链，
赤金的宽手镯带在手腕，
接过宫女递来的盛红粉的铜盘。
皇后亲临到御苑中。
这时，“伊曼”曲中的笛声急促威严。

凯撒尔·卡说：
“凝望着您的亲临，我差点瞎了双眼。”
皇后说：“我也有同感。”
一百个宫女不禁大笑，
突然帕坦将军的额头上飞来皇后手中的铜盘。
血光四溅如喷泉，帕坦将军真的瞎了双眼。

有如晴空霹雳一声，
响起了战鼓咚咚。
星空中升起战抖的月亮，
飘散着冷森森的剑光。
唢呐在园门中雄赳赳声音嘹亮，
御苑里一棵棵的树下响起了战鼓咚咚。

长裙脱下，
披肩被风吹起在空中。
是谁念了声咒语，
脱下了女人的华衣。
仿佛花丛中蹿出了百条毒蛇，
百名英雄立刻包围了帕坦。
长裙脱下，
梦幻般被风吹去了披肩。

帕坦从那条路上前来，
他们再不能由原路返回。
春夜中沉醉了的杜鹃不断啼鸣。
凯撒尔·卡的酒红节结束于凯杜那的御花园。
帕坦从那条路上前来，
他们再不能由原路返回。

婚礼

宁静夜晚响起了喜庆的法螺声。
新郎新娘如画像般衣襟相连羞涩地站在礼堂。
女人们掀开面纱的一角，在窗外偷偷地观看，
雨季的夜晚响起了阵阵雷声，
雷声中吹起了结婚的法螺。

清爽的东南风不再吹起，
阴沉的天空中彤云密布。
礼堂中的烛光辉煌，
珍珠项链闪闪发光。
是谁突然冲进了礼堂?
大门外还响起了咚咚的战鼓。
人们全都惊诧起立，
聚拢起围绕着新郎新娘。

向戴着花冠的麦特里王子禀报的是马鲁瓦的使者。
拉姆辛格陛下亲临战场，
亲自统军与异族敌人交战。
他召唤你们前去参战。
动身吧！勇敢的拉其普特。
“万岁！拉姆辛格万岁！”
马鲁瓦的使者高呼。

“万岁！拉姆辛格万岁！”
麦特里的王子高呼相应。
新娘的心惊吓粉碎，

一双大眼闪烁泪水。
“万岁！拉姆辛格万岁！”
伴郎们异口同声，齐声高呼。
拉姆辛格的使者大声疾呼：
“麦特里王子，时间不许你再延误停留。”

为何还空吹口哨？
为何在空响法螺？
解开永结同心的衣衫，
新郎凝视着新娘的脸说：
“亲爱的，这是死亡的邀请，
破坏了你我快乐的结合。”
如今突然空吹着口哨，
如今突然空响着法螺。

穿着礼服戴着花冠，
王子上马飞驰而去。
满脸惆怅，温柔地低垂着头，
新娘返回自己的绣阁。
灯火慢慢熄灭，
宫廷的礼堂变成漆黑一片。
穿着礼服戴着花冠，
王子上马飞驰而去。

妈妈哭着说：“脱下结婚的礼服。
唉，你真是命苦。”
女儿安静地对妈妈说：
“别哭，妈妈，我求你。
让我穿着结婚的礼服，
我愿为他前往麦特里堡。”

妈妈听了手捶着额头，哭着说：
“唉，命苦的女儿。”

皇家的司仪送给她祝福，
在她头上洒满了吉祥草和米谷。
新娘坐上华美的彩轿，
女人们吹起吉祥的口哨。
彩衣鲜亮的男女仆从，
一队队走来陪她上路。
妈妈走上来给她亲吻，
爸爸亲抚着额头送给她祝福。

深夜中，火炬照亮天空，
是谁来到了麦特里的城门前？
有人呼喝：“喂，停下轿子，
禁止吹奏，停下吹笛，
麦特里的居民正在一同准备，
为麦特里王子举行火葬。
麦特里王子今天在战场上牺牲，
在这不幸的日子是谁来到了麦特里？”

“吹起笛声，奏起喜乐！”
新娘在花轿里面吩咐。
如今的神圣时刻不再失去，
衣襟上的同心结不会再解开，
在火葬场熊熊的火光中，
念诵婚礼中最后的曼荼罗。
“吹起笛声，奏起喜乐！”
新娘在花轿里面吩咐。

戴着珍珠项链，穿着新郎礼服，
麦特里王子躺在火葬场中。
花轿中走出王子的妻子，
衣襟和他的血衣牢牢结起。
新娘坐在王子的头前，
新郎的头被抱在她的怀中。
深夜里，穿着血衣，
麦特里王子躺在火葬场中。

响起了一阵阵高声的口哨，
女人们一队队走到近前。
“善品行！”皇家司仪婆罗门赞颂着，
颂赞师说：“啊！你这征服死亡的女人。”
新娘盘膝端坐在焚尸的柴堆上，
风吹着熊熊的烈火在燃烧。
火葬场上一片胜利的欢呼，
女人们吹起结婚的口哨。

审判官

拉胡那特·拉奥，马拉塔皇家的英雄。
他登上王位后在普纳城宣布：
“我要减轻人间苦难的负担，
我要征服麦索尔王海德拉里，
打消他的气焰。”

转眼间集合了八万雄兵。
四面八方，川流不息地从马拉塔所有的高山中，
英雄们如雨季的山洪般汇聚在普纳城。

胜利的旗帜在天空中飘扬，
千百个法螺在共鸣齐响。

女人们吹起了尖声的口哨，
普纳城在光荣里战抖，
毁灭的战鼓动人心魄地敲打着，震动四方。

朝阳躲藏到旌旗遍布的树林，
马蹄扬起了滚滚灰尘。
震聋天空的胜利欢呼之中，
拉胡那特骑上了血色战马。
突然，好像谁念了一句咒语，
军乐停止了前进的喇叭。

是谁在前方，使国王变得如此谦恭?
是谁在指挥，宫门外刹那停止了兴奋奔赴战场的士兵?

婆罗门拉姆·沙斯特里，公正的最高审判官。
他高举着双臂，
大声疾呼：
“拉胡那特·拉奥，离开城市奔赴战场，在没有受到惩罚之前？”
停止了军乐，
停止了胜利的欢呼。
拉胡那特说：
“为什么偏偏在今天阻挡我的去路?
我正为使阎摩的宴席丰盛而去歼灭异教之徒。”

拉姆·沙斯特里说：
“你谋杀了嫡亲的侄儿！
在未接受审判之前，
你在这期间失去自由。
按照法律的规定，你需要被严加看管。”

拉胡那特·拉奥脸上含笑，心中怒恼：
“国王的行动谁可约束?
刀剑之下我来去自由，
今天我不是来到路中听人讲解法律。”

沙斯特里说：
“拉胡那特，去吧，尽管去征战。
我也即刻辞职，返回自己的家乡。
绝不容许自己坐在这无视法律的法庭之上。”

吹着法螺，敲响战鼓，
出征的队伍再次启程。
舍弃了高贵的职位，
抛弃了所有的财宝，
清贫的婆罗门回到了乡村中的草屋。

践誓

“注意，马拉塔的强盗已经来到，
大家握好武器！”
阿吉密堡中将军杜姆拉吉高呼。
正午时分，家家户户正烤着粗面饼，
人声鼎沸中碉堡上传来战鼓的咚咚声。
登上城头，看到南方的遥远天际，
马拉塔骑兵的铁蹄下扬起了一片灰尘。
“这批马拉塔的蝗虫今日在扑入我们的剑火，
彻底消灭不容一个人回去。”
杜姆拉吉怒吼着。

从马鲁瓦来的使者说：
“何必准备迎敌？
这是陛下的旨意，看看吧，将军杜姆拉吉。”
信德人来了，同来的还有法国的将领。

恭敬的将城堡交给他们，你必须服从命令。
幸运之神如今抛弃了国王为佳耶辛哈，
阿吉密堡不用血战抵抗，奉送给马拉塔吧。
“国王的命令，英雄的职责，
到底该如何选择？”
长叹了一声，杜姆拉吉痛苦地低语。

马鲁瓦的使者宣布旨意：
“全部放下武器。”
杜姆拉吉如同石像呆立。
天色已晚，牛羊蹒跚在暮霭中的田间，
树荫下牧童的笛声悠扬婉转。
“阿吉密堡交付于我时，
我曾在暗中发誓，
国王的堡垒绝不会失陷于敌，
今天难道因国王的命令就将誓言背弃？”
辗转反侧，主意不定，
杜姆拉吉长叹着。

拉其普特的军队羞愤地放下武器，
堡垒门前杜姆拉吉默默呆立。
赭色的黄昏悄悄降临在西方的田野，
马鲁瓦的军队扬起灰尘停止在堡垒门前。
“躺在门前的是谁？
起来，打开大门！”
没有回音，失去生命的躯壳再不会能回答询问。
君王的旨意，英雄的职责，
如今再不会令他忧虑。
阿吉密堡的大门外，
英雄杜姆拉吉开始长眠。

《游思集》选

1

你在无形中向前奔涌，永恒的游思，

哪里有你无形的冲击，那儿死寂的空间便会荡漾起逡巡的波光。

是不是你的心灵向往着在无法估量的寂寞中向你呼唤的情人?

你缠绕的发辫散落，飘洒如同暴风雨般纷乱，

你前行的道路上火珠滚滚，如同碎裂的项链散落开点点火星。

这是否因你的心情急促，步履匆忙?

你疾走的步履将世上的尘土亲吻得甜美芳香，将腐朽之物扫除干净；

你舞动的四肢是暴风的中心，将死亡的霖雨哗哗地洒落地上，更新了生命气象。

假如你突然之间因为疲倦而停留片刻，世间将会滚成一团，

变成一团障碍，阻止自己前进。

如此一来，即便是最微小的尘埃，也会因为无法忍受的沉闷而划破无涯的天空。

光明的镯子戴在你看不见的脚上，摇荡的节奏使我的思想满是活力。

它们在我心脏的跳动中回响，全身的血液激荡起古老海洋中的歌声。

我听见雷鸣般的浪潮震荡，将我的生命从此世冲到彼世，从一种形式变为另外一种。

我听见它们的悲叹和欢歌中，抛洒着无数飞溅的礼物，使我的躯体四处飘荡。

浪涛卷起，疾风怒吼，扁舟一叶如愿在风浪中舞蹈，我的心灵！

请把聚敛的财宝抛弃在海岸之上，扬帆起航，

穿越这目不可测的黑暗，向着无尽的光明前行。

2

夜色已浓，我问她：“我现在到达了哪片陌生的土地？”

她的双眉低垂，当她离开时，坛子里将要溢出的水吱吱作响。

堤岸上，树林影影绰绰，依稀可见，这片土地仿佛已属于昔日。

水默默无声，竹林忧郁地静止不动，小巷中传来一只手镯撞击水潭的声音，叮叮当当。

不要再前行，把小舟系在树上，因我深爱这片土地的景色。

夜晚的星星在教堂的圆顶边下落，埠头的大理石台阶的苍白与流水的黝黑相映成辉。

夜色中赶路的旅人长叹，遮掩的窗中透出光亮，透过了路边密集交织的树林和灌木，被撕成碎裂的星光融入夜色中。

手镯仍在撞击着水坛，归去的脚步声还在遍地落叶的小巷中发出响声。

夜晚渐渐深沉，宫殿的高塔如同幽灵般显现，小镇在疲惫中呻吟。

不要再前行，把小舟系在树上。

让我在这片陌生的土地上休息，朦胧地躺在月光下，

这儿的夜色里震动着手镯撞击水坛的声音，叮叮当当。

3

如果在迦梨陀娑做御前诗人的时候，我恰好生活在皇城乌贾因，也许我会认识某个马尔瓦的姑娘。

她音乐般的芳名会萦绕在我的脑海，她或许会将慌忙的一瞥从眼帘中向我投来，

任素馨花遮住她的面纱，找一个借口停留在我的身旁。

这样的事儿只能出现在往昔，如今学者们你争我夺，为了那些捉迷藏的日子。

我不会难过伤心沉迷于这些逝去的岁月，

但是，我一声声的叹息，马尔瓦的姑娘已随岁月而去。

我不知道，她们将与御前诗人的短笛共鸣的时日，用花篮提到了第几重天际。

今天黎明，一阵由于降生太迟而不能与她们相会的分离之情，令我心事重重，愁眉不展。

然而，四月的鲜花，仍是曾经点缀过她们秀发的鲜花，

今天在玫瑰上细语的南风，也仍是曾吹拂她们面纱的南风。

是这样，今春的欢乐并未少，尽管迦梨陀娑不再歌唱。

但我却知晓，倘若他能从诗人的圣殿见到我，他将会嫉妒。

4

我暂时忘记了自己，所以我来此。

请你抬起双眼，让我看看是否仍有一丝往日的阴影尚未消散，

宛若天边残留的一片被夺去雨水的白云。

请暂且宽容我，如果我忘却自身。

玫瑰依然含苞待放，它们仍不知晓，今年夏日我们无意采摘鲜花。

晨星身怀着同样的惶恐而不安沉默，晨曦被垂下在窗边的树枝缠绕，一如过往岁月。

我暂时忘记了时光流逝，所以我来此。

我不记得我向你袒露心迹，你是否转头避开，令我羞愧无言。

我只记得你颤抖的嘴唇上欲言又止的话语，

我记得你乌黑眼眸中热情的影子闪过，

仿佛暮色中觅食归巢的翅膀。

我忘了你已不再记得我，所以我来此。

5

在水一方并无埠头，姑娘们从不来此汲水。

河滩边长满了密密麻麻的矮小灌木，

嘈杂的沙里克鸟在陡峭的堤坝上挖土筑巢，

河岸的神情皱眉不语，在这里渔船找不到任何庇护。

你坐在这无人会来的草地上，清晨随之流逝，

告诉我你在这干燥龟裂的堤坝上做什么?

她凝视着我的脸说:“不，我什么都不做。”

在河的这边堤坝荒凉。没有牛儿来此吃草，只有几只从村庄跑来的离群山羊，整天在这里吃着稀疏的草。

那只孤独的水隼，栖息在一棵倾斜在泥中连根拔起的菩提树上，正四处张望。

你独自坐在那棵希莫尔树的吝啬阴影下，清晨随之流逝。

告诉我，你在等谁?

她凝视着我的脸说:“不，我谁也不等。”

6

“为什么你不停地做这些准备？” 我问心灵，

“难道将会有人来？”

心灵答道：“我忙于搜集东西建成楼宇，无暇回答这样的问题。”

我温顺地返回忙碌自己的工作。

当材料已经成为一堆，当他的大厦建成了七座翼殿，

我对心灵说：“难道这还不够？”

心灵回答：“还不够容下。”说着便停下了话语。

“容纳什么?

心灵装作没有听见。

我猜是因心灵也不知道答案，才用无止的工作来压抑疑惑。

他的一句口头禅是：“我必须充分准备。”

“你为何定要如此？”

“因为这非常了不起。”

“是什么如此了不起？”

心灵转而沉默无语，但我定要他来回答。

带着轻蔑和愤怒，心灵说道：

“你为什么老追问这些不着边际的东西?

去注意你眼前的重要大事——格斗与战争，砖头和砂浆，还有无法统计

的劳动者。”

我想:“也许心灵方是明智。”

日复一日，他的大厦翼殿不断增加，他的领域也越发开阔。

雨季早已结束，乌云变得洁白稀疏，

明媚时光在雨水冲洗的天空中流逝，仿佛许多彩蝶在看不见的鲜花上舞蹈。

我变得痴迷，逢人就问:“微风中飘荡着什么乐曲？”

一个流浪汉从路上走来，他的衣衫和他的举止一样落拓不羁，他说:

“听，那是降临者的乐声。”

我却相信了他的话语，脱口说:“我们无需久等。”

“就在眼前。”疯子说。

回到工作之地，我大胆对心灵说:“什么都不要再做。”

心灵问:“有了什么消息？”

“有。”我回答:“降临者的消息。”但我却无法解释。

心灵摇着头:“没有旌旗，也没有华丽的仪仗。”

夜色即将降临，星光在空中变得暗淡。

突然，晨曦的试金石将世间染成一片金黄，众人的呼唤不断传来。

“使者来了。”

我俯首问：“他来了？”

回答仿佛从四面八方传来：“来了。”

心灵气愤地说：“我还没有封上大厦的圆顶，一切仍是杂乱无章。”

天空中传来声响：“将你的楼宇推倒。”

“可是，为何？”心灵问。

“只因今日是降临者之日，你的楼宇实在碍手碍脚。”

这高耸的大厦倒于尘埃，一切都变得破碎凌乱。

心灵四处张望，又能看到什么？

唯有启明星和沐浴朝露的百合。

除此之外，还有什么？一个孩子脱离母亲的怀抱，大笑着跑进空旷的晨光。

“难道仅仅为了这些，人们就说是降临者来到的日子？”

“是的，就为这些，人们才说空气中飘荡着乐章，天空中闪现光芒。”

“难道仅仅为此，人们才要求拥有这个世界？”

“是的。”传来这样的回答：“心灵，你铸造围城囚禁自我，你的仆人们辛苦劳碌。

世界和无限的空间，却是为了这孩子，为了新生而创造。”

“孩子带来了什么？”

“整个世界的希望和快乐。”

心灵问我：“诗人，你是否理解？”

“我放在了我的工作。”我说：“正因为我需要时间来理解。”

7

将军走到沉默不语怒气勃发的国王身前，向他禀报："村庄已受到惩罚，男人们被打倒在地上的尘土里，女人们战抖地躲藏在没有灯光的屋中，害怕得不敢放声哭泣。"

祭司长站起向国王祝福，并放声大笑说："愿神的恩宠与陛下您永远同在。"

小丑听到这句话，忍不住放声大笑，笑声中满朝文武不知所措，国王低沉的眉头更加紧皱。

小丑的笑声愈加响亮，国王怒斥说："岂能不分场合的欢笑？"

"神灵赐予陛下那么多的恩宠。"小丑说："赐予我的只是笑的天赋。"

"这种天赋会使你丢掉性命。"国王右手抽出了他的锋利宝剑。

然而，小丑却站起身放声大笑，直到再也无法发出笑的声音。

恐怖的阴影笼罩着殿堂，因为它们听到了小丑的大笑回响在神灵沉默之处。

8

这一天到来，庙宇中的神像被安放在光辉的圣辇中，绕着圣城游行。

皇后对国王说："我们去参加喜庆圣典。"

全部人都去顶礼膜拜，只有一个人例外，

他的工作是收割茅草的茎秆，为皇帝的宫廷制作扫帚。

总管怜悯地对他说："你可与我们同行。"

他低着头说："这可不行。"

他的房屋就在国王的仆从的必经之路上。

大臣骑着象经过这里，向他高喊："和我们一起，去瞧瞧坐在圣辇中的神灵。"

"我怎么敢效仿皇帝去拜见神灵。"他说。

"你下次怎么有机会再次拜见圣辇中的神灵？"大臣问。

"等到神灵亲自来到我的门前。"他回答。

大臣放声大笑："傻瓜。说什么等神灵亲自来到我的门前。连国王他都不会屈驾前往。"

"除了神灵，还有谁会来看望穷人。"他说。

9

房屋在它财富消失之后，依然恋恋不舍地站在街边，仿佛一个疯子只剩下点缀补丁的破衫。

日复一日，岁月无情的利爪将这房子撕得满目疮痍，雨季在赤裸的砖头上留下了疯狂的名字。

楼上一间凄凉屋中，两扇对合门中的一扇因为铰链锈蚀而脱落，另外一扇独自的门则在疾风中日夜响个不停。

一天深夜，房子中传来女人们痛哭的声音，她们在悲伤家族中最后的儿子的死亡。

这孩子不过才十八岁，在一个巡回剧院中依靠扮演女角而谋生。

几天后，屋子中已失去声音，门上都已落锁。

只有楼上那房间向北的一面，孤独的房门不愿休息倒下，也不愿静止不动，来回在风中摇摆，仿佛一个自我折磨的灵魂。

一段日子后，孩子们的声音又回荡在房子之中。

阳台的栏杆上晾晒着妇女的衣服，遮盖的笼子里，传来鸟儿的啼鸣，还有一个男孩在阳台上放起风筝。

一个房客来租用了几个房间，他的收入微薄，孩子众多。

劳累的母亲责打孩童，他们哭泣着在地板上打滚。

一个四十岁的女仆，整日忙碌单调乏味的工作，与女主人的拌嘴中总是威胁要辞职，却从未实现过。

小修补每日在进行。纸张贴在无玻璃的窗棂上，栅栏中插上了竹子。

空空的箱子顶住了没有门闩的房门，陈旧的污渍在新粉刷的墙壁上依稀可见。

荣华富贵本已在荒凉颓废中找到了合适的纪念，

但，这新来的一家却在财力微薄下，试图用暧昧的办法来掩盖凄凉，结果却损伤了荒芜的颜面。

他们没有注意到北边那个凄凉的房间，被遗弃的房门依然在风中作响，仿佛绝望之神在捶打着胸膛。

10

森林深处，苦行的隐士紧闭双目开始修行，他希望能够悟道进入天堂。

来了一位拾柴的姑娘，用裙子给他兜来水果，用绿叶编成的杯子带来清溪中舀出的水。

日子逐渐过去，他的修炼日益辛苦。

最后，他不吃一个水果，不喝一滴清水，拾柴的姑娘悲伤难抑。

天堂的神王听说有凡人妄图修成神灵，虽然神王曾一次次打败他的敌人，并将他们赶出疆域。

但他却害怕具有承受苦难的力量之人。

按照他熟悉的终生秉性，神王安排计策诱惑这个凡人放弃他的修行。

一阵微风从天空中吹过，亲吻着拾柴姑娘的四肢。

她的青春因为沉浸于美妙之中而充满渴望，她的思绪仿佛蜂巢受到干扰的蜜蜂纷纷作响。

时辰来到，苦行的隐士离开森林，前往山洞中完成艰难的修行。

当他睁眼正要动身时，姑娘出现在他的身前，宛如一首熟悉却难以回忆的诗篇，增添了韵律变得更加陌生。

苦行的隐士缓缓站起，告诉她将要离开森林的时刻已经来临。

“你为什么要夺取我侍奉你的机会？”她眼含着热泪问。

他再次坐下，沉思许久留在了原来的地方。

当日夜晚，悔恨的心情使姑娘难以入睡，

她害怕自己的力量，痛恨自己的胜利，她的内心在骚动的欢乐波浪上飘荡。

清晨，她前来向苦修的隐士礼敬，告诉他，她即将离他远去，希望能够得到他的祝福。

他默然注视着她的脸庞，然后说：“去吧，如你所愿。”

年复一年，隐士独自修炼，直到功成圆满。

众神之王从天上降临，邀请他进入天上王国。

“我已不再需要。”他说。

神王向他询问，他想要得到什么更加珍贵的报酬。

“我想要那个拾柴的姑娘。”

11

人们惊讶地倾听着青年歌手卡希的演唱，
他的嗓音仿佛怀有绝技的宝剑，
在无望的纷扰纠缠中摇摆，
将它们劈碎成片而欢呼。
听众席上，老普拉塔普王忍耐着静坐，
他的生命曾为巴拉杰拉的歌声哺育培养，
仿佛幸福的土地被美丽河流点缀。
绵绵细雨夜，
静静秋风日，
通过巴拉杰拉的歌唱，向他的心灵述说。
以往的欢乐夜晚在歌声的伴随中，妆点起各色灯盏，回响着叮当的银铃。

卡希停止了他的歌唱，
普拉塔普微笑着向巴拉杰拉眨眼，低声对他说：
“大师，现在让我们享受些音乐，并非这种模仿着小猫的跳跃追逐猎物般的歌曲。”
戴着洁白头巾的老歌手向观众深深鞠躬，
他坐下来双目紧闭，用纤细的手指弹起了琴弦，犹豫中开始了他的演唱。
大厅宽敞倒映了他歌声的微弱，普拉塔普高声喝彩：
“太好了！”边在他的耳旁低语：“大声些，我的朋友。”

听众们躁动不安，有的打哈欠，有的瞌睡，有的在抱怨天气炎热。
大厅里心不在焉的纷乱声音嘈杂一片，
歌声仿佛一只随时沉默的小舟，徒劳地在波浪上颠簸，
最后，终于淹没在这喧哗之中。

老人因为心灵的创伤而忘记了歌词。

他的声音痛苦探索，仿佛盲人在集市中摸索着寻找他失散的引路人。

他师徒用音乐的曲调来填补这个缺口，但这缺口依旧张开嘴巴。

受尽折磨的音乐拒绝继续下去，它们改变了旋律，爆发出呜咽之声。

大师的头无力低垂在乐器上，情不自禁地爆发出婴儿降生般的第一声啼哭。

普拉塔普轻拍着他的肩膀，说："走吧，我们的聚会之地在别处。

我知道，我的朋友，没有爱的真理唯有孤独。

美不会与人们同在，也不和人们片刻同行。"

12

黎明的晨曦伴随中，

他独自漫步在雪杉遮掩的一条山路上，

这道路盘山绕岭，仿佛难舍难分的情侣。

他手里握着新婚的娇妻从家乡寄来的第一封信，思念他回到她的身边，

加快了他回程的脚步。

当他漫步的时候，一只看不见的纤手轻轻抚摸，令他的心潮澎湃，

天空中响起了信中的呼唤："亲爱的，我亲爱的，我的天空挂满泪珠。"

他惊讶地询问自己："是什么让我值得她如此？"

太阳突然从葱葱的山岗中跳出，四个女郎迈着轻快的脚步，从陌生的海岸走来。

她们打闹嬉笑，一旁跟随着一条吠叫的狗。

年龄稍长的两个女郎，看见他魂不守舍的样子，不由得转过头去，掩盖她们被逗笑的容颜。

那年幼的两个，则大笑着相互拥抱，高兴地飞奔而去。

他停下脚步，低垂着头，

他忽然感受到手中的信笺，打开了它，再重新读上一遍。

13

我顺着一条遍布绿荫的小径行走，突然听到有人在后面呼唤："喂，你还认识我吗？"

我转身看着来人，对她说："我记不起你的名字。"

她说："我是你年轻时遭遇过的第一次巨大的哀伤。"

她的眼睛仿佛饱含着朝露的清晨。

我默默站立一会，开口说："你已经卸下了泪中的所有负担？"

她笑而不答，我感到她的眼泪已经学会了从容说出微笑的谎言。

"曾经你说过，"她喃喃地说："你会把痛苦永远铭记心田。"

我的脸红了："是的。可岁月流逝带它去了忘却世间。"

于是，我握着她的手说："同样，你也已经改变。"

"昔日的感伤，变成了今日的漠然。"她说。

14

画家在集市上兜售画卷。

不远处，走来了前呼后拥的大臣之子。

他的父亲曾在年轻时用敲诈将画家的父亲骗得伤心而死。

孩子在画家的作品前流连忘返。

他选中了一幅，却被画家匆忙用布遮盖，“这幅画不再售卖。”

这一天后，孩子因为心病而变得憔悴。

他的父亲愿意为那幅画付出高价。

可画家宁愿将画卷挂在自家墙头，也不愿出手。

他阴沉地坐在画的前面，自言自语说：“这就是我的报复！ ”

每天清晨，画家都会画一幅信奉的神的画像，这是他祈祷的虔诚方式。

可是如今，他总觉得神像与昔日的作品逐渐不同。

这件事令他苦恼不已。

画家茫然地寻找原因，终于有一天，他惊恐地丢下画笔，难以自禁地跳起。

那刚刚画好的神像之眼，竟然如果大臣的眼睛一般，嘴唇也是如此的相似。

他将画撕成碎片，高喊：“我的报复回到了我自己的身上。”

15

昏昏欲睡的村子之中，正午安静得仿佛阳光灿烂的午夜，我的假期却已经结束。

整个早上，四岁的女儿始终跟在我的左右，从这一间来到另外一间。

她一本正经地默默看着我收拾行囊，直到她疲倦地依靠着门柱坐下。

静默之中，她喃喃自语："爸爸一定不能走。"

午餐的时间来到，困倦睡意每天按时向她袭来，可是她的妈妈却将她忘记，孩子闷闷不乐却不说一句抱怨的话。

最后，当我张开双臂向她告别，她却一动不动。

她的眼睛伤心地注视着我："爸爸，你一定不能走。"

这句话差点让我笑出眼泪，这个小小的孩子，竟然想要挑战这个生计所迫的世界。

而她的战术不过是寥寥数字："爸爸，你一定不能走！"

《再次集》选

泰戈尔诗文彩图馆

昆虫的天地

卡弥亚树木的枝条上悬挂着被露水打湿的坚韧蜘蛛丝。

花园弯曲小径的两旁，星罗密布着小小的棕色蚁蛭。

我于上午和下午在其间穿行，忽然发现素馨花绽放了花苞，达迦尔树被洁白的花朵点缀。

地球上，人的家庭看似很小，其实并非如此。

昆虫的巢穴却也是这样。

它们难以看清，却营造了创造的思想。

祖祖辈辈，它们有忧虑，难处和需求，

这些一切构成漫长的历史。

日复一日中，显露难以阻止的生命活跃。

我在它们中间徘徊，听不到它们的生老病死。

永恒的情感在流淌。

我低吟着诗篇，斟字酌句，用以完成这未完的歌曲。

对于蜘蛛的世界，蚂蚁的社会，我的斟酌增添了费解、奇怪和毫无意义。

在它们昏暗的天地之中，是否回荡着婆娑的柔声，呼吸的妙曲，听不清的喃喃低语，无可表达的沉重的足音?

我是个凡人，但自信可周游世界，甚至能够去除飞往彗星、被天狗吞噬的日月的道路上的障碍。

然而，蜘蛛的王国却向我关闭大门。

充满我痛苦、怨恨和喜悦的世界尽头，

蚂蚁的心灵帷幕始终低垂。

上午和下午，我在它们的狭小无限以外的路上往返，目睹素馨花绽放，达迦尔树被洁白的鲜花点缀。

美艳

仿佛白金钻戒上镶嵌的钻石，阳光穿透漫天阴霾的空隙，斜照于原野上。

风儿呼呼地吹，木瓜树惊魂未定。

北面的原野上，木楝树显出对抗的气势，棕榈树则嘟囔着发出牢骚。

时间大概到了一点半，在潮湿的树木闪光的中午，跳进了南墙北墙敞开的窗户，

在我的心头涂抹上一层缤纷迷离的色彩。

瞬间，不知为何，我觉得今天仿若昔日的那天。

那天无需承担责任，那天不再忙于急迫的事情，

那天是扯断了现在的枷锁，悠然逍遥的一日。

我看见它是昔日的海市蜃楼，那昔日是怎样的现实？

在哪里？属于哪个时代？难道说已经超越永恒？

那是，我的爱人仿佛在前世便已相识。

那时有天堂，是纯真的时代，绝不是其他时代能够感悟。

同样，畅饮了翡翠般的树荫和金子般的阳光混合的余下鸡尾酒，

畅饮了田原上挥舞薄纱的迷醉雨天的甜美，

我也感到若有似无，

仿佛天上琴弦奏动了婉转的古代孟加拉的萨伦曲调，

从一切时间的帷幕之后音乐前来。

人类的儿子

为了使前来问询的人们感悟，

耶稣在十字架上奉献出不朽生命。

自那一日起，逝去了多少时光。

今天，他从天国重临人间，

张目四望，看到了旧日刺入肌肤遍体鳞伤的罪恶凶器。

狰狞的长矛，狡诈的匕首、短剑，残忍狠毒的巨斧。

在悬挂着一面乌黑旗子的工坊中，飞速地霍霍磨砺，溅射炫目的火花。

新造的死亡箭羽，在刽子手的手中闪耀寒光，教徒用尖利的指甲在上面刻下姓名。

耶稣手捂胸膛，恍然大悟，原来死刑的执行期尚未结束。

科学的殿堂正在试制新式的武器，用来刺入他的关节。

那天站在宗教庙宇的阴影中残害他的凶手，正一批批复活，

如今站在庙宇神坛的面前，诵读般命令行刑的刽子手："斩尽杀绝！斩尽杀绝！"

人类的儿子悲伤地仰天长叹："啊，上帝，世人的上帝，你为何将我抛弃？"

最后的赠予

孩子们的游乐园全是干热的泥土，无法长出一根小草。

游乐园旁的一棵康基那树，看不到什么颜色与自己相同，

见到它我不禁想起家里门廊中的黑毛狗。

厨房四周，一群野狗在打转，怀着信心等着食物施舍。

它们争夺、挨打、惨叫，却享受快乐的天性。

我的宝贝黑毛狗戴维不时兴奋跃起，身子剧烈抖动，

它饥渴的眼神注视南方，怀着期望的激情放声大叫，想要加入它们的行列。

康基那树并非独立在自己的绿色世界，

它正站下人类碾成的贫瘠土地上。

它眺望远方，那里的草叶上画着林木的画像。

春天到了，无人知晓春风的情感是怎样渗入到骨髓之中。

不远的地方，顶天立地的檀树向南方海上新来的使者通报新春到来的消息。

高涨的绿色的喧闹之中，寿命即将完结的使者打开了康基那树的心扉。

在它的耳边讲述了那天最后一刻阳光的降临，将在嫩叶的最后一场孩童的活动中舞蹈。

它没有迟疑，微笑的表情在几朵淡紫色花瓣上显现。

萌发的新叶全部凋落，它的手中一无所有。

一个春天，它送出了全部的礼物，然后向灰褐色的尘土默然地告别。

分离

今天阴雨连绵，并非是写出流传千古的诗篇《云使》的日子。

今天被禁锢在静止之中。

风儿不吹，云儿不动，细雨如同薄纱垂直落下，遮盖住白昼的面孔。

时光仿佛被静止，四周只有无边的尘寰，痴傻的闲暇。

大诗人迦梨陀娑创作《云使》的那一日，闪电照亮青山，乌云划过地平线，

疯狂的东方摇撼苍翠的森林。

药叉的爱妻惊叫："天啊，飓风卷起了高山。"

云使飞走了，离别愁苦没有碾碎贞洁女郎的心，离别的自由战胜了悲伤。

飞流直下的瀑布，奔腾急促的江流，欢呼咆哮的林涛，

这一天世界被惊醒。

离人的心音旋律雄壮地升腾。

团圆不应被阻挠的时代，偏偏天各一方，人世间奇怪的无形壁垒环绕在凄冷的洞房。

分离的时日，无羁的愁苦飞渡江河，飞渡山岗，飞渡森林。

屋角中的哭泣被路途上的熙熙攘攘所淹没，

最后它抵达了盖拉莎山，露出缠绵的真相。

雄壮的宝库中，保存了等待时的坚贞不渝的感情。

还缺少一块块欢乐的里程碑，那应该是走向圆满的时候，在离愁的路上竖立。

团圆在静静地等待。

花儿常开，月儿常圆。

药叉独居此地，心中怀有离别之情。被他征服的美人踩着蒺藜欢快地走来。

啊，可是有些错误。

团圆并非静止不动。他在吹奏短笛，期盼的低声，笛音在幽暗的路上向前飘荡。

贞女的脚步和心上人的召唤，正以同样的节奏相互接近。

这就是为什么古往今来江河以行走的韵律奔腾，大海在呼唤中翻腾。

一个人

一个已经到了暮年的北印度人，身材瘦高，嘴唇上的胡须已经是银白色。
脸上因为剃光了胡须犹如干瘪的水果。
上身穿着一件方格背心，下身围着围裤。
脚上穿着土布鞋，右手拄着一根拐棍，左手撑着布伞走进城里。
正是八月天气，朝阳绚丽，轻抚着云彩，
围裹黑布的夜晚早已气喘吁吁地逃走。
被雾气染湿的风漫不经心地摇晃着阿穆拉吉树的嫩枝。
我的世界中飘荡着幻影，在尽头处出现了一个旅人。
我只知道他是一个人，没有姓氏、意识、感情和需求，
就是一个八月的上午蹒跚走向集市场的人。
他也看到了我，在他的世界中，在大漠的尽头吹拂的紫岚之中，
人与人之间并无关系，我也只是一个人。
他家里有牛犊，笼中有鹦鹉，他的妻子带着粗陋的铜手镯，推磨磨麦。
他有洗衣服为生的邻居，与杂货店的老板相识，欠着喀布尔商人的钱。
我不在他们中间，我，仅仅是一个人。

悲哀的世界

在消沉的岁月，我乞求着我的笔：不要添加我的愧疚。

别让无法震撼人心的作品被人们看到，

黑暗中不要蒙着脸，别把门关死。点亮五彩的花灯，啊，你不要吝啬。

世界如此辽阔，它的荣誉永不褪色，它的性格如此温和。

挺立在看不见的阳光下，它不眨眼的目光安详和坚定，胸膛上陈列着河流、山脉、平原。

它不只属于我，属于无数的人。

它的鼓声响动四方，它的火焰照亮黑暗，它的旌旗在天空中飘扬。

在世界的面前，不要让我愧疚，我失去的，我的苦恼，对它而言简直微乎其微。

当我依靠自制力忘却自身的苦痛，苦痛就用世界的面貌出现。

于是我看见，悲伤的河流通过密密麻麻的支流在岁月的胸膛上流淌，

浩荡的心灵之河在千万户人们生活的河床上奔腾，

眼泪的布拉马普特拉河水波涛汹涌，在各国家庭的河滨孕育沧海桑田。

永恒不变的人们的悲哀音乐刹那间进入我的胸膛，如洪水般使我的肋骨颤抖不断，

随后在大地的一声悲鸣中消失于无穷，无法知晓它的用意。

今天，我请求我的笔：不要令我感到愧疚。让你的共享如同河水蔓延出堤坝，让我的哀伤因为你的恩赐而被掩藏，让我哀痛的哭泣融合世界上千百万种的乐章。

闲暇

给我闲暇，让我描绘我要的去处。

在那里，小路上飘荡着希里斯的花香，蜜蜂终日飞舞。

无边无涯的天空漂浮着云朵，夜晚的星星升起之前，小溪轻声唱着歌谣。

在那里，停止了一切咨询。

雨夜，寂静的寓所之中，往事的回忆不会再打搅酣睡。

在那里，心神就好像村庄外牧牛的田野中一颗安静的榕树，供人们走到下面片刻休息。

令人困乏的晌午，有人放下了新娘的彩轿，席地而坐吹响了情笛。

二十六日夜晚，下弦月微弱的清光在蛰鸣中于树木的影子相互交融。

在那里，往返的河水日夜川流不息。

没有停留的兴致，没有被流放远方的怨恨。

晨光中，夜晚的星星放下了梦的灯火，独自离去，没有留下可以追寻的痕迹。

信

我寄给你一本写满诗歌的书籍。

密布的诗拥挤在一个笼中。

你可以得到所有的诗，却无法得到它们的缝隙。

降落在广阔的闲暇场所的诗篇，如今被冷落在身后。

如果摘取午夜的明星编织一条项链，在造化的店铺中或许能高价出售。

然而，审美情趣的拥有者，知晓它贬值的缘由。

贬值的虚幻天空，无法称量精确的重量，但却弥漫着情思。

放飞你的想象，奏响轻柔的乐章，无语的时光胸膛上，是一颗蓝莹莹的宝石，

何必非要将它放在首饰盒中观赏。

毗迦罗玛迪德耶的宫殿中，诗人天天吟诗作赋。

那时没有印刷厂这个魔鬼抹黑诗的时空，没有水力磨盘磨出诗的汁液，

一口口在口腔中沉淀，诗歌的味道须得在饭后茶余中聆听品尝。

唉，聆听的诗终于戴上了视觉的枷锁，

诗被流放在图书馆之中，爱不释手的永恒的珍宝在出版的市场上蒙受羞辱。

无计可施！这个时代尽是文学团体，诗歌不得不乘坐公车去和读者见面。

诗的灵魂喟然长叹："唉，倘若我生在迦梨陀娑的时代，倘若你是毗迦罗玛迪德耶，那将会是什么情形？"

我生在那个时代又怎样！恐怕也是向印刷屈服的迦梨陀娑，你们是他作品中的女主角玛尔碧佳，买了诗集坐在转椅上翻看。

不会闭着眼睛听着朗诵，听了也不会给诗人戴上茉莉花环。

只要花一元两角钱买本诗集就万事大吉。

《最后的星期集》选

我完整地得到了你

我深深地知道，你已属于我，我从未想到应该明了你赠予的价值。

你却也不提如此要求。

日复一日，夜复一夜，你清空了你的花篮，我看了一眼，随手扔到了仓库中，第二天再没有一点印象。

你的赠予中融合了新春枝叶的嫩绿和秋夜圆月的清辉。

你用黑发的波浪淹没我的双脚，

你说："我的赠予不足以缴纳你的王国的税赋，贫困的女子再无可赠的东西。"

话音未落，泪水模糊了你的眼眸。

你匆匆离去，日复一日，夜复一夜，再不见你返回。

多年后我打开仓库，看到你赠予的宝石项链，用手捧在胸前。

我冷漠的高傲颓废地瘫倒在刻印你足迹的地上。

回忆中的爱恋昭显了爱情的价值，失去你之后我才完整地得到了你。

创造之海——死亡之海

青春的边界，残存有暗淡的殷红。

消逝吧，它的迷恋！

清明之中，肃清吧，我浑浊的双眼。

用记忆和遗忘的颜料绘成的悲与欢的浓雾，消散吧，仿佛轻轻的暮云。

我沉浸于残花遗香的心灵左右，梦魂的蜜蜂嗡嗡飞舞，寻找无踪无迹的芬芳。

从阴暗枷锁住的日子里，出来吧，我的心！

走进明媚阳光的淳朴。

目光飘向了无语、无痛、无愁的创造的海洋。

我将会踏上没有目标的旅程，在流年的纷扰之中，冷静地观赏万物，聆听乐章。

我要隐没在庄稼收获后的辽阔原野的空阔走廊。

我要将我的冥思苦想与娑罗树融合，那里埋葬了千年冷寂的生命。

乌鸦在罗望子树上聒噪，苍鹰飞入烈日炙烤的高天的碧空，渔夫在沼泽中垒坝，驾船捕鱼。

沼泽那一面的古老村落若隐若现，天空淡蓝的边际飘荡着缨络丝带般的紫岚。

秃鹰在渔网上空盘旋，鸬鹚静坐在竹顶，无风无浪的水中倒映纹丝不动的影子。

湿润的风中飘散着水藻的清香。

四周的生存河流，每日都融入无数支流。

天然的河水融合和世代生灵繁多生命，凌驾于人类的兴衰之上奔腾不休。

在生机勃勃的春天的最后，我如今疲倦地沉湎于生存之河的深处，

波浪按照血液流动的节奏，在我胸膛上潺潺鸣奏。

让我的知觉映射在它的光影之上，飘向没有典籍没有争执没有烦恼的死亡海洋。

夏雨

没有收到请柬的夏雨降落在原野之上，遮暗了一行行的棕榈树梢，在堤内的湖水中注入了躁动。

我期望地呼唤着雨滴滋润我的心田。

我旅游了一些时日，异域的语言难以与我的心灵语言沟通，心灵的殿堂无法举行灌顶的仪式。

没有了雨云晦暗的流动，生活将会变得孱弱。

好像树木结果的时间随着年份增加，在圆形的年轮上留下了痕迹，每年降雨的欢乐在我的骨髓之中增添了乐趣的财宝。

在生活的画布之上涂抹浓厚的色彩，艺术家手中的示意，将我的心里上刻下痕迹。

每当我坐在宁静的窗口，任由无所事事将时光放逐，留下了一些赠予在我的祭坛之上。

生活的秘密仓库中，聚集了被遗忘岁月的财富。

多支彩笔将我的躯壳勾画，包裹着全部财富的继续，在哪个时代观察入微的目光下完全暴露?

它看着洞悉的苦修，像昏暗的黄昏星和夜晚尽头的晨曦般呼唤:“来呀，展示你自己。”

在它完全显示真相的那天，
我也在我的光照中认清了自己，
如同心中填满了恋爱的时候，
将离愁编织成项链的时候，
将贫苦赠予荣光的时候，
死亡并非意味着终结。
情欲中真实地认识自己，
真实地展示自己。

创造的幼稚

痴情的心说："我把整个王国送你。"

如此幼稚而不切实际。王国该如何赠送？我又能如何接受？

它是被七大海洋分隔的一个大洲，

辽阔、无声，却不可跨越。

昂然翘首于被云遮挡的山巅，双脚踏入了幽暗的地洞。

我的身躯好像是不可登陆的星球，依靠望远镜只看到了一些光环的孔隙。

我口中的整体，还没有具体的名字，它的解剖图该如何画好？

谁能跟他保持直接的交往关系？

从开始的地方搜集的碎片，拼接成整体，才有个名字。

四周的天空中遍布着失败和成功的愿望的光与影，

复杂情感的缤纷影子里，降落在心间。

风中包含着春天与冬天的摩挲，

无法看见的生动游戏，谁能够说得清楚？

谁用语言的手指将它捉住。

生活的边界需要一条界线，因为工作的复杂而无法实现，

另外的一条边界上，受挫折的摸索变为空中的云雾——绘画的海市蜃楼。

个人世界出现在人间生与死狭窄的交汇之地。

在没有光的区域，广泛的愚昧中积累着陶醉的力量和没有获取价值的荣光。

尚未萌芽的成功种子埋在土中。

那里有胆怯的羞射，隐藏的自卑，平淡无奇的经历，

有戴上了自怨自艾面具的各种素材，

浓烈的幽暗鄙夷地看着死亡手中的宽恕。

这是未成熟的未绽放的自我，这是为谁？

有何用？携带来这些开端和隐喻。
无法倾吐情思中遭受束缚的言语，无法忍受创造的幼稚，
只能在庸碌的深处毁于一旦。
贤者拽下了奥秘的面纱，
花儿隐藏在蓓蕾的掩盖下，
艺术家未完的事业隐藏在暗处，
有些线索表明，
被幽禁的整体已经在被发现的路上。

他在我中间的参禅尚未完结，所以凝重的沉寂环绕着我。
我不可得，不可识，
他在未知的世界中开始创造，还没到可以昭告天下的时候。
大家站在远处——说了解的人并不了解。

一个人是一个谜

一个人是一个谜，人乃不可知。

人孤独地在自己的秘密中流连，没有旅伴。

在拥有家庭烙印的框架之内，我划定人的界限。

被定义出的高墙内的住所中，他重复工资固定的工作，额头上写着平凡。

不知风儿从哪里吹来，爱的风将界限的篱笆吹散。

永久不可知走出来。

我看到他的特殊、神奇、不凡、无与伦比。

与他亲近需要建造诗歌的桥梁，用花朵的语言致意新词。

眼睛说："你超越了我曾经见的东西。"

心儿说："视觉、听觉的对岸满是玄妙。你是来彼岸的使者，好像夜晚降临，在地球面前显露的繁星。"

于是，我忽然看清了内在的不可知，我从未找到的感觉，无时无刻不在更新。

不可知的鸟儿

街头走来一个游方僧，站在你的门口唱：

“不可知的鸟儿飞入牢笼。”

于是愚昧的心儿说，我捉住了无法捉住的东西。

你披散这沐浴后的湿润头发，站在窗前。

“捉不住的东西”本就在你远眺的眼睑上，

“捉不住的东西”本就在你带着手镯的手腕的柔嫩中。

你让它去乞讨，它却一去不返，你不知道游方僧在唱你的故事。

你像乐音，在琴弦上往返，

单弦琴是你容颜的牢笼，在春风中飘荡。

我捧着琴在胸口漫游，为它染色、折花，将它融入心中。

我弹奏时忘记了它的形状，琴弦跳动中消失。

“不可知”走出大门迈向世界，在森林的碧绿中游戏，在金色的芳菲中隐居。

你啊，不可知的鸟儿，栖息在团圆的笼中，装饰一新的笼子。

离别之情充盈着翅膀和延迟的飞行，不知道鸟巢在何方，

它的约定在世界的另外一边，所有景色消逝之中。

那一瞬间

林中鸟儿的最后一首歌唱，隐没在漆黑的夜色中。

空气凝滞，树叶不再晃动，透明的星辰仿佛降落在楝树蝉鸣突然停止的秘密上。

这时你突然非常激动地握住我的手说："我永生不会忘记你。"

没有灯光的窗前，我的身子模糊不清。

在阴影的掩护下，你没有了倾吐衷肠的忧郁。

那一瞬间，你爱情的仙宫，屹立在我无尽的回忆的地基之上。

那一瞬间，悲伤，由光阴的琴弦奏起，飘向无尽的来生。

那一瞬间，我的小我，从你真挚的感情中获得了无限。

你颤抖的声音令我生命的苦修得以品尝成功的琼浆。

相比起世界的无数万物，我更加充实，更有朝气。

那一瞬外的万物，微不足道。

那一瞬间外的死亡，某日我将会退出形象辉煌的舞台。

在可察觉的悲与欢的世界中，我记忆的影子，向有形的无垠认输。

门前的火焰树下，你每天亲手浇水，这无比重要。

今后你将我推到枝叶外面混沌的无边宇宙之中，也不再重要，我等待着。

劫

新的劫数。

开辟之始，在浩瀚宇宙中，光定下了时间的刻度。

从最广阔的亿万年的光圈之中，飞出了星辰的飞蛾，不计其数。

它们迎接第一抹的晨曦，一群群飞出洞穴，展开翅膀循环飞翔，从一重天飞向另一重天。

最初它们潜伏在混沌之中，进入光明后便开始舍弃生命飞行。

它们不知为何难以舍弃赴死的冲动。

不知道哪里的中心燃烧着熊熊烈火，促使它们如疯子般渴望地飞去。

它们在漫无边际的奥妙中寻找寿命的虚耗。

直到劫数的黄昏，火焰黯淡，飞行艰难，翅膀脱落，它们湮灭在永恒却无形的光明之中。

在星系延伸的视线外，地球的版图上，光以微笑的时间，确定了人类时代的范畴。

星系的一刹那，完成了创造与毁灭。

广阔的限界内，短促的时间轨迹，画了又抹掉，抹掉又画出。

泡沫般升起的穆罕陀贾罗无声消失于沙海。

撒玛利亚、亚西利亚、巴比伦、古埃及，壮丽地跃上低矮的时光围墙内的历史舞台，仿佛淡墨书写的作品，留下了淡淡的痕迹，然后逐一消失。

它们的愿望如同昆虫，飞向无边际的朦胧。

英雄们都在发誓：让宏愿演变的工业的雕像，永垂不朽！

他们建造了雄伟的凯旋门。

诗人们表示要把实现愿望的痛苦，写成隽秀的诗篇。

宇宙中无涯的纸张上，闪光的灼热字母正在书写遥远的星体上祭火的咒语。

念一句咒语的功夫，时代的凯旋门倾塌，诗人书写的史诗无声无息，彪悍民族的历史在傲慢中消逝。

今夜，面对永恒的星光，我在藤架下向伟大时空膜拜。

让向往的不休，如同儿童松开的小手中的玩具，掉入尘埃逝去。

我不断获得溢出的甜美蜜浆的时刻，谁来确定它的界线?

它无限的真实，不会纳入生存亿万年的星系中。

在劫数的末端，它所有的光明将熄灭，创造的舞台寂灭入暗，在毁灭的后台，它静待着下一个劫数。

我爱

我极目远眺，啊，苍天也没有片刻的休息。

悠久时空庇护的星辰在无声地低语。

它们射出的光芒，惊扰了参禅的静谧的思想。

我的心灵负担着无尽的重担，四周一群匆忙的乞丐，

将无限的闲暇剁碎，抛入到恼人的喧哗声中。

狭隘的生活中，我的嗓音惶恐万分。

缺乏了真情实意的言语毫无光彩，重复的话语枯燥无味，毫无意义。

我的言语好像浓雾侵袭的秋日的乐章，憋在胸中。

心灵无法如同纯净的霞光般坦然地昂首说："我爱。"

言语中的吝啬参杂了疑惑。

仁慈的原野啊，我为此整日坐在你的面前，我要借用你的绿荫使我的咽喉通畅。

我看见你的枝叶轻易地跨越枝干的堡垒，战胜了四周沉闷的停滞。

你无声的振奋穿越辽阔的天际，前往东升旭日的壮丽景象。

创世之初的生命的魔咒，在天空上南风的水流中涌来，涌入了你新叶的心里。

立刻迸发出宇宙中心的欢呼：

“我爱。”

无穷的好奇心带着我飞向远方，如今的刹那消失于无时。

一双看穿世界的眼睛从彼世凝视着我的脸庞，

将我心中充满的奇妙的情感思想，运送到一切界限的另外一侧，高空中传来创造的永恒福音：我爱。

时代之夜过往的一天，阳光的光辉使者在天幕上镌刻了太初的预言。

在创造的第一个时光中，生命之海的巨大波浪中飘荡着咒语，在落日寂灭晦暗的海滨，幽静的天空中，创作渴求的神像。

在今天的暮霭之中，让我今生的愁思、情怀升华为深沉的认识，凝聚成黄昏星一般的晶莹的遗言：我爱。

《尘埃集》选

恩赐的高傲

苍苔抬起头："池塘，记载下，我又赐予你一滴甘露。"

敌对的自豪

蝙蝠时常大声叫嚷："你们是否知道我的敌人是太阳？"

生死

生死一同做生活的戏耍，
好像走路，脚刚触地又复抬起。

强者中的强者

肆虐的大风挑起争战。
结局怎样？和风缓缓凯旋。

灰尘

灰尘，你将万物洁净的面容弄脏，

你可认罪？

门第差异

芒果树说："药西瓜，兄弟，

原始森林中，你我平等，

人们凭借自己的兴趣选择。

平等消失则是因为有了价值差异。"

批评者

瞎眼的硬币驼着背对卢比说：

"你不过16安那，不是5塞格。"

卢比回答："这是我真正的价值，你的身价早不如你宣称的那样多。"

平等原则

乞丐的褡裢叫嚷："喂，钱袋，咱们兄弟间只有微笑的不同。

来，互通有无。"

钱袋生气道："微笑的不同理应首先消灭。"

惊人之美

“美好”问：“啊，至美，你住在天上的哪座宫殿？”

“至美”含泪说：“唉，我呀，住在无能的骄傲者徒然的妒忌中。”

信徒

车水马龙，人声鼎沸，非常热闹。

信徒们跪下，虔诚叩拜。

路想：“我即神。”

车想：“神即我。”

偶像想：“我方为神。”

命运的主宰活活笑煞。

贫者的报答

荒漠说：“你降下了充足的雨水，

我该如何回报您的恩德？”

雨云说：“我不需要回报，荒漠，只要你能长出我赠送的绿色欢乐。”

人生三部曲

“长大成人”，孩童想：“我会买下所有的玩具。”
成年后对游戏不屑一顾，
梦想要收敛金银财宝。
垂暮之年看一切淡泊，
人世的游戏场抛在脑后。

自由

箭矢说：“飞翔吧，我拥有自由，只有弓才愿意死守一隅。”
弓笑着说：“箭啊，你忘记了你的自由归我掌握？”

花与果实

花儿焦急地问：“啊，我的果实，告诉你可曾成熟？告诉我！”
果实说：“先生，你叫嚷什么，我始终在你的心窝。”

永恒真理

我是一束光芒，
照耀着极短的时光。
我寂灭于刹那间，
可无始无终的昏暗啊，你永驻人间。

不必要的必要

绿草和庄稼都不生长的海洋啊，
你占据了地球的大多部分，
你整日整夜地舞动，
你有什么脸面活在世间?
大海辩解说：
“假如我如你所说的无所事事，
是谁从陆地丰满的乳房中引出了甘甜的江河? ”

情爱与离愁

情爱感叹：“离愁，唉，看不到你的本性。”

离愁说：“啊，情爱，你属于雅致的幻梦，我却奉劝你走自由的道路，隔断绵绵的情丝。”

情爱说：“若如你所言，我将与你融为一体。”

《抒情集》选

泰戈尔诗文彩图馆

太阳颂

啊，太阳，我的挚友，
绽放你的光耀金莲。
举起闪亮的巨斧，
劈开充满泪水和苦难的黑色云团。
我知道你端坐在莲花的中央，
披散的头发金光灿灿，
唤醒万物的梵唱，
飞舞自你怀中的燃烧的琴弦。
今生今世，第一个黎明，
你曾经亲吻了我纯洁的额头。

你热切的亲吻点亮了光的细流，
在我的心潮中奔腾着灿烂的浪涛。
永远不会平静的火焰，
在我的歌声中奔腾呼啸。
带着吻痕的我的鲜血，
在韵律的洪水中跳舞。
痴癫疯狂的音乐，融合了炽热的情愫飘向四方。
你的亲吻也引起了心灵无端的哭泣，莫名的忧伤。

向你熊熊的烈焰之中，我追寻真理的形象敬礼，昔日的诗人。
昏睡的海滨你吹响了驱除黑暗的芦苇长笛是我的心，
笛孔中袅袅飘出了天空云彩的缤纷，
森林中绽放开素馨花的潋滟，泉水的叮咚。
韵律的起伏中活力的溪水涨满了我的四周。

我的灵魂是迷失的乐音。
你登上了乐曲的方舟，
好奇地怀抱着苍茫大地，
微笑着在岁月的河流上飘荡。
阿斯温月温暖的阳光下，
我羁縻的灵魂不甘寂寞地躁动，
好像被露水打湿的素馨花折射出的阳光。
波峰上你皎然起舞的光芒将惊诧照射到我的眼眶。

灼热的宝库中有什么财宝是你的恩赐?
在我灰暗的心中编织出什么梦想参杂了五颜六色?
你派遣的女使者在田原的殿堂中作画，
刹那间昔日无形玄妙的幻想隐匿起来。
啼笑、悲欢恢复了正常，不再将我囚禁。

斯拉万月的女使者们，躲藏在摇动的绿叶丛中。
她们的脚镯和翻越山岩的淙淙泉水唱和，

维沙克月畅饮着风暴的美酒，
微醉地跳着舞，
天地随之摇动。
别绪依依的春天馈赠了全部的财富。
匆忙过后，她们消失在清贫的天际不留下脚印。

啊，太阳，你的宫殿中，
秋的金笛吹奏神曲。
拥有朝阳、清露、眼泪和笑容的世界有时快乐，有时忧愁。
不知道我的歌声听从了谁的呼唤，
忽然有了疯狂的热情，
好像游方僧沿着天空的道路专注地向你奔走，提着花篮。
光的乞儿，梦中是否能够进入你的圣殿？

啊，太阳，打开大门。
将我久等的歌声搂在怀中，
火泉的一旁举行着静谧的洗礼，
洗掉彷徨和惊恐。
黄昏用晚霞的朱砂将她的分发线涂抹红色，
黎明时用启明星在她娇嫩的眉心上点下吉祥痣，
用海水雄壮的乐章走向暮歌。

露珠

露珠泪盈盈地说：
“我的生命如此短暂，仿佛孩童的幻想，
刚出生就要命归黄泉。
唉，我只不过是苏醒的朝霞仙子欢喜的泪滴，
只要她的笑容收起，立刻便会枯萎消失。
玫瑰花抬起粉红色的脸颊，
露出了甜美动人的笑容。
茉莉花奉献出生命的甘饴，风儿失魂地畅饮。
蝴蝶没有主意，跟谁成为一生伴侣。
拍打着翅膀在花丛中来回飞舞。
啊，我为什么不能和他们一同享受欢乐。
为什么就在睫毛睁开兴奋而短促的一刹那，
就要带着舍不得的微笑凄凉地别离美丽的人间。”

躺卧在无忧花的绿叶上，
奄奄一息的露珠悲叹：
“唉，欢乐还没有结束，生命为什么就要尽早凋谢。”

年轻的诗人叹气说：
“我为何不是一颗朝露，
每天睁眼的黎明，生命即可枯萎。
啊，上帝，你创造了我露珠般的命运，
却为何不赐予我露珠一样的寿命。”

奇梦

填满了时间，填满了辽阔的天空，
酣睡的神灵做着壮丽的梦。
虚渺的梦中，
广阔的大地仿佛一个水泡在心海中飘荡，
升起了日月，升起了暮霭和晨曦，
升起了数不清的灿烂星系。
一簇簇行星和卫星旋转不停。
昼夜在天穹下沉浮不定，
孤独的大海终日里吟咏，
脚下聚集了千万条河流的精灵。
江水潺潺，泉水幽幽，
云声沉闷，海啸雄壮，
狂笑的风走出了旧日的楼宇，
无数粗犷的大手弹着树木的琵琶。
如同妖怪凝结的笑声，
冰川嚎叫着奔向山谷的深处，
森林的脑袋摇晃得头发蓬乱，
四处回响着的歌谣声凄惨哀婉。
一块块大地发射着美妙的音波，
汇聚成博大心怀的赞歌。
这梦中的王国的景色和生灵，
不断地变换着形象。
花儿结出果实，果实变为种子，
森林中繁衍的新树多种多样。
水汽凝结成云朵，云朵降下成甘霖，
瀑布冲破了群山的桎梏。

夏日里融化的雪水降到焚尸场中，
浇灭了焚烧实体的冲天火焰。
夏天的雨水变成了白发苍苍的冬季，
又像朱查迪送回春天的山花烂漫。
除了亘古的心灵，一切都那么新颖。
亘古的心中酝酿了新的梦境。
不完整的梦中创造出了习惯的奴隶之人，
为了得到清醒的完整而努力不懈。
他唯一的心愿：
领悟撕裂混沌的幔布。
至善的灵魂何时脱离昏睡？
人间的缺憾的梦可会慢慢变圆？
日月星辰的梦魔阴影消逝在闪光的心中。
地球杂碎，一个个星球像水泡一样相继破裂。
比星宿更为光亮的灵魂也像水泡一样消逝。

嫣笑

身居在异国他乡，仍旧莫名其妙地时刻想起她迷人的笑容。
不知何时夕阳坠落在山下，
不知何时海浪停止了咆哮。
纤巧的唇上露出的微笑
仿佛世界边境玛达毗花树的嫩枝和新叶遮掩的尚未绽放的花朵。
没日没夜流淌的泪水创造了令人爱抚的机会。
谁不远万里将笑颜接来，
让思慕的他人成为单相思?
笑容何时能够不顾生死顾惜我淳朴亲吻的华彩?

思念

我每天都用充实的心来思念你，
坐在宇宙形成的地方等候你，
你无处不在，掌管着我的生与死。

我看不到你的边际——蕴藏着的情与爱，
我找不到一件东西可与其媲美。
我的全身心好像从东山升出的一轮红日，
凝望着转瞬即逝的一对明眸。
目光深邃、远大和冷峻，没有限界。
你是玉宇，澄清辽阔，
我是无尽的沧海碧波，
中间的皎洁明月使二者世代缠绵。

你是昼夜间永远的宁静，
我是周期性无尽的躁动，
放眼望去，地平线上你我浑然一体。

黄昏

你啊，变成黄昏吧！
在遥远的西山，在金光灿烂的傍晚，
静静观看，不眨眼。
宁静的秀美，忧郁的妩媚，
仿佛沉思中默然的女子。
迈着轻盈的步伐，登上了我的生命之舟，片刻伫立。
起航，将自己送到时光的极地——尘世的彼岸。
终止了节日的活动，听不到嘈杂的喧闹，看不见人烟。
来吧，无声无息地化为倦意，渗透入我的眼中。
来吧，苦笑着走到了目光焦虑的暮年，一如死亡的诺言。
干枯无泪的眼睛睁大，我凝望着地表上的羁縻，
松散的发髻用昏暗的浓密将我层层包裹住。
将你温柔凉爽的手掌像酣睡中的甜美一样按在我的眉头。
无语地轻柔，将你霓裳盖在我麻木的身上。
不知不觉间，湿润的哀伤出现在你的瞳孔，
我的身心俱已明了，你沉默的烦恼，沉重的离愁。

告别青春

再见，美丽的青春小舟，
从此后重担将由中年承担。
船桨驶过了许多码头，穿过了多少缤纷的幻梦。
温暖的南风年年岁岁吹送走你跃动的风帆。
惊涛骇浪将你颠簸，
涌动的暗流将你冲打，
明月照耀的海洋上，
疯狂的浪涛将你戏弄。
此刻，浓密的彤云漫天笼罩着迷蒙对面。
七月的江水暴涨，看不到沙滩和堤坝的影踪。
复杂的人生游戏，一点一点终结。
伫立在四十岁的码头上，
啊，青春之舟，永别。

啊，青春之舟，
让我装些锦绣年华最后的几首颂歌。
昔日里偷偷的哭泣和爽朗的笑声，
狡黠、真实和虚假，请全都带走，一个也不要留下。
不要下锚停留，不要回头东张西望，
也不要在渡口四周打转，犹豫不去。
潮水已经开始退去，
扯起那千疮百孔的风帆，飘向梦境般的夕阳落下的西山。
多年承载的沉重负担最终卸下载金色霞光的港湾，
那是你长眠千古的理想之地。

心灵之灯

啊，探索者，啊，有情人。
你降临人世间，充满激情，
是哪一种春节的光点燃了你的心灯?
茫茫人海，
悲伤敲打着你心弦。
笑迎困境，
你受到哪位慈母笑颜的影响?
为了寻找谁你宁可烧堕欢悦?
哪个恋人令你黯然神伤?
转而神情欢快，是因为有了情侣?
忘掉了死亡，在哪片生命的海洋上你快乐游荡?

当生活凋零

当生活凋零，
来吧，变为慈爱的甘露。
当甜美消失，
来吧，变为喜悦的醇酒。
当琐事用可怖的形象发出遮蔽天地的狂吼，
来吧，神，稳步地走进我的心灵。

当贫贱的思想在心灵安稳睡卧，
使自己变得吝啬，
变为君王的威严，
神，来吧，打开心扉。
被尘埃欺蒙的憧憬在愚顽的黑暗中耳目不灵，
崇高伟大，从不休眠的神啊，
来吧，变为燃烧的光之轮。

苏醒

跃起，耻辱的床上的爱神！
辉耀的阳光中恢复了光芒的真身。
让该死的死去！
苏醒吧，重现你使人迷醉的坐姿。
只是烧掉你的鲁莽和愚笨，
重新生长无尽的新颖。
爱神，从寂灭中醒来。
啊，无形无相，变还你原本英雄的风姿。

死神用手杖敲打你不死的头颅，
你从死亡中提炼出甘露，
从仙界圣洁的烈焰中引发出一股清冽的活泉。
将离愁变为不堪的美，
爱神，从寂灭中苏醒。
啊，无形无相，变还你原本英雄的风姿。

爱情的胜利战车，
翻越过苦与乐结成的坎坷，
长夜的黑暗的门前，
车轮带起雷霆般的巨响。
无法压抑的高昂激情，
驱散了渺小的羞涩和惶恐。
爱神，从寂灭中苏醒。
啊，无形无相，变还你原本英雄的风姿。

《吉檀迦利》选

我旅行的时间很久，路途也十分长远。

天色破晓，我就驾车开始旅行，踏遍了辽阔的世界，在许多星球上，都留下了车辙的痕迹。

距离你最近的地方，路途最远，最简单的音符，需要最辛苦的锤炼。

旅人要在每个生人的门口敲门，才能找到自己的家门，人需要在外面四处漂泊，最终才能走到最深处的宫殿。

我的眼睛向空旷的地方张望，最后才闭上眼说："你原来就在此处。"

这疑问和呼唤，"啊，在哪里？"消融在千股泪水的泉中，

和你保证的回答"我在这儿"的洪水，一同在世界泛滥。

我想要唱的歌曲，直到今天还没有唱出。

每天我总是忙于调整乐器的弦。

时间还未来到，歌词尚未填好，唯留愿望的苦痛在心中。

花蕊未曾开放，只有风走过在叹息的身旁。

我没有看清他的脸，也未听到他的声音：我只听见他轻轻的足音，从我屋前的道路上走过。

漫长的一天消磨在为他在地上铺设座位，然而灯火还未点燃，我不能邀请他前来。

我生活在和他相会的愿望之中，但这相会的日子还未到来。

我的欲望众多，我的哭泣可怜，但你永远用坚定的拒绝救赎我，这刚强的慈悲已经严密地在我的生命中交织。

你使我日渐有资格领受你自然的简单，伟大的授予——这天空和光明——这身躯和生命与心灵——把我从极欲的危险中拯救。

有时我因懈怠而迟延，有时我匆忙警惕地寻找我的方向，但却你忍心躲藏起来。

你不断地拒绝我，从软弱动摇的欲望的危险中拯救了我，使我一天天更有资格获取你完全的接纳。

我来为你歌唱，在你的厅堂之中，我坐在屋角。

在你的世界中我并没有事情可做，我无用的生命也只能演唱毫无目的的歌。

在你黑暗的厅堂中，半夜响起祈祷的钟声的时刻，命令我吧，主人，站起来在你面前唱歌。

当金琴在晨曦中调整就绪的时刻，恩宠我吧，命令我来到你的面前。

我接到了世界节日的请柬，我的生命领受祝福。

我的眼看到了美丽情景，我的耳朵听到了醉人乐音。

在宴会中，我负责奏乐，我也尽力而为。

现在，我询问，那时刻是否来到，我能否进去瞻仰你的容颜，并献上我宁默的礼敬?

我只是在等候爱，要最终将我交给他的手中。这是我迟误的缘由，我愿对这迟误负责。

他们要用法律和规程，来将我牢牢束缚，

但是我总在躲避他们，因为我只是在等候爱，要最终将我交给他的手中。

人们对我责难，说我不去理人，

我也清楚他们的责备并非无理。

市集散了，忙人的工作全都结束。

对我的呼叫没有回应的人们含怒离开。

我只是在等候，要最终将我交到他的手中。

云雾密布，黑暗笼罩。啊！爱，你为何让我独自守护门外?

在午时的最繁忙时刻，我与大家一起，但在这黑暗寂寞的日子里，我只能寄望于你。

若是你不肯与我相见，若是你完全将我抛弃，真不知要怎样才能度过这漫长的雨天。

我不住地凝视着遥远的阴沉天空，我的心和不安静的风一同彷徨叹息。

如果你不说话，我就忍耐，用你的沉默来填满我心。

我要静静地等候，像黑夜在星光中不眠，低头忍耐。

黎明必将到来，黑暗一定消散，你的声音将会划破天空从金泉中降临。

那是你的言语，要在我的每一个鸟巢中生翅发音，你的音乐，要在我森林繁花中盛开怒放。

莲花开放的一日，唉，我不自觉地心神荡漾。

我的花篮空放，花儿我未去理睬。

不时有一段幽香袭来，我从梦中惊醒，觉得南风中藏有一阵异香的芳踪。

这茫然的温柔，令我想念得心痛，我觉得这好像是夏天渴求的气息，追求圆满。

我那是不知道它距离我如此之近，而且属于我，这完美的馨香，却是在我自己的心灵深处绽放。

我必须将我的小船驶出。时光都已在岸边消磨——不堪的我啊！

春天在花开后道别，如今满地落红，我在等待中逡巡。

潮声逐渐喧闹，河岸的绿荫沙滩上黄叶飘下。

你凝望着的是怎样的空虚！

你是否察觉到有一种惊喜和彼岸遥远的歌声从空中一起飘来？

《园丁集》选

泰戈尔诗文彩图馆

1

驯养的鸟儿在笼中，自由的鸟儿在林中。

时间到了，他们相见，这也是命中注定。

自由的鸟说："啊，亲爱的，让我们飞翔到森林中。"

笼中的鸟低声说："到这儿来，我们同住在笼中。"

自由的鸟说："在栅栏当中，哪有展翅飞翔的空间？"

"真可怜，"笼中的鸟说："在天空我不知道该去哪里休息。"

自由的鸟叫唤说："我的宝贝，唱起山林的歌谣。"

笼中的鸟说："坐在我的身边，我将教导你学者的言语。"

自由的鸟叫唤说："不，不，歌谣是无法传授。"

笼中的鸟说："可怜的我啊，我不会唱山林的歌谣。"

他们的爱情因为渴望而炽烈，但他们却永不能双飞比翼。

他们隔栏相望，但他们相知的愿望尽是虚幻。

他们在依恋中展翅，唱着："靠近点，我的爱人。"

自由的鸟叫唤："这无法做到，我怕这笼子紧闭的门。"

笼中的鸟低声说："我的翅膀毫无力量，它们早已死去。"

2

当我独自在夜间赶赴幽会，鸟儿不鸣，风儿不吹，街道两侧房屋默默伫立。

是我自己的脚镯随走随响令我羞怯。

当我站在露台上倾听他的足音，树叶不摇，河水静得仿佛熟睡士卒膝上的刀剑。

是我自己的心在狂跳，我不知该怎样使它平静。

当吾爱亲来，静坐在我身边，当我的身躯颤抖，我的眼睫垂下，

夜深沉，灯被风儿吹熄，云朵在繁星上面笼罩轻纱。

是我自己胸前的珠宝发出光明，我不知道该怎样将它遮盖。

3

你在腰间挎着灌满的水瓶在河边岸堤上行走。

你为什么快速地回头，从飘起的面纱里向我偷望?

这个从黑暗中投来的目光，仿佛凉风在粼粼水面上掠过，一直微颤到树荫的旁边。

它向我飞来，如夜晚中的小鸟快速地穿越无灯的屋子洞开的窗户，又消失去黑夜。

你像一颗隐藏在山峰后的星辰，我是路上的旅人。

但是你为何站立一会，从面纱中窥视我的脸，当你腰间挎着灌满的水瓶在河边岸堤上行走的时候?

4

他每日都是来了又走。

去吧，将我头上的花朵赠送给他，我的朋友。

假如他问送花的人是谁，请不要将我的名字告诉他，因为他总是来了又走。

他坐在树下的地上。

用繁华密叶为他摆设一个座位吧，我的朋友。

他的眼神饱含忧愁，它把忧郁带到我的心头。

我没有说出他的心事，他只是来了又走。

5

不要将你心灵的秘密藏起，我的朋友！

讲给我听，秘密只对我一人说起。

你的笑容如此温柔，你的声音如此糯软，我的心将聆听你的言语，而不是我的耳朵。

夜渐沉，庭院安宁，鸟巢上笼罩着睡梦。

从踌躇的泪中，从沉吟的微笑着，从柔美的羞怯和痛苦中，将你心中的秘密告诉我。

6

“从你慷慨的手中来的赠与，我都接受，别无所求。”

“是的，是的，我了解你，谦卑的乞丐，你在乞求一个人的所有。”

“如果你给我一朵残花，我也会将它佩戴心上。”

"假如花上带刺？"

"我可以忍受。"

"是的，是的，我了解你，谦卑的乞丐，你在乞求一个人的所有。"

"如果你只在我的脸上投过一次怜悯的目光，就会让我生命直到死后仍有甜美。"

"假如那眼神残酷？"

"我会让永远刺穿我心。"

"是的，是的，我了解你，谦卑的乞丐，你在乞求一个人的所有。"

7

跟我说，亲爱的，用言语告诉我你在唱着什么。

夜晚是黑色的，繁星躲藏在云中，风儿在叶丛中叹息。

我将我的头发披散，我青蓝色的披风如黑夜般紧裹着我。

我将我的头在胸口紧抱，在柔美的寂寞中在你心头倾诉。

我将闭目静听，我不会看望你的脸。

等你的话音不再，我们将沉默静坐。只有林木在黑暗中低语。

夜将发白，天将破晓。我们将彼此凝望眼睛，然后各走走路。

对我说话吧，我亲爱的！用言语告诉我你在唱着什么。

8

我的心，一只野鸟，在你的双目中找到了天空。

它们是黎明的摇篮，它们是晨星的国度。

我的诗歌在它们的深处消失。

只让我在天空中高飞，在宁静的空间中翱翔。

只让我冲破它的云层，在它的阳光中展翅。

9

灯为何而熄？

害怕它被风吹熄而用斗篷遮住了他，因此灯熄了。

花为何而谢?

热恋的爱情将它压紧在我的心头，因此花谢了。

泉为何而干?

筑起一道堤坝拦住泉水为我而用，因此泉干了。

琴弦为何而断?

强要演奏它不能胜任的音节，因此琴弦断了。

10

你是何人? 读者，百年后朗诵我的诗歌?

我不能从春天的财富中增你一朵花，天边的云彩里送你一片影。

打开门四处远望吧。

从盛开百花的园中，采摘百年前消逝了的花儿的记忆芬芳。

从你心灵的欢乐中，希望我感受到春天清晨的欢欣歌唱，把快乐的声音，传递百载光阴。

《流萤集》选

泰戈尔诗文彩图馆

1

花儿对虫儿爱惜，
虫儿却不是蜜蜂，
花儿的情意是个大错也是个包袱。

2

羽毛满意地懒散地躺在灰尘中，
忘记了天空。

3

为生存的权利支付了足够的价格，
我们才获取自由。

4

世界是浮在宁静的海面之上的，
那变化莫测的泡沫。

5

我还在路上犹豫不前，
终于你的樱花树花朵落尽，
可是，我的亲人，杜鹃花将你对我的宽恕带来。

6

生，就是从夜晚的秘密进入到白昼的更大的神秘。

7

流浪的歌声在我心中飞翔而出，
在你情意缠绵的声音中寻找栖息的巢穴。

8

爱情给予宽恕时也给予惩罚，
同时用它可怕的沉默伤害了美。

9

神灵的世界因死亡而重生，
泰坦巨人的世界总是被巨人的生存所毁灭。

10

痛苦的火焰，
为我的灵魂照耀出一条璀璨的小路，
穿越哀愁。

《爱者之贻》选

1

我的果园之中，硕果累累占满了枝头，

它们在阳光下因为自己的丰满和多汁而犯愁。

我的女王，请骄傲地走进我的园中，坐在树荫下，从枝头摘下成熟的果实，

让它们尽量将它们甜蜜的负担推卸到你的唇上。

在我的果园中，蝴蝶在光下飞舞，树叶轻轻地摇动，果实喧嚷着，它已成熟。

2

如果我占据了天空和漫天星辰，

如果我占有了世界和无穷宝藏，

我还会有更多的追求。

但是，我一旦拥有她，

即便在这世上只剩下了立锥之地，

我也会心满意足。

3

我已所剩无多，

其他的都已经在夏天的无忧无虑中漫不经心地挥霍掉。

现在，它只够谱写一曲短歌供你倾听；

只够编成一个小小的花环，轻轻戴在你的手腕；

只够用一朵小花做成一只耳环，像一粒圆润的粉红色珍珠，一声羞涩的低呼，悬挂在你的耳边。

只够在黄昏的树荫下，小小的赌赛中，孤注一掷，彻底输光。

我的小舟简陋，容易损坏，无法胜任在暴风雨中迎着

风浪前行。

但是，只要你愿轻轻地踏上它，我愿慢慢滑动双桨，载着你沿着河岸行进。

那里，深蓝色的水面碧波荡漾，如同被幻梦揉搓的睡眠。

那里，鸽子在垂下的树枝头咕咕鸣叫，给正午的树荫笼罩一层忧伤。

日落入倦时分，我将采一朵露珠晶莹的睡莲，插在你的秀发，然后向你道别。

4

昨晚，我在花园中向你献上了青春洋溢的美酒。

你举起杯子放在唇边，闭上双眼浅笑。

我掀起你的面纱，披散你的长发，将你安静又充盈着柔情蜜意的脸蛋贴在我的胸口。

昨晚，月光如梦般照洒在沉睡的大地上。

今朝，晨露晶莹，黎明寂静。

你刚刚沐浴而还，身穿洁白的长袍，手提着满是鲜花的篮子，前往神庙。

我伫立在通向神庙小路旁的树荫下，在静悄悄的黎明中低垂着头。

5

如果你定要向我倾心，你的生活将会布满忧愁。

我的家位于十字路口，房门敞开，我心不在焉，只因我的歌唱。

如果你定要向我倾心，我全然不会用心来回报。

假若我的歌曲是爱的山盟海誓，请你谅解，但乐曲平息，我的誓言也不复存在，

因为在寒冬时节，谁会谨守五月的信约?

如果你定要向我倾心，请不要将它时刻放在心上。

当你笑语盈盈，一双明眸闪耀爱的欢欣，我的回复必定是狂热且草率，一点也不符合实际。

你应将它铭记于心，再将它永远忘掉。

6

经书上说，人过半百，理应远离尘世喧嚣，隐居于林中度日。

然而，诗人却宣告：静修林只应属于年轻人。因那儿有百花故乡，蜂与鸟的家园。

在那里的幽静角落，等待着情侣们私语的震颤。

月华亲吻着素馨花，倾诉着情愫深深。

只有距离半百尚远的人才能来领略其中深意。

啊，风华年少，既无历练且任性！

因此他们才该隐居于密林，经受情爱参杂的锤炼，而让老人们去管理世间蝇营。

7

你站在半掩的窗前，面纱微微撩开，等着货郎来卖手镯和脚铃。

你懒散望去，笨重的牛车在尘土四溅的土路上嘎吱嘎吱地转动车轮。

远方的河面上，天水一色之处，船帆慢慢飘动。

世界于你而言，就如同老妇人摇着纺车时轻吟的曲调，毫无意义和目的，却又充满随心所欲的幻想。

但又有谁知，也许久在这闷热令人疲倦的正午，那个陌生人提着满篮奇妙的货物悄然上路?

他响亮地叫卖着路过你的门前，你就会从朦胧的梦中惊醒，将窗户打开，抛下面纱，走出房门迎接命运的安排。

8

如果你偶尔想起我，我会为你歌唱。

雨后的傍晚将她的影子洒落河上，

将她淡然的光芒慢慢拖向远方，

斜晖脉脉，不再是劳动和游戏的时候。

你坐于南向的露台，我在黑暗的屋里为你歌唱。

暮色苍茫，从窗儿飘入了湿润的绿叶清香，预示雷雨将要来临的狂风在椰林中狂啸。

掌灯时分，我将离去。当你倾听着夜间的天籁，那时或许你能听到我的歌谣，虽然我已经停止歌唱。

9

多少次，

春天叩响了我们的房门，

我在为工作繁忙，你也不作理睬。

今日，只留下我独自神伤，意气消沉时，

春天再次来临，我却不知该如何驱赶它。

当春天给我们献上快乐的冠冕时，我们却将大门紧闭，

但是现在，当春天带来了忧伤的礼物，我却不能不让它畅行地走进门来。

10

混沌初开，从造物主不安的梦境的升腾中，出现了两个女人。

一个是天堂乐园的舞姬，男人追逐热恋的对象。

她欢笑着，从智者冷静的沉思，愚者空虚的蒙昧中，攫取他们的心灵，

把它们如同种子般新手散落在三月豪放的东风中，五岳狂喜的花丛中。

另外一个是天国的皇后，是母亲，她坐在金秋丰饶美丽的宝座上。

在收获的季节，她把那些飘零的心，带到如泪水般温柔甜美，如海洋般宁静壮丽的地方，

带到神圣的生与死交汇处那冥冥未知的殿堂。

《渡口》选

泰戈尔诗文彩图馆

1

在大地沉眠，风儿在枝叶不动的森林中瞌睡的时候，独自清醒的是谁？

在宁静的鸟巢里，在花蕾的密室中，是谁还未沉睡？

在闪烁摇动的群星的夜空，在我沉重的痛苦中，是谁在独自守望，尚未入睡？

2

从尘埃中将我的生命拾取，

将它安放在你右手掌心，凝视着它。

让它沐浴阳光，避开死的影子，让它与夜空的星辰结为伴侣，让它等到黎明时，

与敬神的百花一齐绽放。

3

阴雨连绵，天地昏暗，

怒吼的雷霆穿透支离破碎的云朵闪烁。

森林仿佛囚笼中的雄狮，绝望地抖动着颈鬣。

在这阴雨的岁月，狂风扇动翅膀的时刻，让我在你的身边获取安宁平和吧。

因为，悲伤的乌云笼罩着我独自的小屋，拨动我的心弦的你的爱抚更加意味深长。

4

你是以我悲伤的身份来到我的身边吗？若如此，我将会紧紧拥抱你。

夜色仿佛面纱笼罩住你的脸庞，我反而看你

看得更加清晰。

死神借你的手袭击了我，反而让生命如灯焰炽烈燃烧。

我眼中泪如泉涌，让泪水围绕着你的双足流淌，表示崇敬。

让胸中的痛苦向我证明，你仍然属于我。

5

我是夏日中被烈日炽烤的大地，

倦怠、饥渴，生命即将耗尽。

我等待着，夜深沉，你的甘霖降下，我将敞开胸膛，静静地吸吮。

我渴望用鲜花和歌声将你回报，但是我却一无所有，只能通过枯萎的草儿传递我心中的叹息。

然而，我却知道，你将会静待黎明到来，那时我会生机勃勃，富饶美丽。

6

如果我的生命中没有爱情，那是什么使黎明的空中充满阵阵歌声，使它心碎？

为什么南风要在新生的绿叶林中，传递着私语呢？

如果我的生命没有爱情，那么为何午夜要在渴求的沉默中承受着星辰的悲伤呢？

为什么这颗痴愚的心还要不顾一切，驾起希望的小船，在无边无际的海上航行呢？

7

在人间，我拥有的财富只有是一部分，其余的都被放在梦中。

你，一直躲避着我的抚摸，请悄声地来到梦中，掩藏你的灯火。

在黑暗的恐慌中，在看不见的万物的私下低语中，在未知的海岸的清风里，

我将认识你。

我会在由心中迸发的快乐融入到悲伤的浪花中认出你来。

8

有人在我的手中悄然地放下一朵爱情的鲜花。
有人偷走我的心，将它抛弃在天涯。
我不知道，我是找到了他，还是仍在四处找寻他，
也不知道这是莫大的快乐，还是无尽的悲伤。

9

许久也无人来我家中作客，我的屋门紧缩，窗户紧闭，所以我以为，我的夜晚将会与寂寞为伴。

当我睁开双眼，却发现黑暗已经流逝。

我起身奔向房门，看到了折断的门闩，你的晨风与光耀正在敞开的门外挥动旌旗。

当房门紧闭时，我是自己屋中的囚犯时，我的心无时无刻不在谋划逃脱，四处漫游。

如今，在敞开的门侧，我安静地坐，等待你的前来。

你用我的自由将我拘束。

10

他在门外等候，像一个生命宴席上前来乞讨的乞丐，
直到你张开双臂将他拥抱，用死亡给他加冕。
他历经失败，你却用右手为他祝福，平静地亲吻，平息了生命狂乱的渴求。
你使他如帝王般高贵，如古时的哲人般睿智。

《采果集》选

1

黎明，鸟儿在啼鸣。

晨曦尚未带来黎明的晓月，巨龙“夜晚”冷酷且黑暗地将天空团团缠绕，他是从哪里寻觅到清晨的歌词呢?

请告诉我，黎明的鸟儿，他是如何跨越了天空和绿叶的双重遮盖的夜幕，走上你梦中的道路，知道到了来自东方的使者。

世界对你信任还不够，当你叫嚷:“太阳升起，黑夜逝去。”

啊，沉睡的人啊，醒来吧。

露出你的额头，等待第一线晨曦的祝福，怀着喜悦的信念和黎明的鸟儿一同唱歌吧。

2

我心中的乞丐举起了瘦骨嶙峋的两手伸向没有星星的天空，

向黑夜的耳朵吼着饥饿的呼唤。

他向看不见的黑夜乞求，这失明的黑夜就像是一个堕落的神祇，瘫倒在希望不再的凄凉天堂。

欲望的呼叫沿着一条绝望的裂隙盘旋，仿佛一只哀鸣的鸟儿绕着空巢飞旋。

但是当黎明在东方的边际抛下锚的时刻，我心中的乞丐欢呼雀跃:

“万幸昏聩的夜晚拒绝了我的乞讨，它的保险箱中已经一无所有。”

他喊道:“啊，生命!啊，光明!你是最珍贵的。我终于认识了你，这种喜悦也无比珍贵!”

3

我一次又一次来到你的门前，伸出手要求你再给我多一些，再多一些。

你一次次赠与，时而迟慢和稀少，而是快速而过多。

有些我保存，有些我遗失，有些被我沉重地放在手上，有些我将它做成

玩具，玩腻后将它砸碎。

直到你赠与我的礼物，打碎的和保存的，多到不计其数，最后遮盖住你，而我则因为永无休止的期望而垂头丧气。

拿走吧，唉，拿走吧，现在已经成了我的呼唤。

将这个乞丐碗中的东西全部砸碎，吹熄了这盏讨厌的守夜人的灯火，

握住我的手，将我从这堆日积月累的你的礼物中拉出，放到你所在的广阔而显露的无垠之中。

4

你将我位于失败者之中。

我知道我不该胜利，也不能离开这赛场。

我将跳入深渊，即便结果只能沉没在水底。

我将参加这将我毁灭的比赛。

我将我的一切押作赌注，当我输掉最后一分钱的时候，我会以我为赌注，

我想这样，我将会从我彻底的失败中赢得这场比赛。

5

一丝欢快的微笑从空中飞过，当你给我的心穿上褴褛的衣衫送她去乞讨的路上。

她挨家挨户前去乞讨，无数次每当她的碗将要积满，就会被人抢劫一空。

疲惫的一天过去，她举着可怜的碗，来到了你的宫殿门前，

你走出来握着她的手，让她坐在了你身边的宝座上。

6

我不认识我的国王，每当他要求交纳供奉的时候，我都想躲藏起来，不去偿还债务。

我在逃走，在白天的工作和夜晚的梦中逃走。

但他的要求每时每刻都在追捕着我。

于是我发现他原来认识我，并且不会为我留下一块属于我的领土。

现在我愿将我的全部奉献于他的脚下，从而换取在他的王国中我的一席之地。

7

我们之间不仅是爱情的游戏，我的爱人。

咆哮的暴风雨的夜晚，一次次向我吹打，将我手中灯火吹熄，

于是暧昧的猜疑如乌云般聚拢，遮盖了我的空中的星辰。

河堤一次次地裂开，任由洪水冲走我的庄稼，哀嚎和绝望将我的天空撕成粉碎。

如今我已经领悟，在你的爱里拥有痛苦的捶打，但这并非是死亡的冷酷无情。

8

啊，火焰，我的兄弟，我向你歌颂胜利。

你是令人敬畏的鲜红的自由之像。

你在空中挥舞双臂，你用你灵巧的手指划过琴弦，你的舞曲是如此美丽动听。

当我的岁月已经完结，大门业已打开的时刻，你就来将束缚我的羁绊全部化为灰烬。

我的身躯将与你融为一体，我的心将进入到你狂热的漩涡之中，

我的生命，燃烧的炽热，也将在刹那间迸发光热，与你的烈焰融合。

9

人间世的细小细流中，我紧守这生命的筏——我的身躯。
当我到达彼岸时，才会将其舍弃。
此后又该如何?
我不知道彼岸是否有光明，是否有同样的黑暗。
未知的是永恒的自由，他的爱却无情。
珍珠在黑暗的监狱中黯然无语，
他为了获取珍珠打碎了贝壳。
你为那逝去的岁月沉思和哭泣，可怜的心。
为将来临的时光而欢呼吧。
时钟已敲响，啊，朝拜者!
现在是你在歧路的选择之时!
他的脸将再次出现，你必将会邂逅。

10

处于你我之间的时光，在向我们作最后的鞠躬以道别。

夜晚在她的脸上蒙上面纱，也遮掩了在我的我卧室中那盏燃烧的灯火。

你的沉默仆人无声地走来，为你铺上新娘的红毯，以便你在默然的寂静中和我独自坐在那儿，直到黑夜离开。

附 录

郑振铎译泰戈尔诗拾遗

采果集

2

我少年时候的生命如同一朵花一般——当春天的微飔来求乞于她的门上时，一朵花从她的丰富里失去一两瓣花片也并不觉得损失。

现在少年的光阴过去了，我的生命如同一个果子一般，没有什么东西耗

费了，只等着完完全全地带着她的充实甜美的负担，贡献她自己。

4

我醒过来，于晨光中找到他的信。

我不知道它里面说的是什么，因为我不会读它。

让那聪明人一个人读他的书吧，我不去惊扰他。因为谁知道他能不能读信中所说的话呢?

让我把它擎在我的前额，把它印在我的心里。

当夜天渐渐地静默了，群星一个一个出来的时候，我要把它展开，摆在我膝上，静悄悄地坐着。

沙沙的林叶要高声对我读它，潺潺的溪流要曼吟它，七颗聪明的星也要从天上对我歌唱它。

我不能找到我所要找的，我不能知道我所学的；但是，这封不能读的信却减轻了我的担负，却使我的思想转而为歌。

15

你的话是简单的，我的主人，但却不是谈论你的那些人的话。

我懂得你的群星的语言，懂得你的树林的静默。

我知道我的心开放起来如一朵花；我知道我的生命自己充满着，如一条伏泉。

你的歌，如同从寂寞的雪地飞来的鸟一般，飞来在我的心里筑巢。在四月温热的时候，我满足地等待这个快乐季候的来临。

23

诗人的心于风与水的声音中间，在生命之波上浮游而且跳舞。

现在太阳西下了，黑暗的天空降落在海面，如垂下的睫毛落在倦眼上一样。这是他把笔搁下，在这沉默的永久秘密当中，使他的思想沉入深渊之底的时候了。

24

夜间黑漆漆的，你的微睡深沉在我身的安慰里。

醒吧，喂，爱情的痛苦，因为我不知道怎么样去开那扇门，我只好站在门外。

时间等着，群星守着，风静止着，沉默很沉重地压在我心里。

醒吧，爱情，醒吧！倒满我的空杯，用歌的呼吸激扰夜间吧。

25

晨雀唱着歌。

在晨光未露之前，在如毒龙之夜还把天空握在他的冷黑圈子里的时候，他什么时候有早晨的语言呢？

告诉我，晨雀呀，由天与树叶盖成的两重夜里，东方的使者他怎么会找到他的路来到你的梦中？

当你叫道“太阳正在走来，夜要过去了”时，世界是不会相信你的。

喂，睡着的人，醒醒吧！

显露你的前额，等着光的第一次祝福，在快乐的忠实里，与晨雀一块唱歌吧。

爱者之贻

4

她接近我的心，如草花之接近土地；她对于我之甜蜜，如睡眠之于疲倦的肢体。我对于她的爱情是我充溢的生命的流泛，如河水之秋涨，寂静地迅速流逝着。我的歌与我的爱情是一体，如溪流的潺湲，以他金色波涛的水流歌唱着。

5

如果我占有了天空和他所有的星星，占有了地球和他无穷的宝藏，我仍是要求增加的。但是，如果她成了我的，则我虽仅有这个世界上的最小一隅，即已感到很满足了。

9

妇人，你的篮子很重，你的肢体也疲倦了。你要走多远的路？你所求的是什么呢？道路很长，太阳下的尘土太热了。

看，湖水深而且满，水色黑如乌鸦的眼睛。湖岸倾斜而衬着绿草。

把你的倦足伸到水里去。午潮的风，把他的手指穿过你的头发；鸽子咕咕地唱他的睡歌，树叶微语着那安眠于绿荫中的秘密。

时间逝了，太阳落了，有什么要紧？横过荒地的道路在朦胧中失去了，又有什么要紧？

13

昨夜我在花园里，献我的青春的白沫腾跳的酒给你。你举杯在唇边，开了两眼微笑着；而我掀起你的面纱，解开你的辫发，让你的沉默而甜柔的脸贴在我的胸前，明月的梦正泛溢在微睡的世界里。

今天在清露冷凝的黎明的静谧里，你走向大神的寺院去，沐过浴，穿着

白色长袍，手里拿着满篮鲜花。我在这黎明的静谧里，在到寺院去的寂寞的路旁的树荫下面，头低垂着。

20

我的歌呀，你的市场在什么地方呢？夏天的微风里杂着学者鼻烟的气味；人们不休地辩论那“油依赖着桶或是桶依赖着油”的问题；黄色的稿子对于逝水似的无价值的人生蹙着眉峰；你的市场是在这些地方么？我的歌叫道：唉，不是，不是。

我的歌呀，你的市场在什么地方呢？幸福的人住在云石的宫殿里，十分骄傲，十分肥胖。他的书放在架上，皮装金字，且有奴仆为之拂去尘埃，他们的洁白的纸上写着的是奉献于冥冥之神的；你的市场是在这个地方么？我的歌喘着气答道：不是，不是。

我的歌呀，你的市场在什么地方呢？青年学生，坐在那里，头低到书上，他的心飘荡在青年的梦境里；散文在书桌上巡掠着，诗歌则深藏在心里。你的市场是在这个地方么？你愿意在那种尘埃满布的无秩序中捉迷藏么？我的歌迟疑不决地沉静着。

我的歌呀，你的市场在什么地方呢？新妇在家里忙碌着，当她一得闲暇，便跑到卧室里去，急急地从她枕下取出一本小说，这书被婴儿粗忽地玩弄着，而且充满着她的头发香。你的市场是在这个地方么？我的歌叹息一声颤震着，意思未定。

我的歌呀，你的市场在什么地方呢？禽鸟的歌声，宏纤毕闻；溪流的潺湲，也能清晰地听到，世界的一切琴弦将他们的音乐倾注在两个翱翔的心上。你的市场是在这个地方么？我的歌突然地叫道：是的，是的。

23

我爱这沙岸。这里有寂静的池沼，鸭子在那里呷呷地叫着，龟伏在日光底下曝着；黄昏时，有些飘游的渔舟，藏在茂草中间。

你爱那有树的对岸。那里，阴影聚在竹丛的枝上；妇人们捧了水瓶，从弯曲的小巷里出来。

同是这一条河在我们中间流着。它对它两岸唱的是同样的歌。我在星光底下，一个人躺在沙上，静听着水声；你也在早晨的光明里，坐在斜坡的边上，静听着。然而，我从它那里听得的话你却不知道，而它向你说的密语，对于我也永远是一个秘密。

25

我握住你的双手，我的心跃入你眼的黑睛里，寻求你这永远避我而逃出于言语之外者。

然而我知道我必须满足我的变动与易灭的爱情。因为我们有一回曾在街道中遇见。我有力量带你通过这个众多世界的群众，经过这个歧路百出的旅程么？我有食粮能供给你经过架着死亡之桥的黑暗的空罅么？

28

我梦见她坐在我头的旁边，手指温柔地撩动我的头发，奏着她的接触的和谐。我望着她的脸，晶莹的眼泪颤动着，直到不能说话的痛苦烧去我的睡眠，如一个水泡似的。

我坐了起来，看见窗外银河的光辉，如一个着火的沉默的世界。我不知道她在这个时候，有没有和我做着同韵律的梦。

29

我想，当我们的眼光在篱间相遇时，我有些话要对她说。但她走过去了。而我对她说的话，却如一只小艇，日夜在时间的每一个波浪上冲摇着。它似乎在秋云上驶行着，在不住地探问着；又似乎变成黄昏的花朵盛开着，在落照中寻求它已失的时间。我对她说的话，又如萤火似的，在我心上闪熠着，于失望的尘中，寻觅它的意义。

30

春花开放出来，如不言之爱的热烈的苦痛。我旧时歌声的回忆，随了他们的呼吸而俱来。我的心突然长出欲望的绿叶来。我的爱没有来，但她的接触是在我的肢体上，她的语声也横过芬芳的田野而到来。她的眼波在天空的忧愁的深处；但是她的眼睛在哪里呢？她的吻香飞熠在空气之中，但是她的樱唇在哪里呢？

36

我的镣铐，你在我心上奏着乐。我和你整日地游戏着，我把你当成我的装饰品。我们是最好的朋友，我的镣铐。有些时候我惧怕你，但我的惧怕使我爱你更甚。你是我漫漫黑夜的伴侣，我的镣铐。在我和你说再会之前，我向你鞠躬。

38

我漂浮在上面的川流，当我少年时，它迅速而湍急地流着。春风微微地吹拂着，林花盛放如着火；鸟儿们不停息地歌唱着。

我旋晕地疾驶着，被热情的水流所带走。我没有时间去看，去感觉，去

把全世界拿到我身边来。

现在，那个少年是消失了。我登到岸上来，我能够听见万物的深沉的乐音，天空也对我展开了它缀满繁星的心。

42

你不过是一幅图画而不是如那些明星一样的真实，如这个灰尘一样的真实么？它们都随着万物的脉息而搏动着，但你则完全固定着你的静止的画成的形象。

你以前曾和我一同走着，你的呼吸温暖，你的肢体吟唱着生命之歌。我的世界，在你的语声里找到它的话语，用你的容光来接触我的心。你突然地停步不进了，伫立在永久的荫旁，剩我一人向前走去。

生命如一个小孩，它笑着，一边跑着，一边喋喋地谈着死：它招呼我向前走去，我跟随着那不可见的脚步；但你立在那里，停在那些灰尘与明星之外，你不过是一幅图画。

不，那是不能够的。如果生命之流在你那里停止了，那末它便也要停止滚滚的河流，便也要停止具有色彩绚烂的足音的黎明的足迹了。如果你的头发的闪熠的微光在无望的黑暗中暝灭了，那末夏天的绿荫也将和她的梦境一同死去了。

我忘了你，这会是真的么？我们匆匆地、头也不回地走着。忘了路旁篱落上开着的花。在忘掉一切的情景中，它们的香气不知不觉进入我们的呼吸，还充满着乐音。你已离开了我的世界，而去坐在我的生命的根上，所以这便是遗忘——回忆迷失在它自己的深处。

你已不再在我的歌声之前了，但你现在与他们是一个。你偕了晨光的第一条光线而到我这里来。到了夕阳的最后的金光消失时，我才不见了你。就是这时以后，我也仍在黑暗中寻求你。不，你不仅仅是一幅图画。

44

当你死的时候，你对于我以外的一切，算是死了，你算是从世界的万物里消失不见了。但却完全地重生在我的忧愁里。我觉得我的生命完成了，男人与女人对于我永远成了一体。

45

携了美丽与秩序到我的艰苦的生命里来吧，妇人，当你生时，你曾携过他们到我的屋里。请扫除掉时间的尘屑，倒满了空的水瓶，备补了所有的疏忽。然后请打开神庙的内门，点燃明烛，让我们在我们的上神之前沉默地相遇着。

48

我每天走着那条旧路。我携果子到市集里去，我牵我的牛到草地上去，我划我的船渡过那条河水，所有这些路，我都十分熟悉。

有一天清晨，我的篮子里满装了东西。许多人在田野里忙着，牧场上停息着许多牛；地球的胸因喜米谷的成熟而扬起着。

大气中突然起了一阵颤动，天空似乎和我的前额接吻。我的心警醒起来，如清晨之跳出雾中。

我忘记了循原路走去。我离开原路走了几步，我看着我的熟悉的世界，而觉得奇异，好像一朵花，我以前所见的仅是它的蓓蕾。

我日常的智慧害了羞。我在这万物的仙国里飘游着。我那天清晨的失路，寻到我的永久的童年，可算是我生平最好的幸运。

50

“来，月亮，下来吻我爱的前额。”母亲这样说着，她把她的小女孩抱在膝上。那时，月亮如梦似的微笑着。夏天的微香在黑暗中偷偷地进来；夜鸟的歌声也从芒果林的阴影密蔽的寂静里送过来。在一个远处的村间，从一个农夫的笛里，吹来一阵悲哀音调的泉源。年轻的母亲坐在土阶上，孩子在她的膝上，她温柔地咿唔道：“来，月亮，下来吻我爱的前额。”她有时抬头看天上的光明，有时又低首看在她臂间的地上的光明。我诧异着月亮的恬静。

孩子笑着，学着她母亲的话：“来，月亮，下来。”母亲微笑着，明月照澈的夜也微笑着。我，做诗的人，这孩子的母亲的丈夫，隐在看不见的地方，凝视着这幅图画。

51

早秋的时节天上没有一片云。河水溢到岸沿来，冲刷着立在浅水边的倾侧的树的裸根。长而狭的路，如乡村的渴舌，没入河水中去。

我的心满盈盈的，我朝四周观望着，看着沉默的天空，流泛的河水，觉着快乐正在外面展延着，真朴如儿童脸上的微笑。

57

这个秋天是我的，因为她在我心头震撼着。她的闪耀的足铃在我的血管里叮呤地响着，她的雾色的面纱，扰动着我的呼吸。我在所有我的梦中知道她的棕色头发的接触。她走出去，在颤抖的树叶上，那些树叶在我的生命的脉搏里跳舞；她的两眼从青的天空上微笑着，从我那里饮啜他们的光明。

歧路

12

我的心呀，紧紧地握住你的忠诚，天要黎明了。

“允诺”的种子已经深深地埋在土里，不久便要发芽了。

睡眠如一颗蓓蕾，将要向光开放它的心，沉静也将找到它的声音。

你的担负要变成你的赠赐，你的痛苦也将烛照你的道路，这日子是近了。

16

你黎明时走到我的门口，唱着歌；我被你从睡梦中惊醒。我很生气，你便悄悄地走开了。

你正午时走进门来，向我要水喝；我正在做事，我很恼怒，你便遭到斥责地走出去了。

你黄昏时，带了熊熊的火炬走进来。

我看你好像是一个恐怖者，我便把门关上了。

现在，在夜半的时候，我孤寂地坐在黑漆漆的房里，却要叫被我斥走的你回来了。

20

天色晦暝，雨淅沥地下着。

愤怒的电光从破碎的云幕里射下来。

森林如一只囚在笼中的狮子，失望地摇着鬃毛。

在这样的一天，在狂风虎虎地扑打他们的翼膀的中间，让我在你面前找到我的平安吧。

因为这忧郁的天空，已荫盖着我的孤独，使你与我的心的接触的意义更为深沉。

77

“旅客，你到什么地方去？”

“我沿着林阴的路，在红色的黎明中，到海里沐浴去。”

“旅客，那个海在什么地方？”

“它在这个河的尽处，在黎明开朗为清晨的地方，在白昼没落为黄昏的地方。”

“旅客，同你一块儿来的有多少人？”

“我不知道怎样去数他们。

“他们提着点亮了的灯，终夜在旅行着；他们经过陆与水，终日在歌唱着。”

“旅客，那个海有多远？”

“它有多远，正是我们所要问的。

“它的波涛的澎湃，涨泛到天上，当我们静止不言之时。它永远地似乎在近，却又在远。”

“旅客，日光是灼炀的热。”

“是的，我们的旅路是长而艰难的。

“谁精神疲倦了便歌唱，谁心里懦怯了便歌唱。”

“旅客，如果黑夜包围了他们呢？”

“我们便将躺下去睡，直睡到新的清晨偕了它的歌声而照耀着，及海的呼唤在空中浮泛着时。”

世纪末日

1

这个世纪的最后的太阳，在西方的血红的云与嫉忌的旋风中落下去了。

各个国家的自私的赤裸裸的热情，沉醉于贪望之中，跟了钢铁的相触声与复仇的咆哮的歌声而跳舞着。

2

饥饿的国家，它自己会在自己的无耻的供养里暴烈地愤怒地烧灼起来。

因为它已把世界当做它的食物而舐着嚼着，一口气吞了下去。

它膨胀了，又膨胀了。

甚至在它的非圣洁的宴会中，天上突然落下武器，贯穿了它的粗大的心胸。

3

地平线上所现的红色的光，不是和平的曙光，我的祖国呀。

它是火葬的柴火的光，把那伟大的尸体——国家的自私的心——烧成了灰的，它已因自己的嗜欲过度而死去了。

你的清晨则正在东方的忍耐的黑暗之后等待着。乳白而且静寂。

4

留意着呀，印度。

带了你的信仰的祭礼给那个神圣的朝阳。让欢迎它的第一首颂歌在你的口里唱出。

“来吧，和平，你上帝自己的大痛苦的女儿。”

“带了你的惬意的宝藏，强毅的利剑。”

“与你的冠于前额的温和而来吧。”

5

不要羞馁，我的兄弟们呀，披着朴素的白袍，站在骄傲与威权之前。

让你的冠冕是谦虚的，你的自由是灵魂的自由。

天天建筑上帝的座位在你的贫穷的广漠的赤地上，而且要知道庞巨的东西并不是伟大的，骄傲的东西并不是永久的。

花环

我的花如乳、如蜜、如酒，我用一条金带把他们结成了一个花环。但他们逃避了我的注意，飞散开了，只有带子留着。

我的歌声如乳、如蜜、如酒，他们存在于我跳动的心的韵律里。但他们，这暇时的爱者，又展开翼膀，飞了开去，我的心在沉寂中跳动着。

我所爱的美人，如乳、如蜜、如酒，她的唇如早晨的玫瑰；她的眼如蜂一般的黑。我使我的心静静的，只怕惊动了她。但她却也如我的花、我的歌一样，逃避了我，只有我的爱情留着。

有许多次，春天在我们的房外敲着门，那时，我忙着做我的工，你也不曾答理他。现在，只有我一个人在那里，心里病着，而春天又来了，但我不知道怎样才能叫他从门口回转身去。当他走来而欲以快乐的冠给我戴时，我们的门是闭着的，现在他来时所带的是忧愁的赠品，我却不能不开门让他走进来了。

无题

静听，我的心。他的笛声，就是野花的气息的音乐，闪亮的树叶、光耀的流水的音乐，影子回响着蜜蜂之翼的音乐。

笛声从我朋友的唇上，偷走了微笑，把这微笑蔓延在我的生命上。

泰戈尔传

一

许多批评家都说，诗人是“人类的儿童”。因为他们都是天真的，和善的。在现在的许多诗人中，罗宾德拉纳特·泰戈尔（Rabindranath Tagore）更是一个“孩子的天使”。他的诗正如这个天真烂漫的天使的脸；看着他，就知道一切事物的意义，就感得和平，感得安慰，并且知道真相爱。著《泰戈尔的哲学》的S.Rabhakrishnan说：泰戈尔著作之流行，泰戈尔之能引起全世界人的兴趣，一半在于他思想中的高超的理想主义，一半在于他作品中的文学的庄严与美丽。他的著作在现今尤有特殊的价值；因为这个文明世界自经大战后，已宣告物质主义的破产了。

二

泰戈尔是彭加尔（Bengal）[①]地方的人。

印度是一个“诗之国”，诗就是印度人日常生活的一部分。新生的儿童来到这个世界上所受的一次祝福，就是用韵文唱的。孩子大了，如做了不好的事，他母亲必定背诵一首小诗告诉他这种行为的不对。在初等学校里，教了字母之后，学生所上的第一课书就是一首诗。许多青年的心里所受的最初的教训就是：“两个伟大的祝福，能消除这个艰苦的世界的恐怖的，就是尝诗的甘露与交好的朋友。”许多印度人写的书，也都是用诗的形式来写的；文法的条规，数学的法则，乃至博物学、医学、天文学、化学、物理学，都是如此。结婚的时候，唱的是欢愉之诗；死尸火葬的时候，他们对于死人的最后的说话，也是引用印度的诗篇。

在这个“诗之国”里，产生了这个伟大的诗人泰戈尔自然是没有什么奇怪的。

① 即孟加拉。——编者注

三

泰戈尔的生辰是一八六一年五月七日。他的家庭是印度的望族；他的长辈，出了许多名人；他的同辈和晚辈也出了好些哲学家、艺术家，他自己曾说道：“我小的时候所得的大利益，就是文学与艺术的空气弥漫于我们家里。”他的接待室里，每天晚上灯都亮着，客人来往不绝。他的兄弟 Ganendra 在家里搭起戏台，演过 Pandit Taskaratna 作的戏；他的侄子 Jyotiprokash 也教过他作诗。他的父亲 Dabendranath Tagore 更是当时的一个天才。泰戈尔在此优越的环境中长成，他的伟大的诗才受了不少的灌溉，自然是要出芽、生枝，而且开花结果。

泰戈尔的母亲死得很早。他在儿童时代，寂寞而不快乐，很少出外——到街上，或园林里——去游玩。离了家塾以后，他进了本地的东方学校，师范学校，又进了英国人办的彭加尔学校，又被送到英国去学法律。但是对学校里的刻板而无味的生活，他十分憎恶。无论到哪个学校，都不过一年就退学回家。他父亲很知道他的性情，并不强迫他去服从学校里的残酷而不明了儿童个性的教师，只在家里请了人教他。

但他还有两个大教师呢！一个是自然界，一个是平民。泰戈尔他自己告诉过我们：自然界就是他的亲爱的同伴；她手里藏了许多东西，要他去猜。泰戈尔的猜法真是奇怪！凡是她给他猜的东西，他没有不一猜就中的。这因为他与自然界相处已久而且很深了，他很小的时候就爱她。他家里有一棵榕树，他少时常到树下洗澡游玩，到了后来，还记住它：

绕缠的树根从你枝干上悬下，呵，古老的榕树呀，你日夜不动地站着，好像一个苦行的人在那里忏悔，你还记住那个孩子，他的幻想曾同你的影子一同游戏的吗？

以后，刚格（Ganges）河[①]的风光，喜马拉雅山的景色，几乎无不深深地印在他明澈的心镜里。

他与他父亲的工人交际得很密切。他在 Salaidah 地方管理他父亲的农产

① 即恒河。——编者注

时，除了帕德马河，他的最好的朋友就是一般农民了。所以他竟成了他们内在的精神的表现者。

在泰戈尔二十三岁的时候，他与一个女子结了婚。这个婚姻是理想的快乐的结合。到后来小孩们降临他家的时候，他又得了新的教师了。《新月集》就是在那时写的。在世界文学家里，没有一本诗集比他这个《新月集》描写儿童更好而且更美丽、真切的了。母亲的永久的神秘与美，与孩子之天真，都幽婉地温和地达出了十二分。且看：

谁都知道你是十分喜欢糖果的——这就是他们所以称你做贪婪的原故么？

呵，呸！我们是喜欢你的，那末他们要叫我们什么呢？

这句母亲对她孩子说的话是如何诙谐而慈爱呀！总之，天真烂漫的儿童世界，教导他以不少的真理。在他三十五岁前后，他的夫人死了。他的爱女、他的爱儿也都相继而夭亡。这个可怕的殷忧笼罩在他身上，使他做出世界上最柔和甜美的情歌，使他的灵魂更有力，更尖锐。他的诗，在这个时期所写的也很优美。后来遂转其笔锋去做颂神之歌，不复作情诗。

这蔓延的痛苦，因爱与欲望更深邃而成为人类家庭里的悲哀与快乐，这就是永远融合、流溢在我诗人心中发出来的歌声中的东西了。

这是他《颂神诗集》[①]（Gitanjali）中的一句，我们读了觉得他还有余痛浮绕在笔端呢。

一九〇二年，他创办了一个“和平之院”——山铁尼克当（Shantiniketan）学校——校址在Bolpus，离加尔各答不远。在那个地方，他的两个大师——自然界与儿童——已融合在一起了，这个学校的教法，用印度的古法，而参以西方的方法，是一种森林学校。凡是到那里参观过的人，都以为泰戈尔的计划非常成功。以前只有二三个学生，现在[②]已经增加到二百人。

① 即《吉檀迦利》。——编者注
② 这里指20世纪20年代。——编者注

他得的诺贝尔文学奖金，已捐入此校为基金。听说，他的著作所得的利益也都消耗在这个学校里。Macdonald 君做了一篇关于这个“和平之院”的游记，说：“无论什么东西在那个地方都是和平、自然而且快活。”任何好争斗、好烦恼的成人，一到了这个“和平之院”，听见早晨的儿童的清脆抑扬的歌声，没有不忘记他的困恼的生之担负的！

他的著作多自己译成英文。最初出版的是《园丁集》。此诗集一出，凡是说英语的民族与懂得英语的民族，无不大为惊讶。以前泰戈尔的名字，除印度外，知道的人极少。自此以后，这个白衣的和平天使的威力立刻弥漫于全人类之间，瑞典的文学会，也立刻把一九一三年的诺贝尔文学奖金，置之于他的座前。

一九一五年，他到了日本，受日人极狂热的欢迎。一九二〇年，他到了美国，这个国家的国民也是非常鼓舞地去迎接他。一九二一年，他到了德国。德国受欧战之刺激，思想大变，对于这个东方的“自然之子”，更表示出一种特别的敬意。据柏林通信说：他讲演的地方，德国人特别布成森林的景色，因为大家都知道，泰戈尔不仅是“人类的儿童”，且是“自然的儿童”。

在一九一九年，法郎士、巴比塞、罗素、爱伦开诸人，在法国巴黎发起了一个“光明团”，提倡永久和平的、非战的运动，泰戈尔也在里边。他又尽力倡导印度的独立，曾向英国政府请愿许印度的自治，竟因此被他们把他的“勋爵”（Sir）头衔取消。

四

泰戈尔的文学运动，开始得极早。在他十四岁的时候，即已开始做剧本。十九岁时，他做了第一篇小说，因此著名。后来继续做了不少的剧本，当时即已在彭加尔及加尔各答各剧场演出。到了现在，加尔各答还在那里演唱他的戏。

他的著作，初时只传布在家庭内，后来才刊登于 Gyanankur 月刊上。他们同他定约，做诗的投稿者。他的散文著作，最初也登载在这个杂志上。

他的著作，最初都是用彭加尔文写的；凡是说彭加尔话的地方，没有人